RONIN

RONIN

THE LAST REINDEER

TONY BERTAUSKI

Copyright © 2022 by Tony Bertauski

All rights reserved.

No part of this book may be reproduced in any form or by any electronic or mechanical means, including information storage and retrieval systems, without written permission from the author, except for the use of brief quotations in a book review.

1

A white blanket covers the world.

Stretched beneath a dark and starry sky, it grips the top of the world. Icy veins cut across it, a network of watery leads where the Arctic Ocean meets the wintery air, a jigsaw floating in slow arrangement as far as the eye can see.

A dark figure is down there.

It contrasts with the icy surrounds, a black dot on a white backdrop, waddling toward the mainland. Short, fat and low to the ice, he slides on wide feet—

"Thirsty?"

Ryder snapped awake. Eyes wide, it took several moments to remember where he was and who the person was smiling at him. The dream was back, so convincing like he was there. The colors so vivid. The air so cold. It was stress that brought it back.

And moving was always stress.

His mouth was cotton-dry, his throat hot. He was totally thirsty. He just didn't want a drink. Every new experience was like this. He'd overheat, feeling nauseous and gross. It always worked best to keep an empty stomach until the first day was over.

He stared out the window.

"That's good." Mindy held a bottle of water. "Pensive. A little worried. Turn a little towards me... that's perfect. You're a natural."

He'd never been inside a limo. He'd slept in bedrooms smaller than this. Technically, they were closets. Mindy whispered to the guy next to her, who was pointing a camera.

This is totally new.

He'd been driven to a dozen homes but never like this. It was usually a social worker driving a compact car with a cracked windshield. Mindy didn't know anything about social work.

The window was icy against his forehead, the landscape buried in snow. He hadn't seen a house for miles. The road was winding and the hills steep. He unzipped his new coat. He was wearing new jeans, too, and a brand-new shirt, sweater, socks, and boots. Even his underwear.

"We'll be there in twenty." Mindy patted his knee. "Just be yourself, okay. If you feel nervous, be nervous. It's perfectly okay. Not many kids like you get a chance like this. Just enjoy, okay?"

Kids like you. How many times had someone told him that? Ryder looked at the guy next to her.

"Don't look at the camera," she added.

Mindy gently lowered her companion's camera and whispered they had enough footage. Maybe it was the look on Ryder's face that did it. She fixed a newly painted smile and turned on a television monitor to take his mind off the countryside and concentrate on things to be grateful for.

You know, for kids like me.

While Mindy and the cameraman talked about film angles and editing, drone footage of snowcapped mountains soared on the monitor. It zoomed toward an isolated building nestled in a tree-filled valley, a sprawling, U-shaped ranch. A fire was roaring in a large courtyard bracketed by the two wings, and a fountain was showering a stack of antler out front.

Kringletown.

It looked more like a resort than a foster home. And the name, it sounded more like an amusement park. This made him more nervous than usual. It wasn't the cameras or Mindy telling him he looked pensive and pensive was perfect for the camera that turned his stomach. He bounced from house to home all of his life and now he was in the back of a limo on the way to some winter wonderland called *Kringletown*. Ryder didn't trust her.

To be fair, he didn't trust anyone.

"Big change," the television reported, "needs Big Game."

Ryder was looking out the window again. At least it was cold, where he was going. He could trust the weather. The weather never pretended to be something it wasn't. It was hot or cold, rainy or dry, and that was that. He couldn't say the same for people.

The limo began to slow. Around the turn, gates were opening. A man tipped a cowboy hat as they passed. Another man pointed a camera.

"Did you get it?" Mindy put her finger to her ear.

Ryder rolled down the window. It was getting stuffy. Snowflakes stung his cheeks and melted on his lips. He closed his eyes and could hear Mindy whispering that this was a spontaneous moment. She was so proud.

They went around a steep bend before the road straightened out. The valley was below. In the distance, Kringletown was nestled in the trees. Mindy buttoned her coat but kept the footage rolling with the window down. The winter wind was biting his nose.

"All yours," she said. "The mountains and streams, forests and hills. Airplanes don't fly over Kringletown. This is private land. Nothing comes out here unless BG says so. It's a half-million-acre playground, Ryder."

It was probably the same line she gave to every kid she delivered. This didn't happen, not in real life.

Not to kids like Ryder.

The limo descended into the valley. It was several more minutes before they were level. From the ground, the ranch looked every bit a resort. The fountain was a geyser bursting from a tangled stack of antlers and dripping into a circular basin.

A group of teenagers were waiting on a wide set of steps. They looked more like a choir than a welcoming committee, wearing brand-new black coats and leather gloves. The boys wore stocking caps like the one Ryder had in his pocket. The girls wore earmuffs.

"This is it." Mindy crossed her fingers then silently mouthed *your big day.*

A boy and girl stepped down to the driveway. They were the oldest, as far as he could tell. Their smiles were expectant, hands clasped in front. Snow began to fall, big flakes drifting from a gray sky.

"Remember," Mindy said, "don't look at the camera."

This was beyond surreal. Resorts weren't houses, and fountains weren't made out of antlers, and kids didn't stand like that or welcome him with creepy smiles, and people with cameras didn't wait around like a reality show—

"Ryder?" Mindy whispered. "Open the door."

His hand was on the handle. He never thought he would ever wish for one of his previous homes (well, not all of them).

I can't do it.

Mindy put her finger to her ear. The boy outside the car pulled the door open. The sound of the fountain crashed inside. Mindy's elbow was in his back. Ryder leaned into her before she shoved.

Snow had settled on everyone's shoulders and caps. The whiteness matched their teeth. Stranger than that was the horde of drones. Ryder had seen quadcopters before, had even flown one in the park once with a friend. These weren't quadcopters. They didn't have propellers, didn't make a sound.

Just hovered silently.

He'd never experienced a sky so big and land so vast. The resort suddenly seemed small. Kringletown was a half-million-acre playground. The welcoming committee's grins were starting to fade.

"I'm John," the boy said. "This is Jane."

Ryder stuck out his hand. John observed it. Jane put her hands to her chin adoringly, her gloves frilly at the cuffs. Her eyes glittered with tears that never fell.

"You're family," John said.

He pulled Ryder in for a crushing hug, pounding his back like he was trying to dislodge something from his throat. Jane was next, her fragrant blond hair splashing across his face. Her embrace was more delicate but deeply meaningful. The welcoming committee cheered.

The drones swarmed like flies.

"It's a lot," John said. "We all remember the day we arrived, and we all felt the same, that this is a dream, it can't be real. But you're not sleeping." He flashed a dazzling smile. "It's time to meet the rest of your family."

Twenty of them came down the steps and introduced themselves and hugged him—the boys slapping his back and the girls holding him tight. Ryder was used to invisibility, not celebrity. He was just a fifteen-year-old boy, not a pop star. But maybe they all got the same treatment the day they arrived. They were just making up for his previous fifteen years.

It didn't explain the smell.

He couldn't describe the strange odor they all possessed. It wasn't body odor or fragrance or smoke from a fire. Ryder couldn't quite place it. Even John and Jane. Like they'd been hanging out in a pottery kiln.

"All right, everyone. Give him some space," Jane said. "No need to rush, we've got all the time in the world. He's with us now. He's home."

She took his hands. Ryder's new brothers and sisters gathered around with their white smiles and sparkling eyes. The drones tracked over them, one per person. Ryder looked up, and everyone paused, their expressions frozen. A drone was recording the final moment of arrival.

"Don't look at it," John whispered.

When Ryder looked at Jane, it was like someone hit play. Her frozen expression thawed. "You didn't win a lottery, Ryder," she said. "You were found by someone with a big heart."

There was another pause. The drone lifted higher.

"We good?" John asked.

Ryder didn't know what that meant. Mindy gave a thumbs-up

after consulting someone. The crowd dispersed, muttering to each other. A few of them waved, but most of them wandered toward the front doors.

"When we're rolling," John said, "don't look at the drones."

"I told him," Mindy said.

"We can edit, but it throws off the flow. Got it, champ?"

Ryder stared.

"It's weird, I know. All of this. But you'll forget the drones, and all of this is for good reason. Now we go inside, show you around, get you situated. You'll have some alone time in a few minutes. How's that sound?"

Jane dropped his hands just before John playfully threw his arm around his neck. But not too playfully.

"Let's shoot in the office," Jane said.

"We'll start in the foyer first," John said, "walk him to the office, do the interview, and then take him to his room."

"It's too slow, John. We never use the footage."

"BG wants to start in the foyer."

The two stared; neither smiled. A warning stiffened Ryder's short hairs. This was the rumble before the storm, Mom and Dad digging their trenches. But they weren't much older than Ryder.

Mindy and a few assistants made their way through the front doors, their footsteps printing the freshly fallen snow. The fountain suddenly stopped. It was mostly quiet, water dripping from the tips of antlers. Jane hooked her arm around Ryder's elbow.

"Let's go to the foyer, then."

Ryder followed. He wasn't asleep, that was clear. Dreams weren't this weird.

DRONES WERE WAITING.

A snowplow could fit through the front doors and half a dozen of them could park in the foyer. It wasn't the decadence that made

Ryder dizzy, it was the vaulted ceiling and the massive windows on the back wall that displayed the white-capped mountains.

The space swallowed him.

A few from the welcoming committee were down the hall on the left, shucking their coats. Ryder recalled the U-shaped building, and the two wings formed a horseshoe that enclosed a courtyard where a fire was burning. John and Jane took their positions at his shoulders and waited. Mindy pointed at them.

"Your room is that way." Jane gestured to the right. It was the opposite direction of the others. He assumed that was the other wing. "You'll meet your roommates tonight at the bonfire, but first things first."

John started toward a small section of solid wall in the center of the glass wall. There was a normal-sized door in the middle. He went inside and closed the door behind him. After the drones took new positions near the glass, Jane led Ryder forward. He wondered if the door would shrink Willy Wonka style.

It did not.

"Go ahead," she said, "open it."

Ryder pulled it open slowly, peeking inside. Jane smiled like it was a present. The room was a normal-sized one. It was an office. The kind of office with a massive oak desk and photos on the wall to impress the occasional visitor.

A drone dropped down from the ceiling. Ryder did his best to ignore the green eye. It wasn't hard to be impressed, if that was what they were expecting.

The photos were of faraway places, mostly snow and ice. Interspersing the pictures were racks of antlers taken from deer and elk, moose and ram. Awards hung in display cases, the kind that recognized excellence and achievement—trophies, diplomas, statues and glass orbs.

There was a man in the photos, tall and slender with shoulders made for chopping wood and a beard built to withstand the cold.

"I know," Jane said. "Not what you were expecting."

Was she talking about the office? The office was normal.

Compared to everything else. The green-eyed drones hovered out of the room. Silence remained.

"When you're ready," she nudged.

John looked like a child behind a desk that could hold a king-sized mattress. There were no papers or folders on it. Not even a pen. Hands folded on the shiny surface, he nodded at the empty chair. The office was void of drones, but based on John's and Jane's stiffly rehearsed expressions, they were still being recorded. A banner was attached to the wall.

Big Change Needs Big Game.

When Ryder sat down, the desktop lit up. John was obscured by holographic images of three-dimensional monitors. Ryder could see through them. From his vantage point, the words were backwards and the images flipped. He recognized his own face and name. John slid his finger on the desk and the images parted.

"Where did you get a name like Ryder Mack?"

Ryder looked around. No one had ever asked him that question, and he was certain the answer was on those ghostly monitors. Jane's hand slid over his shoulders. Her fingers were icy.

"You don't talk much," John said. "I get it, but this is a conversation. You need to participate."

John stared at Jane and nodded. He leaned back and slowly weaved his fingers behind his head. His expression turned stony.

"You've seen the show." Jane squeezed Ryder's shoulders. "I'm going to let you in on a secret. On TV, it looks like we're all about entertainment, telling stories about all the drama in a big family of misfits. It's more than that. We're chronicling life, Ryder.

"You lose a little bit of privacy and gain a lifetime of opportunity. That's a small price to pay, given where you've been—all of us, honestly. So forget the cameras and the millions of people watching. Act natural. You're at home now, and we're family. All the people out there watching are family. They want to know you."

She knelt next to him and whispered. Her breath was humid in his ear. "We want to hear your story."

She patted his arm. Ryder licked his lips. The attention was a thousand spotlights. She stood up with her hands on his shoulders.

"Let's try again."

John sat forward, elbows on the desk like a director had shouted action. There was no clapper. Just the expectation of paying for all of this wealth with a little bit of freedom.

"Where did you get a name like Ryder Mack?"

Ryder cleared his throat. "It's the name of a truck."

"Truck?" John raised his eyebrows.

"A, um, a moving truck."

"Right, I get it. Mack truck. Why would you be named after a truck?"

Tension pulled Ryder's eyebrows together. His cheeks flushed. John's gaze flicked up to Jane.

"Not a big deal," John said, "you don't have to tell me. We're not like the rest of the world. It's why we're here. If you think you're special because someone found you in a moving truck, not around here you're not. That's just another day."

Jane squeezed his shoulders gently. Then they waited. The silence drew out. There was no escape. Not from half a million acres.

"That's the name they gave me," Ryder finally said. "It was a Mack truck owned by the Ryder moving company."

A smile widened on John's cheeks. "Ryder... Mack. Now that's a story. And an original name for an Alaskan. Do you think you're Inuit?"

"What?" Ryder shook his head, but he remembered someone once saying, *You got Eskimo in your blood. It's why you didn't freeze in the truck.*

"How many homes have you been in?" John asked.

A facial tic poked Ryder in the eye. He couldn't read the reports on John's fancy monitors, but he knew where this was going. He'd never seen the reality show he was currently starring in, didn't know exactly what they did, and had assumed it was like all the other bright lights.

"Ten."

"Ten? That's a bunch."

"How many for you?" Ryder said.

John stiffened, the question unexpected. "Three, including this one."

"Three is a lot."

"Why have you been in so many?" John asked.

Ryder clutched the armrests. The tension rippled up his arms. Jane let go and came around the desk. This was an impasse. He wasn't going to tell the world why he'd been in ten homes. And they'd better not read them out loud, either. Half-million-acre playground or not, he'd hike out the way he came in.

Jane read the monitors over John's head. "You have a history of property damage. Is that right?"

A rapid tapping echoed in the room. The toe of his brand-new boot was bouncing on the floor. The muscles in his jaws flexed. He gave a quick nod. He'd been in awful situations at school and in homes. Rooms were trashed, buildings wrecked, and a few people were hurt. They were the sorts of things a troubled young man would do.

Only he didn't do it.

No one believed it. No matter what he said, they added it to the growing record that was in front of John and Jane. Someone once said he had a guardian angel. If that were true, the angel let his mom leave him in the back of a truck.

Nothing angelic about that.

"We're all imperfect," John said. "Some of us more than others."

Playfully, Jane swatted John on the arm. "You're in the right place, Ryder," she said. "You're home. You'll help us build a better world by building a better you. How does that sound?"

All for the low, low price of my freedom and soul? Golly, a deal.

"Let's start with your phone." John held out his hand.

"I don't have one."

They both laughed. He was sure they'd practiced it. "That's a first. No, seriously. Let me have it."

"No, seriously. I don't have one."

"Okay, we'll talk later." He looked at Jane. She nodded and he frowned. Someone didn't tell him that Ryder was the only kid in the world without a phone. "Let me have your hand, then."

John's grip was firm. He put a sleeve over Ryder's index finger. There was a slight sting followed by mild numbness. When he took it off, there was a red pinprick at the tip of his finger.

"We take a blood sample," John said, "for health reasons."

"Welcome to the family," Jane said. "Nothing here is free. You'll earn your place. We value hard work and serious play." Laughter, on cue. "There's a lot a fun and honor out here, but ultimately, there's only one person responsible for Ryder Mack."

Ryder nodded along. The questions were piling up. He was overloaded and in need of space. *Why did they take my blood?*

"You'll see him tonight," Jane said.

"What?"

"That's when you meet BG. I know you're wondering."

It was weird that he was being interviewed by people nearly his age, but that wasn't what he was wondering. He had no idea who BG was. Jane pointed at the banner then one of the pictures.

"That's a wrap," John announced.

Both of them relaxed. The door opened and Mindy walked in. "Fantastic. I could feel the tension through the walls, kids. Well done. The hits will go through the ceiling on this one."

Ryder was dizzy. Mindy mussed his hair and hugged Jane. They discussed the bonfire. It was the beginning of November, but they were going to do Thanksgiving early so they could advertise it. This was reality entertainment.

Not actual reality.

John grabbed Ryder. They were going to his room, where he could clean up and get ready for the bonfire. He was going to meet the man responsible for all of this. Ryder turned around before leaving the office. *Big Change Needs—*

"Big Game," Ryder said.

2

Trees like sculpture.

Conifers set up like snow-laden bowling pins in a sparkling layer of snow. The silence, thick and padded, is broken by a roar and clatter.

The herd's under attack.

A mother reindeer lowers her head and charges. The bear stands with fur bristling, swatting the rack of bony tips with desperate claws. The herd gathers around her, but the predator is hungry.

The fight is long.

Somewhere in the trees, a figure is watching. His beard is braided into two ropes that hang over his belly. Thick eyebrows hide chiseled eyes, and wrinkles fold across his wise features.

Never interfere.

His people let nature take its course. Even the best intentions could have long and lasting consequences. The predator-prey relationship is as important as the sun rising and the ocean tides. But it hurt his heart to see prey so innocent at the mercy of such a beast.

Even if the predator had young of her own.

No one witnesses such violence, not like Gallivanter. He is the ancient *wanderer of his people. It is the risk he takes, to be in the world. To witness the good and the bad.*

And terrible.

The bear gives up. She will find a meal somewhere else. The herd gives chase without losing one of their own. Two newly born reindeer follow. Gallivanter smiles. He remains until a mewling tears a hole in the silence.

His long green coat drags behind him.

Tucked at the base of a tree, a runt is curled up and shivering. The mother gave birth to multiple calves, but only two followed. This one looks up with gluey eyes. Gallivanter searches for their return, but the herd has moved on. It's too dangerous to leave the newborn alone. Perhaps she'll come back for her boy.

Because he can't interfere with nature.

Ryder opened his eyes.

He wasn't in the Arctic surrounded by snow or curled up against a tree. He was lying on a lower bunk, staring at the bottom of a box spring. Someone had carved tiny words on one of the struts.

Don't be nice.

A train was coming from a bunkbed on the other side of the room, a boy with a mop of blond hair and rosy cheeks. His head was in the corner and his feet hung over the mattress, a torrent of wind ripping through him.

Ryder was still dressed.

His coat was on the floor, but he was wearing jeans and a sweatshirt. He didn't remember lying down or taking his boots off or pulling a blanket up to his chin. Jane had showed him to his bedroom with two bunkbeds. No one was there when he arrived.

Now the window was dark.

On the top bunk, a boy was curled up beneath the covers, his head sunk into the pillow. He looked tiny. If the two were combined, they would probably make an average-sized person.

A long desk was below the window. There were three laptops, each of them labelled. Arf was written on one of them. Ryder was taped on the other one. He'd never had a computer before. He'd used one, sure, but never had one with his name on it.

Outside, an orange glow was creeping over distant mountains, and a bright light was on in a barn. Something was smoldering out there, the remains of a fire having melted the snow.

See you in the horseshoe, Jane had said.

He'd fallen asleep. There was no memory of anyone trying to wake him or the sounds of celebration. Just one long dark night and a vivid dream.

Two in a row.

Ryder leaned closer to the window, his breath fogging the glass. Someone was out there. He was bundled in a thick coat, a wide hat tipped toward his face. He walked with a slight hitch, poking a stick, embers floating up like fireflies.

A door closed.

The giant was still chugging down the tracks and the boy on top still curled up like a bean. The bedroom door was closed. Footsteps walked past it. Ryder put his hand on the knob.

Something dropped from the ceiling.

Ryder swatted at it. He'd been in houses that had cockroaches the size of bats and rats that lived in the attic. The giant snorted into silence and the boy on top moaned. A small green light hovered near him.

A drone.

It was the same type as before. There were no spinning propellers, just a silent oblong disk staring at him with a glowing eye. It moved away when Ryder moved near it, hovering over his head and out of reach. There were two more lodged in the ceiling like spitwads, each with a pinpoint of light.

The drone followed him into the hall.

There were several closed doors. To his left, a light illuminated a large board. Someone was in front of it, rubbing a towel on her head. A tiny green light hovered above her. She wasn't there long, going into an open door. The green light followed her. A moment later, it zoomed out of her room like it had been punted.

Ryder looked in both directions.

His footsteps were quiet. Cold seeped up from the hard floor as he crept toward the lighted board. Music leaked from the girl's room. Ryder lingered for a moment, tempted to tap on the door. He didn't know why. He'd always found acclimating to a new home worked best with silence, getting a feel for the people around him before talking. But he'd never lived in a place with so many people, especially his age.

Or with drones.

The board was lit with names and times. On the left side was a schedule. At seven o'clock, it was time to rise. Eight o'clock was breakfast. Nine o'clock was chores. Arf had kitchen duty along with Soup.

Ryder didn't see his name.

On the right side, all the names were listed in scoreboard fashion. They were numbered beneath a heading in bold letters that said *NICE*. There were forty names. Ryder was at the bottom. Soup was number thirty-eight. Arf, thirty-seven.

No one had explained the board. Maybe that was supposed to happen at the bonfire. He was used to figuring out the rules on his own. Keep quiet and do what everybody else does. Blending in was survival.

And he was a master.

A door opened. It was the girl with the towel. Her hair was short and her eyes dark. She stopped suddenly and stared. A drone dropped in front of her and she slammed the door. The sound echoed to the end of the hall and seemed to set off a dozen alarms. They beeped behind closed doors. One by one, they turned off. Then the first door opened.

The walking dead shuffled out.

Drones followed them like magnetic balloons. Boys emerged from one side, girls from the other. Partially dressed, some muttered good morning. Scratching their heads or butts, they wandered to the other end of the hall toward bathrooms—girls on one side, boys on the other. No uniforms, no smiles or sharply pressed shirts.

This wasn't the welcoming committee.

Several journeyed toward the board. A few of them sighed, a girl with a pixie haircut let out a little *weee*, and a boy with thick curly hair groaned. They all, however, ignored Ryder until a little girl wrapped in a comforter looked up at him.

"Move."

Ryder made his way through the slow hustle. Music was beginning to bleed through the doors, a variety of country, rap and pop. A roll of socks fired out of the boys' side and into a girl's open door. A moment later, a return volley.

There was no music coming from Ryder's room, only the rich timber of snoring. The giant was sprawled across his mattress; his sheet had been pulled off him. The small boy was streaming a video on the laptop. His hair was closely shaved. What Ryder thought was a headphone cord was a small disk attached to the side of his head, just above his left ear.

"You good at games?" the kid said without turning. "I bet you are."

Ryder wasn't sure if he was talking to him then noticed the video he was watching. The limo pulled around the fountain, and the well-dressed welcoming committee was waiting. The view was from one of the drones, capturing Ryder's reluctant exit from the car, the clench of his jaws. It zoomed on the half-moon birthmark on his cheek.

Ryder's face heated up.

"We didn't get a limo," the kid said. "We got an Uber. John and Jane were waiting in BG's office, not on the steps. The lady there"—he smudged Mindy with his finger—"never looked up from her phone. She definitely didn't do that."

Mindy's eyes were wet and her hands clasped below her chin as she watched them hug Ryder.

"We did chores that night."

He turned the laptop. The opening credits of the reality show were playing, the same view he'd seen in the back of the limo—the flyover of the resort, the confident, square-jawed profile of the man running this place, and scenes of adventure.

Big Game.

"You know where you're at?" He clapped the laptop shut. It was labelled *Soup*. "This is Kringletown, bo. This is every misfit's dream.

You're in Billy Big Game's house, and he's here to give you everything you ever wanted for the low price of your privacy."

The sun still wasn't above the mountains and there were already two million views on the episode. Two million people who watched him arrive.

"You Eskimo?" Soup said.

"What?"

"That's what Jocko John said, but I got to admit he was right. You look Eskimo. I'm Swedish, mostly. That's what my blood test said, plus the blond hair, vanilla ice cream face. I look Swedish and you look Eskimo."

"What's an Eskimo look like?"

"You."

"Is that a problem?"

"You narco?" Soup waited. "Someone who falls asleep all the time. I knew someone like that, would fall asleep standing up. Once he went down, you couldn't wake him. That was you."

Ryder couldn't remember falling asleep.

"The bonfire was for you. It's on the stream, Sweet Jane all worried and Jocko making an executive decision to let you sleep. It's a tearjerker."

He scooped a shirt off the floor and threw it at the giant kid.

"Arf put the blanket on you. Thought you were cold."

The giant snarfed through the shirt and dragged it off his face. He looked up with a hollow expression, details of who and where he was slowly loading. He propped himself up, careful not to hit his head.

"Smells nice in here." His voice was deep. Ryder wondered if he was still a teenager.

"He's right," Soup said. "You smell nice."

Ryder nodded. No one had ever told him that.

"No, you smell like them." Soup pointed out the window at the other wing. Where the welcoming committee went.

Arf might be huge, but Soup was running the show. Ryder knew one thing, if he didn't push back, he was going to end up on the bottom rung. It was better to be a punching bag than a welcome mat.

Arf stood up and stretched. He was well over six feet tall with a frame that probably exceeded the bunkbed's capacity. He scratched his butt and shuffled into the hall.

"What'd the board say?" Soup said. "The one in the hall, the one everyone's looking at?"

Ryder stared. He wasn't getting in line with the pack. Not yet.

There were four sets of drawers beneath the desktop. Soup made a pile of clothes at his feet. He threw a sweater over his shoulder and grabbed a toothbrush. He was wearing furry slippers.

"Please tell me you shower," he said.

"It doesn't smell like anyone showers."

"I don't because I don't sweat. I do brush my teeth. We got forty-five minutes before breakfast. Then chores. You'll probably go suntanning with the nicies." He threw a towel. "Follow me."

"I'm good."

Ryder dropped the towel. Soup watched with disappointment. Maybe this worked on Arf, but Ryder wasn't on board. When Arf returned wearing a robe, they were still in a standoff. His hair was damp and wild. A wispy crop of whiskers covered his jaw.

"Arf." Soup waved at him.

The big boy closed the door and let the robe fall. He stood in a pair of boxers and fuzzy-lined boots. His shoulders were bright red from a hot shower. All the lights on the drones turned red.

Ryder tensed.

He'd managed his way out of a few tight spots. You didn't know what people were made of until they got tested. Sometimes they were mean all the way to the core. Sometimes it was hot air.

"Jane tell you the drones would stop filming if you asked?" Soup said.

She hadn't said anything about drones. Not that Ryder could remember.

"She tell you that's your personal spy? Nod once if you understand."

Ryder was about to change the subject when Soup raised his hands.

"Don't shoot, bo. I'm telling you how it is. You have a spy, I have a spy… we all do. Arf named his Drony. Not original, but I'm not judging. Mine is Dingleberry. Come here, Dingleberry. Introduce yourself."

Three identical drones hovered near the ceiling. He waved at one and it didn't move.

"What Jane probably told you was that if you don't want your spy recording, all you have to do is ask it to stop. She's lying. There's only one way to stop them and that's in the bathroom or getting undressed. No one wants to see us half-naked, not even Bill. Someone would sue his jingle bells blue."

The drone lights were still red.

"Honestly, Bill's probably still listening, but whatever."

"Bill?"

"BG, bo. Big Game." Soup whispered, "Billy 'Big Game' Sinterklaas. He gave himself the nickname. That tells you everything you need to know."

"What do you want?"

"Me? I don't want anything. You want something, Arf?"

The giant shrugged. Soup dug through his top drawer. He pulled out a bottle of cologne.

"We just want to make sure you're not one of them."

"Who?"

"The nicies." When Ryder didn't get it, he added, "The goodies, the smilies. Sweet Jane and Jocko John and the rest of the country club that live on the ding-dong wing. They're not welcome over here."

"Why?"

"Because they're robots. Are you serious, you've never seen this stupid reality show? This is the snowglobe, man. No one gets in or out till Billy commands it. It's the most watched reality stream three years running because it's got poor children and crazy talk. Don't get me wrong, this is better than where we were, but Billy is molding us into white-toothed nicies. You should be afraid. You should be very afraid."

Ryder shook his head. *Don't be nice.*

"They're fake, bo. For real."

Soup was skinny and short. Ryder looked down at him, noticed the piece in his left ear was some sort of hearing aid, but was unsure why there was a disk attached to the side of his head.

"You afraid of me?" Soup asked.

"No."

"Arf?"

"I'm not afraid of anything."

"Everybody's afraid." He pulled the lid off the cologne. "Maybe you just don't know it yet."

Ryder appeared relaxed and lazy. Of course he was afraid. Every day was a bobsled through anxiety. But if he admitted it, it would crash on him like an avalanche. It was better to put up a front no matter how heavy the mask.

"Just do what we do," Soup said, "follow the rules just enough. If you're too good, you go to the basement for a white shirt and straight teeth. Too bad and Billy sends you packing. Arf and me are the best you ever met. We'll show you the way."

Ryder was staring at his chipped tooth—it was slightly yellow—and wondering if he got that before he arrived at Kringletown. Arf pulled on a pair of long johns. When he pushed his head through a sweater, Soup snapped his fingers.

"Smile," he said.

The green lights were back. Ryder could feel the heat of a million eyes. This wasn't live but might as well be. He was the new guy.

Arf grabbed his toothbrush. The side of his face was badly misshapen. His ear scarred. As they walked past Ryder, Soup aimed the cologne bottle. He ducked before Ryder could knock it out of his hand. A misty cloud of fragrance hit him.

"Avert your eyes, ladies," Soup shouted. "You're not dreaming."

A roll of socks fired across the doorway.

THE DRAWERS WERE FILLED with neatly folded clothes, brand new and creased. Soup's laptop was still open, the video paused. Ryder looked over his shoulder and listened before clicking play.

"A New Naughty."

That was the title of episode 204. It sounded bad, but it was the same stream Soup had been watching. *Big Game at Kringletown* was the reality show Ryder had signed up for. He looked at the drone. Someone was watching him watch himself—the arrival, the interview then the walk to his bedroom. Ryder didn't realize he was so tall or his hair so black and straight. Was the birthmark always that bright?

My face is round.

Toxic waste spilled inside his brain. He felt contaminated. A hundred thousand people had watched this just in the last fifteen minutes. There were thousands of comments and even more thumbs up and down.

"I think he's sweet." Jane was sitting next to John. "And he's happy to be here."

"How can you tell?" John said. "He hardly talks."

"He just got here. Give him a minute."

"He doesn't own a phone, Janie. Think that's a little weird?"

"Because he doesn't have a phone?" Jane swatted his arm. "It's innocent. And sweet."

"And weird."

Their banter had plenty of snow-white smiles and snorting laughter. They looked like twins but didn't act like it. It made him squirm.

"And no one sleeps like that." John addressed the camera this time. "The bonfire was pointless."

"He was tired. And stressed."

"Maybe he's narcoleptic."

"Stop it." Jane whacked him hard this time. "BG is going to love him."

"Yeah. I know."

A long pause erupted from an inside joke. *Why was that funny?*

How long would it be before his superpower of invisibility kicked in? A week? A month?

A year?

He swallowed a knot. Soup was right. It was a blessing to be here. There was a warm bed and hot food and lots of friendly faces. He looked up at the green-eyed drone. Was it worth it?

To be determined.

Wasn't BG supposed to be running this place? Ryder scanned the sidebar and found a dozen links to related videos. Most were episodes of *Big Game at Kringletown*, but one was a sponsored advertisement.

Finding Claus.

It was a two-minute preview of an upcoming documentary. The scene scanned across a snowy ice cap. A dull red sun hung just above the horizon, snow glittering around three figures. Long shadows dragged behind them.

"We've been lied to." The voice-over was rich and husky. "All our lives."

Captivating scenes of ice floes alternated with night skies and Northern Lights and distant polar bears. The figures camping on the ice. Drones released in snowstorms. Blistering wind whipping a flag that said North Pole.

The largest of the three people took a knee. He dug into the snow and retrieved a round metal bell. It jingled in the gale. The man looked up, his reddish beard knotted with ice, bushy eyebrows knitted.

"He's real," the voice said.

The title faded to black. *Finding Claus*, it said. *This Christmas.*

It was satire, had to be. If that was CGI, the effects were flawless. They looked like they were actually on the North Pole.

Finding Claus? Ryder thought. *As in Santa?*

"What are you doing?" Soup said.

Arf pushed past him. Ryder jumped up as the giant came at him. He was ready to duck a swing and scramble through the bunkbed, but the big boy didn't come for him.

He grabbed a stocking cap from his drawer.

"That's yours." Soup pointed at a different laptop. "That's mine. They're labeled and you can read. I assume you can. Can he read, Arf?"

Arf shrugged.

"It was open," Ryder said. "I was just watching."

"Well, you clicked something, didn't you? Streams don't play themselves."

"Yeah, they do."

"You know about YouTube but not this show? Liar." Soup stripped off his shirt and snorted. "You are a naughty."

Ryder looked through his drawers again. There was no need to change clothes, but he did take note they were exactly the kind of things he liked to wear. Plain sweatshirts and jeans. Half a dozen wool beanies stacked on top.

His laptop was still closed. A corner of paper was sticking out from inside it. Ryder pried it open to find a piece of red wrapping paper with golden bells and green holly leaves. Black lines bled through the back of it.

"Good news," Soup announced. "Your name got added to the board. You're coming to the kitchen with us. Thanksgiving is the worst, so congrats."

Ryder folded the paper and acted normal.

"And just so you know, Dingleberry can read the numbers off a dollar bill. Your drone..." He nodded at it. "What'd you name it?"

Ryder shook his head.

"Well, *Drony Jr* can easily show the world what you got there. There are no secrets in Kringletown. Not for long."

Ryder shoved the paper in his pocket. He hadn't flipped it over, so none of the drones would have seen what it said.

"Come on," Soup said. "Chore time."

"I got to go to the bathroom."

"Don't be late. Bill's keeping a list. Right, Arf?"

The big boy nodded. Ryder waited until they were gone. The rest of the naughty wing followed. The last one was the short-haired girl from that morning. She glanced at him on her way.

When the wing was quiet, he closed the door and stripped off his shirt. His drone looked like a floating rock. When the green light didn't change, he unbuckled his belt. Before he got down to his boxers, the light turned red. It hovered up to the ceiling and docked.

He waited.

When it stayed red, he slid the piece of paper out and held it close to his chest, peeling it back until he could barely see the writing. Maybe Sweet Jane had left it when he was asleep, or Soup was testing him. Neither of those guesses made any more sense than the message.

Why are you here?

When he got dressed, the drone dropped off the ceiling and the green eye returned. It followed him into the hall. His roommates were waiting.

"Did you pee out the window?" Soup said.

"False alarm."

His blond-haired roommate smacked him on the back. "You're catching on."

They caught up with the others and Ryder blended in. No one seemed to care. He wondered, though, who would have put a note in the computer? It didn't seem like a secret message, but he kept thinking there was more to it. Something that worried him when he lay in bed that night, because Soup was wrong about one thing.

There were plenty of secrets at Kringletown.

3

They were misfits.

A mishmash of jeans and T-shirts, untucked and wrinkled, boots with loose laces. Cuss words and dirty jokes, staying up past curfew and banging on the walls, throwing toilet paper through open doors and wrestling in the hall.

The stars of *Kringletown*.

Ryder stayed low and watched, did what the board told him to do. Boring kept him off the stream. Most of the others were happy with the spotlight.

Thanksgiving arrived.

He followed the others to the elevator. Like everything else, it was big—large enough to park two trucks inside. It also went in all directions. Sometimes, Ryder couldn't tell which way it was going.

They arrived at the library.

It was a circular room that went up five stories like the inside of a silo. A flock of drones hovered near the ceiling. Kringletown was only two stories tall.

We're belowground.

A few naughties raced up to the fifth floor. Cheers followed them to the vaulted ceiling and back, laughter ricocheting wall to wall.

Claustrophobia pressed down on Ryder. If the library was this far belowground, what else was down there?

He watched from one of the archways, where stacks of books smelled like old paper. His bandaged thumb pulsed. He'd spent the morning dicing potatoes to be boiled and mashed, the knife nicking his thumb just before he was finished. With all the technology, slicing potatoes hardly seemed necessary.

Billy loves work, Soup had told him. *Pointless, mindless work.*

Apparently free speech was still an option. His clip made the stream. Drama was good ratings.

The nicies were gathered on the other side of the library, their white shirts without wrinkles, slacks pressed and creased. Ties tightly fitted to the boys' necks. The girls wore variations of the standard attire, some in dresses and others in pants. They spoke calmly, laughed like adults, and covered their mouths when it was too loud.

Only one other person was acting quiet. It was the girl with a pixie haircut, the one who lived next to the board. She leaned against one of the arching doorways with a black hardback propped open. She didn't look up, her focus racing from page to page, folds of concentration bunching between her eyes.

His personal spy had joined the others, a bunch of oblong, one-eyed futuristic starlings. Ryder felt the torn wrapping paper in his pocket.

"You know the bunk above yours?" Soup startled him.

"What?"

"The bed above yours, that was Paul's. Paul's not here anymore. Know why?"

Ryder shook his head.

"Paul hooked up with Janine."

A roar of cheers rose up as another race to the top began. Soup cupped his hands and bellowed a name, pumping his fist.

"Who's Janine?"

"Exactly. It would've been on episode 1240, but then you don't watch the stream. Even if you did, you wouldn't have seen it. Billy cut it out. Doesn't want the public to get the wrong idea, you know, girls living across from boys, all hormony and whatnot. Cut them out, too."

"What do you mean?"

"Sent them packing, bo. Reassigned. New home, somewhere else. They weren't fit for Kringletown, couldn't control themselves, pick a reason. One day they were here; the next they were gone."

The race started back down the spiraling staircase. Soup joined the chorus as the drones followed. They'd been listening to what he was saying. If it was true, it wouldn't make the stream.

"I'm just saying," Soup said between hoots, "don't get your hopes up. You'll get used to it."

The girl was still in her book. Ryder knew everyone's name. Just not hers.

"Unless you're a nicy," he added. "They all flirt. I mean, they're all probably getting down, but Jocko and Jane are barely hiding it. Sort of the cookie Billy dangles, you know. *Hey, be nice, you can hook up.* But then you look like that, smell like them."

He pretended to puke. It was loud. The nicies were looking.

"Hi, I'm Jocko John," Soup droned. He did robot arms. "My shirt matches my teeth."

A flush of heat warmed Ryder's cheeks. All the eyes were on them. He wanted to crawl under a table. The race to the bottom was a close one, and the attention quickly dissolved. Jonas won by tripping on the last flight. Arf got between them before a fight started.

The naughties booed.

"You name your tattletale yet?" Soup pointed at his drone.

Ryder had been told to forget it was there, like it was just part of the scenery. Not own it like a pet. It was hard to ignore.

"Kooper," Ryder blurted.

"Like Bradley Cooper?" Soup grimaced.

"No, just... it was a, uh, a name of a dog."

"That thing ain't a pet, bo. It's a traitor, loyal to the great and almighty Billy Big Game. You should name it Turdbird. Fartsmeller's taken. I don't know, Bradley Cooper works. I guess."

"It's not..."

Ryder waved him off. His thumb was beginning to throb. It would calm down when this was over and the attention cooled down. The girl was the only one who hadn't looked at them. She wore baggy clothes and dark colors and stayed buried in her book. He wanted to be like that, around people but not with them. He imagined them standing side by side with a book, even though he didn't read. They wouldn't need to even talk. You know, just hang out.

"Cherry," Soup said. When Ryder turned, he said, "As in 'on top.'"

"Cherry?"

"Her name, bo. Cherry Stone is the oldest naughty on the block, been on the wing longer than any of us. She perfected invisibility, carving the rules like an Olympic snowboarder—just enough boring to avoid the eyes, but not enough to get booted out of Kringletown."

Ryder frowned. They couldn't get thrown out for being boring.

"*Thou shalt entertain*," Soup said.

She could feel them looking. Ryder sensed a hesitation as she turned a page, an agitation of unwanted attention. She snapped the book closed, the pop of heavy pages echoing throughout the library. The drones turned, so did everyone else. Without looking, she dipped out of sight.

"See that?" Soup said. "She made a little scene, but it won't make the stream. She's a Zen master. You should try talking to her. You'll have a great time."

He raised a thumbs-down and mouth-farted. It sounded like he'd tried. Maybe they all did. *Thou shalt entertain.*

The floor lit up.

A spontaneous moment of silence was followed by excitement. The drones suddenly positioned at the perimeter of the room. A large circle of white light glowed in the center of the room and engulfed everyone standing on it. The illumination beamed all the way to the ceiling, throwing sharp shadows.

Everyone backed away, but someone remained. They were a dark form contrasting with the bright light. It looked like he was inflating.

"This is so stupid," Soup muttered.

Arf was next to him, his eyes lazy, mouth open. No one looked rattled by the growing man, who was now as tall as the second floor. They looked sort of bored. At least the naughties did.

"Hallo!" a deep voice called.

The giant figure emerged in full detail—burly and red-bearded, a stocking cap folded just above his eyebrows. Ryder recognized him from pictures. Billy Big Game Sinterklaas.

BG to you and me, Soup had said.

"My apologies, children." His hearty laughter shook the walls. "My expedition took an unexpected turn and I won't be back for Thanksgiving."

The nicies genuinely moaned. The naughties made an effort.

"I can't wait to tell you about my discoveries. In the meantime, I want to belatedly join everyone in welcoming the newest member of the family."

He looked down at Ryder. The heat of attention turned up the thermostat. Every eye was on him, human and drone.

"I hope your arrival has been warm and welcome," he said. "We are so happy to finally have you home."

There was applause. Soup muttered, "He has never said that to anyone ever before."

"This trip has been lonesome," BG added. "And I miss every one of you. The greatest discovery of all is at hand, children. It's so very close. With just a little help, we'll find what we're looking for."

"He literally says *that* every year."

The weird thing wasn't what he said but what he did when he said it. *With just a little help,* he'd said and looked right at Ryder. Did nobody notice? Or was he just imagining it?

"Let's give thanks."

Everyone shuffled to the edge of the lighted circle. The nicies laced their fingers together, forming a long hand-in-hand chain that connected to the naughty side. Arf grabbed Ryder and pulled him up to the circle.

"I want to give thanks for my family," BG started. "Without your hearts and minds, our lives would be cold and empty. Our house would not be a home. It's the people around us that make our lives what they become."

He nodded.

The thanks continued around the circle, each person sending up gratitude. Some were long and thoughtful; others short and poignant. The drones aimed and recorded what would be a spectacularly heartfelt episode. Ryder's heart began to thump.

"I give thanks for being here," Arf said. He totally meant it.

Everyone nodded. Then they waited. A fire was roasting Ryder's cheeks. His throat was dry and his tongue was the size of a Christmas ornament.

"Go," Soup whispered.

Arf squeezed his hand so hard that his knuckles crunched and, for a moment, the pain made him forget the world was watching.

"Thank you."

"I want to thank my socks," Soup blurted out. There were moans and eyerolls. "What? My feet are cold."

That might have come naturally, but he did that on purpose. No one was looking at Ryder anymore. *Thank you, Soup.*

"Happy Thanksgiving, children!" BG bellowed. "I'll see you at the big game."

Hands above his head, the larger-than-life figure winked out. The lighted circle faded back to waxy concrete. A large set of arching doors began to move. The tops brushed the second floor as they split open. There was a long room on the other side with a wide table running the length of it. The smell of food wafted out.

"What game?" Ryder said.

The room was candlelit.

Turkey and yams and turnips and mashed potatoes and pies and fixings covered the table. The nicies spread napkins on their laps and waited for everyone to be seated. The naughties filled their plates and ignored the napkins.

The walls were dark with large oak columns and rough-hewn beams. A chandelier of antlers flickered with artificial candlelight. Heads of various game watched them eat—glassy-eyed antelope and elk, deer and ram.

A moose was mounted at the head of the table, its rack spanning wider than all the others'. Jane sat at one setting and John at the other. The one between them was untaken.

Mouths full, laughter shot food across the table. Silverware clattered on the floor, drinks were spilled and shoulders rubbed. Ryder's plate was still empty when a glass began to ring. Jane stood up and played her cup with a spoon. It took several attempts to get their attention. A fight nearly broke out across the table.

"BG can't be with us," she said.

"But that doesn't mean we're without leaders," John finished. "We lead each other with actions and words."

"To recognize our unity, we'd like to invite a guest of honor up front this year," Jane said.

A wildfire ignited Ryder's belly and raced into his head. The birthmark was burning when his name was called. He didn't hear anything else. He felt encouraging pats on the back and was lifted onto his feet and shoved toward the front, where the moose was watching. John pulled out the chair.

"As Ryder so simply and eloquently put it," she said, "thank you."

There was a long uncomfortable pause before John raised his glass and Thanksgiving commenced. The room was once again filled with laughter and conversation. Jane and John put very little food on their plates. They took small bites and ate with their lips tightly sealed. Mostly, they watched. The naughties slaughtered their side of the table with gravy drips and careless crumbs.

Ryder wasn't hungry.

When he didn't reach for anything, John and Jane filled his plate and insisted. His stomach was knotted. Anything that hit it was going to rebound like a trampoline. He scrambled the mashed potatoes and managed to eat half a roll. He mostly drank water. No one was watching him except the glassy eyes.

"What's the big game?" he asked.

"Teamwork and structure," Jane said, dabbing her lips. "It's why we do chores."

"We also have fun," John said stiffly. Ryder doubted he knew what the word meant. "You seriously haven't seen the stream?"

Ryder shook his head.

They looked at each other and laughed. "Relax. It'll be fun," Jane said.

When plates were empty and everyone was full, a board appeared on the wall. Some moaned; others sighed. It was mostly the naughties who complained.

Actually, it was only the naughties.

Ryder was relieved to see his name next to Soup's and Arf's. They were on cleanup duty. Ryder's plate was a mix of mashed potatoes, turkey and cranberries. He carried it to a nearby tub where everyone was stacking their plates.

"Next time," John said, "only take what you can eat."

Ryder hadn't put the food on his plate, but didn't argue. *Because drama equals attention.*

"Take this." Soup handed him a tub. "Or is it too much? I mean, all the love they're putting on you must be heavy."

"Shut up," Ryder said.

"That's the spirit." Soup dropped more dishes in the tub.

4

Ryder woke before dawn.

The sky above the mountains was starlit. Snowflakes fluttered through the barn's spotlight. A dark figure moved across the horseshoe with a limp and disappeared in the glare. Ryder waited, but the person didn't return.

Bradley Cooper dropped off the ceiling with a mechanical click. The green eye cast an eerie glow and followed him into the hallway. The board was lit up.

GAME ON!

Chores were limited to breakfast. Free time was a larger block than usual, and there was something new on the board.

Introspection. Arf's name was under it.

A bedroom door opened and the sounds of a flute flowed out. A square mat was on the floor with a round pillow. A candle flickered. Cherry abruptly stopped in the doorway, a towel over her shoulder. Her hair was damp, her forehead sweaty, and her eyes were oversized in the dim light. She was staring like she'd been caught doing something. Ryder broke the awkward silence.

"What's introspection?"

She stared a moment longer then closed the door.

Maybe she needed to change clothes or wasn't done exercising. He waited a minute longer and the flute played through an entire song. When it started up again, he went back to his room and gathered a change of clothes.

The shower room was divided into cubicles. The sinks were lined up below a long mirror spotted with toothpaste. Music filled the hallway when he was finished.

Soup was in bed with his laptop. Arf was still snoring. Ryder sat on his bed and thought about lying down, but thoughts of the day nibbled at his attention like field mice. *Game on.*

"How do you sleep?" Ryder said.

"What?"

Ryder repeated the question. Arf had kicked his breathing into a higher gear.

"I turn my ears off." Soup tapped the disc on his head. "You think this was headphones?"

"You're deaf?"

"Not anymore." A cochlear implant, he explained. It took some time getting used to, but it brought his hearing back.

"And you were thankful for socks."

"I thank him every year for the ears, thought I'd mix it up. And I am thankful for socks. Don't forget the little things, bo."

He went back to the stream. Ryder didn't want to see it. The less he saw of himself, the better he would feel.

"What's introspection?"

"Why?" Soup sat up. "Am I scheduled?"

"No. Arf is. What is it?"

He flopped back on the bed. "Oh, man. Never mind that."

"Pretty much what Cherry said."

"You talked to her?"

"Sort of. I said, 'What's introspection?' and she closed the door."

"Huh." He paused the stream and stared at the ceiling thoughtfully, then rolled over and pointed at him. "She's into you."

"Yeah, I don't think so."

"Did she look at you?"

"What?"

"Did she look at you, like right at you?"

Ryder had surprised her. They'd stared at each other for like five seconds before he said something, and then she'd closed the door and never came back out. So yeah, she'd looked at him.

"It was an accident," Ryder said.

"But she still looked at you. You said like five seconds, right?"

"Yeah, but—"

"She's into you, man," Soup said. "Trust me."

Ryder could feel his birthmark glowing. He didn't want to tell him that it was more than a surprise. She had been doing something in her room. Maybe it was just exercise, but she looked like she'd been running and was more than a little guilty about it.

Ryder pried the blinds apart while his laptop booted. A hazy morning settled on the snow. The producers were already in the horseshoe. He hadn't seen Mindy since the first day. They were here for the big game, the most popular episode of the year.

Game on.

Reluctantly, he opened the stream. He couldn't just sit there and think about what was going to happen. And he was the only one who knew next to nothing about what was going on. He fast-forwarded through the opening—the flyover of the U-shaped building, the horse barn and pastures and endless trees.

There was a quick scene of a nicy argument. Peter had grabbed the clothes washer even though Erica was waiting for it. They actually raised their voices. Ryder watched the whole thing.

Most of the action was in the naughty wing, where Jamby, an overweight math prodigy with an annoying habit of counting the letters in words, was caught picking his nose. He studied the end of his finger before popping it in his mouth.

"Does it all the time." Soup was watching Ryder's stream.

Ryder couldn't recall if he'd picked his nose since arriving. He'd definitely farted, but it hadn't made it to the stream. Maybe Bradley Cooper did him a solid. He'd die if he was caught mining for nose gold. Jamby didn't seem to care.

Jane and John began their narration in the interview room.

"This is my favorite time of year," Jane said.

"What?" John said.

"Well, Christmas is my favorite, obviously, but you know what I mean. It's the anticipation. Everything is about to happen. We only have so many holidays to celebrate. It's all in front of us. It's not like we can start over and do it again."

They laughed a little too long. They were always sharing a secret and never let anyone in on it. Even the nicies didn't know what they were laughing about half the time.

"They're in charge," Ryder muttered.

"Mmm," Soup half-agreed.

Ryder had been at Kringletown almost a month, and it was clear they were running things. They'd interviewed him. The producers talked to them. This was supposed to be Billy Big Game's show. It was his ranch, but everything went through Sweet Jane and Jocko John. Ryder hadn't even seen BG yet.

Not in person.

There were segments of him trekking the North Pole and photos in the office. The hologram in the library could've been animated. This was all for show, just one big semi-serious boardinghouse that made millions in the stream. They didn't really need BG.

"He's not real," Ryder said.

"What?" Soup said.

Ryder was surprised by the sudden answer. Soup's eyes pinned him in crosshairs. Ryder wasn't sure what he said. Soup leaped off the top bunk and closed the blinds. He looked in the hall and closed the door gently. He shouted at Arf, telling him to strip down to his boxers. The big boy rolled over and snored.

Soup took off his pajamas.

His skin was white as snow and thinly stretched over his ribs. He crossed his pointy arms, already shivering, and had second thoughts about whatever he was thinking. He put his shirt back on then rummaged through his junk drawer. Pen and paper in hand, he tore the blanket off his bed and draped it over his head.

"Come on." Ryder shook his head, but Soup nodded aggressively. "Get in, man."

"Uh—"

"Just for a second."

Ryder reluctantly peered in. Soup threw the blanket over him. He could feel the drones orbiting around them. There was just enough light to see the pad of paper. Soup scribbled giant letters and held it up.

Ryder squinted. "*BG isn't*—"

"Stop. Just..." Soup frowned. "I'm writing for a reason."

Ryder read the message silently so the room wouldn't hear. Short of stripping down to their boxers, which was guaranteed not to get them on a stream but not necessarily from being heard, this was the only way to tell a secret.

BG isn't real, his message said.

"You've never seen him either?" Ryder said.

"What? No." He shook his head and started writing again. *None of them are real.*

"Who?"

"The nicies," Soup whispered.

"I don't get it."

"They're not right. *Too nice*, know what I'm saying?"

Ryder didn't know how to answer that. But there was something going on right in front of them and they weren't seeing it. The entire world wasn't seeing it. And it wasn't just the way Jane and John laughed or BG having an excuse not to be there in person.

It's like the secret is out in the open.

"What should we do?" Ryder said.

Soup shrugged. That was all he had. Something wasn't right and that was it. He was no help. In fact, he was making Ryder more nervous.

It was hot and suffocating. Soup threw the cover off and wadded up the papers. The snoring had stopped. Arf was looking over his shoulder.

"What?" Soup said. "We're playing fort. Not like you can fit in here."

Arf dropped his man-sized feet on the floor and yawned like an elephant. His hair stood like hay. He grabbed a towel. A sock fight had broken out in the hall. Soup scooped a handful of sock rolls out of the hall and fired them like snowballs.

"You ready for the big game?" Soup screamed at Ryder. "You jacked? Huh? I know I am." He shouted down the hall, "N-A-U!"

"G-H-T!" someone answered.

They did this several times. Ryder didn't want to point out they were spelling it wrong. The naughties didn't stand a chance anyway, but winning really wasn't the point. That was how Ryder had come to see everything at Kringletown. Everything had a secret purpose.

Even a stupid game of football.

❄

THE TABLES WERE DUSTED with snow. Boxes were filled with red flags. The producers were carrying clipboards in thick mittens, their breath streaming through wool scarves.

Jane and John wore black cleats and long-sleeved jerseys with numbers on the back. A yellow belt was cinched around their waists, flags dangling from their hips.

Team Nicy.

The naughties dressed like it was just another day, like they'd rolled out of bed and came outside. Only half of them had flags around their waists. Soup had them around his head. Instead of practicing, they were having a snowball fight.

Arf leaned against the building.

He had never come to lunch. They'd waited for him to come back from introspection, but he'd met them in the horseshoe. He hadn't said much since then, mostly staring at the ground.

"You all right?" Ryder asked.

He nodded, kicking at the snow. His shoulders were slumped a little more than usual. It was cold; maybe that was it. The sky was a gray sheet, the sun a dull disc rising from the mountains. Drones circled like turkey buzzards. A small plane was silently crossing the gray sky. It was the first one he'd seen. He had been told this was restricted airspace, that nothing was supposed to fly over Kringletown, for proprietary reasons. No one got to cash in on the stream without BG getting his cut.

"Ryder!" Mindy was calling from the tables. "Ryder!"

"I think she wants you," Arf said.

The producers were gathered like penguins, their noses bright red. Mindy hopped through the snow, clapping as he approached, like a mother watching a toddler take his first steps.

"How are you?" she sang. She knew exactly how he was doing. "You look great, you really do. These are fun times, right? Are you excited?"

He offered his best shrug.

"It's an annual event, you know that, right? A big deal at Kringletown, bragging rights to the winner for a whole year. You've seen the big game from last year, right?"

He was tired of explaining that, no, he'd never seen the stream before coming there and, no, he hadn't watched anything from the archive.

Mindy hugged the trophy. It was taller than her. The nameplate was engraved with past winners. Team Nicy was stamped on it fifteen times. Since the game was invented.

The year I was born.

"Have you ever played?" she asked.

Ryder shook his head. He was forced to watch it at one of his foster homes every Sunday. It had been dumb then too.

"Don't worry." She put her arm around him. "It's nothing extreme. It's fun, you know. A way to get to know your family, challenge each other, and develop teamwork. Most of them have never played either, so you'll blend right in. Just have fun, okay? Like you've been doing."

Fun? What stream is she watching?

"By the way, you're one of the captains."

"What?" His insides suddenly chilled. "I don't—"

"It's no big deal. Just join the others for the coin flip. They'll tell you what to do. We just want your handsome face." She grabbed his chin. "Go, have fun."

He didn't want to hear the word *fun* ever again.

A small group was waiting in the middle of the horseshoe. Soup was one of them. He was making a snow angel. Mindy walked with Ryder. He really wished she wouldn't.

"Good luck," she whispered.

Jane and John were there and another nicy named Kraig. Kraig —*spelled with a K*, he reminded everyone—was the only nicy close to Arf's size, but beneath that sweatshirt was solid muscle. Arf was just mass.

"Yeah," Kraig with a K said. "Good luck."

They shook hands and pretended to introduce each other. Soup insisted they high-five. None of the nicies went along with it. Bryant was the only naughty who had any idea how to play the game. He was lanky with a protruding Adam's apple. His eyes were always a bit too relaxed.

"Good luck, Campbell," Kraig said.

"That's not my name," Soup deadpanned.

Kraig let a dark smile creep under his nose. "Yeah. It is."

"That's not my name."

"Okay, Campbell."

Soup threw snow in his face and charged. Kraig caught him in a headlock and barely moved, laughing as he spun around. Soup threw swings that just bounced. John wrapped his arm around Kraig. Soup's face was blotchy and bright. Kraig laughed hard and loud.

"All right, all right." Jane got between them. "He's just getting under your skin, Soup."

"That's not my name!" Soup pointed. "Say it! Make him say it!"

Kraig threw up his arms in surrender. It was only after John muttered in his ear did he say it. "Sorry."

"That's not my name, say it." Spittle bubbled in the corners of his mouth.

"But—"

John stopped him.

After another quiet conversation, Kraig said, "Okay. That's not your name."

Soup walked off. Jane went with him, but he shrugged her off. Kraig was muttering back to John. Ryder heard him say, "That's his name."

"Just go with it," John said.

When Soup came back, his cheeks were pink, but he'd calmed down. He stared bullets through Kraig. There was a long pause before Kraig offered a hand. John and Jane brokered peace with a brief handshake. Soup wiped his hand on his pants afterwards.

"We're flipping a coin," John said, "to see who gets the ball—"

A chopping sound echoed in the distance and quickly got louder. Everyone turned toward the mountain. Something soared toward them.

"You all right?" Ryder asked.

Soup ignored him. They watched a black helicopter approach. It landed far from the horseshoe. Snow scattered beneath it as the reflective door opened. A big man climbed out and cupped his hands.

"Not without me, you're not!"

It was followed by cheers and an avalanche of nicies. They raced toward the heroic figure with an enormous black dog at his side. He greeted them with hugs. The naughties were out there too, they just didn't beat the nicies to fresh hugs and hearty handshakes.

"I thought he was on the North Pole?" Ryder said.

"That's what he wants you to think." Soup pointed at the mountain. "Most of the time he's over there."

"Where?"

"Other side of the mountain."

"Why?"

Soup shrugged. "Why does he do anything?"

Billy Big Game allowed the drones to capture his confidence from every angle. His eyes were firmly aimed at Ryder, a visual harpoon that stuck him in place, and he marched toward them. His cologne arrived first. Ryder held out his hand.

"I don't know what they told you about family..." He grabbed Ryder's coat and crushed him.

So he is real.

Billy Big Game wasn't an animated hologram. He was an overperfumed lumberjack who laughed while he squeezed him until he couldn't breathe.

"Let me get a look." Billy Big Game was a little misty. "I've been watching you, son. Welcome home."

He hugged him again. Judging by the awkward silence, this didn't usually happen. Ryder wished he'd watched the stream to know if this was normal. The dog sat obediently at his feet, eyes never leaving BG. The teams gathered around. There was no escape.

"Back up." The dog went to the exact spot where he was pointing.

"I've waited a long time for this day," he muttered.

"What day?" Ryder said.

He shook his head. It was like he was talking to someone else, his eyes slightly unfocused. Ryder tried to pull away, but he held him firmly. The drones captured what Ryder assumed would be all over the morning's stream.

He was so wrong.

"Hold out your hand." When Ryder didn't do it, BG grabbed his hand. "It's him, Figgy. Come say hello."

The dog got up and smelled Ryder's hand then licked it. BG looked like he was about to weep. He scrubbed the dog's ears and began laughing then stood up and did it again, only this time it sounded like Christmas.

"Ho! Ho! Ho!"

And then everyone cheered right on cue. The awkwardness dissolved into a less awkward moment of rehearsed laughter and sitcom comradery.

"I have a feeling about this year." BG took the coin from one of the producers. "This might be the year of the naughties."

Boos cascaded from the nicies.

Was he doing this for the stream? Ryder hadn't done anything to deserve this. In fact, everywhere he'd gone had ended in disaster. Why was BG acting like he was a saint?

"Call it!" The coin tumbled high into the air, the dull sunlight glinting off the edges. Bryant elbowed Ryder.

"Heads," Ryder called just before it landed in the snow with a dull thump.

BG leaned over. "Heads!"

The naughties cheered, sort of. The nicies booed. It was like the intergalactic World Series of coin flipping had been decided. Everyone returned to their sidelines. *What just happened?*

Ryder was happy it was over. He was already guaranteed a starring role in the next morning's stream. Now to engage his disappearing powers. Cherry was leaning against the building. He found a spot near her.

BG was on the opposite sideline, log-sized arms crossed over his chest. The dog was at his side. Ryder felt like they were looking at him.

"Good girls and boys," Cherry said, "do what I tell them."

She was looking at BG and his dog.

"Ryder!"

Bryant waved from the middle of the field. Ryder waved back.

"I think he wants you," Cherry said.

Ryder didn't budge. The game was about to start. He was just being friendly. The naughties came for him. They pried him off the wall.

"Stop," he said quietly, hoping Bradley Cooper wasn't recording.

They didn't stop. Unless he went limp like a five-year-old, he had no choice but to go. He trotted out to cheers from the naughties, all because they didn't want to be out there. Ryder joined the huddle.

"Here we go." Bryant told everyone what to do. He diagramed a play in the snow that made no sense. "Ready, break!"

Ryder followed everyone to the football. Bryant pulled him back and whispered, telling him where to stand. "Just run," he said. "Straight."

I can do that. I can run.

Jane followed him to the sidelines. Her hair was tied back. She looked serious and, honestly, a little intimidating. It was the mouthpiece that scared him a little. Crouched, hands up, she didn't take her eyes off him as Bryant shouted nonsense. The ball was hiked.

Ryder hit the ground.

Jane stood over him, teeth clenched and nostrils flaring. He didn't even see it happen. He was supposed to run and she'd driven him into the snow. The little plane was still soaring in the gray sky above her, a black speck far above.

I thought there wasn't supposed to be planes, he thought.

"That's it, Janie!" Kraig barked.

The football was moved back. Bryant called another play; this one he said was a screen. It didn't change what Ryder was doing.

"Run," Bryant said. "That way."

They went backwards again. When the play was over, Arf was standing over one of the nicies. No one could get past him, but it didn't matter. There were too many of them. Jane didn't knock Ryder down, but he couldn't get around her. She had chopped her feet and hand-checked him until the whistle blew. She was surprisingly strong. And the way she was frowning made him uneasy.

One more play.

Just get this one over with and he could double-down on his invisibility powers. Bryant drew a play. They had to go thirty yards for a first down. Ryder didn't know what that meant, but thirty yards was a long ways. And they had been going in the wrong direction, so this was almost over.

Jane was standing far away this time. She was watching Bryant when the ball was hiked. Ryder did what he was told. He started running. Jane turned to run with him.

She couldn't keep up.

Ryder flew past her and the guy behind her. There was a sudden cheer, and he turned around in time to see a big brown object spinning toward him.

It thumped into his stomach.

Ryder cradled the football. He didn't so much catch it as it stuck in his arms. He didn't slow down. His feet kept moving. The wind was in his ears as the cheers pushed him forward. He went past the orange cones and kept going. The nicies had stopped.

The naughties were chasing him now.

It wasn't just the team on the field but everyone on the sidelines, too. They buried him in a dogpile of bodies, smacking his back, grabbing his hair, and screaming his name. He didn't know how this worked, but it couldn't be the end of the game. Arf picked him up and spun him like a figure skater.

Soup was pretend-crying.

Ryder's face hurt. He'd never worn a smile that big. It sketched his cheeks and dried his gums. His chest inflated like a helium balloon. If Arf let go, he'd float through the sky.

Ryder rode Arf's shoulders back to the sidelines, where they were reminded the score was only 7-0. The celebration continued while the game continued.

Cherry was still against the wall. She was looking at him. Not a glance, but actually looking at him.

The nicies scored and no one seemed to care. Ryder was still floating somewhere in the gray sky. He actually wanted to go back out there. All those years he'd made fun of high school pep rallies and it took one touchdown for him to get it.

"You're up." Soup slapped Ryder on the butt. "Win it for the naughties, bo."

He jogged out to cheers and boos. BG was clapping loudly, his hands coming together in huge wallops. Mindy was leaping next to him, her mittened hands barely making a sound. Ryder tried to kill his smile.

"Here we go," Bryant said.

Ryder was going to block Jane or at least try. Arf would come out and pretend to block. Bryant would throw a short pass to Franken, a tall naughty with long hair. It didn't matter if he caught it, because that wasn't the play they were going to score on.

Jane was guarding him. She was more serious, if that was possible —squatting, scowling and bouncing on the balls of her feet.

"We naught, we naughty. We naught, we naughty." Soup was leading a cheer. "You nice, you nicy."

When the ball was hiked, he did like he was told. Jane shoved him down. Snow went up his shirt. When the play was over, Arf helped him back to the huddle, brushing his back.

The second play was a lot like the first—a short pass and nothing. Arf picked up Ryder again and wiped the snow out of his hair. His head was ringing this time. Jane barked like a dog.

Sweet Jane was gone.

"Here we go," Bryant said.

He changed the play. It was genius. The first two plays were setting up the third one. Jane's face was red as coals and not from the cold. Rage melted the snow off her cheeks; it came out in long steamy breaths. She stomped the snow down to bare ground.

"We are naughty; you are nice. We get totaled; you get lice. We eat cake; you get rice. We ride cheetahs; you get mice—"

The ball was snapped.

Ryder pretended to block. Jane pursued the short pass. Arf came around full gait when Franken caught the ball. He took two steps. Just before his flags were stripped, he tossed the football. Jane recognized the play, but it was too late.

She was bounced off the ground.

Arf didn't do it on purpose. His momentum was a fully loaded freight train and she stepped on the tracks. The football sailed over her, but she was seeing stars.

Ryder caught it in stride.

The last thing he saw were the bottoms of Kraig's shoes. He'd tried to cross the tracks like Jane, and Arf the Unstoppable was right on time. Ryder wrapped the football with both hands.

And the naughties came screaming.

Soup led the way and the others trailed behind him. The entire naughty wing was going to form another dogpile. Even Cherry was walking toward them. But Arf wasn't.

He was still on the field.

The nicies had formed a circle around him. They were trying to hold Kraig back. The drones were divebombing, hungry for drama. Arf was all alone while the nicies took turns shoving him.

"Hey!" Ryder shouted.

He ducked around the oncoming naughty avalanche and sprinted up the field. They turned to follow him and saw what was happening. Ryder's face was cold, his chest burning. He pumped his arms and closed the gap just as Kraig tossed John off him. Arf held his hands out, shaking his head. His cheeks were bright red.

"I'm sorry, I'm sorry," he was saying.

Snow still dusted Kraig's uniform. He shoved through two more of his teammates and balled up a fist.

"No!" Ryder jumped on his back. "Leave him—"

Kraig turned his hips and threw an elbow before Ryder could latch his arms around his neck. It caught him in the temple and lit up the sad sky.

A high-pitched whine filled his head.

Lightning flashed behind his eyes. White pain flooded his forehead. Voices went underwater and distant. The ground was below him, but the world shimmered. Dark forms blotted out the dull light.

And then they heard it.

Ryder was looking up from the bottom of a huddle when they all heard it.

Something cried from deep in the trees. It was long and lonesome, starting out low and guttural and peaking with a howl that shook snow from limbs. The hairs on his arms rose. It was an animal, but it wasn't in pain or frightened. Ryder had heard it before.

It's a warning.

Everyone looked at the mountains. The howl went on. And when it stopped, silence grabbed them. BG glanced at the nicies, squinting. He nodded.

John and Jane took off.

The other nicies followed. The drones swarmed in formation, a spearhead soaring for the trees. A few minutes later, the roar of four-wheelers shattered the silence. The nicies roared out of the barn, two on each machine, leaning into the cold wind, some with flags still attached to their waists. BG watched them lay tracks into the forest, snowy rooster tails in their wake.

"What was that?" someone asked.

"Come on," BG said. "Get him inside."

"I'm good." Ryder sat up. The planet was still spinning too fast.

BG put his hand on his shoulder. "Boys, give him a hand."

Arf lifted him up. Ryder stopped him from holding him like a toddler and grabbed his shoulder. His cheek was numb. Pain radiated through his face to the other side of his head. A few molars felt loose.

One at a time, the naughties patted his back and shoulder. Two of the girls hugged him. He was one of them now. It was a touching moment, guaranteed to be mopped up and edited for public consumption. But there were no green eyes in the sky.

We're off stream.

"Everybody inside," BG said. "Free time until dinner."

"Is the game over?" Soup asked. "Did we win?"

The producers kept their distance. BG separated himself from the group, staring at the mountains. The whir of all-terrain motors called from somewhere in the trees.

"We all did."

"What?" Soup said.

But BG wasn't talking to him. He was sort of talking to himself.

Arf kept an arm around Ryder, and the naughties went back to their wing. The secret that Ryder felt was coming to the surface. It had something to do with whatever was out there. It wasn't the pain that bothered Ryder the most or the strange sound. It was the smile crawling across BG's face.

5

Exhaust fumes hung in the trees.

Low branches were knocked clean. Knobby tracks ran through the snow, taillights glowing in the dense canopies. Ahead, all-terrains were parked side by side, engines off.

Billy Big Game stopped in a puddle of sunlight.

Figgy sat next to him, her tongue hanging loosely. Above him, a small gap of gray light punched through the trees. It was wide enough for a turkey vulture to fly through. He searched for tracks. There were no scuff marks on the trunks, no broken branches from a bony rack of antlers.

It's him, my boy.

Sometimes his thoughts were so vivid, his compulsions so strong and undeniable that Billy Big Game heard his thoughts like a whisper. He trusted his thoughts. They were his guide to all his success. No one would doubt that—a half-million-acre ranch, the highest rated stream on the internet, and one of the largest privately funded children homes in the country.

If this was insanity, he was all for it.

It might have been a mistake to let the nicies be so aggressive. His thoughts wanted him to be assertive but patient. He was overwhelmed with excitement and didn't hear what he was thinking. If there were tracks, they might have been trampled by the all-terrains. Still, he had to act quickly before they were gone.

He's still here.

The children were gathered in a straight line. Some were sitting on their vehicles; others standing. All with their backs to him, not hearing him approach. Tracking was a tedious pursuit best done on foot.

He slipped through a narrow gap, putting a hand on their shoulders as he passed. They bowed their heads. John and Jane were at the edge of a clearing. Green-eyes circled overhead. He pulled his favorite ones closer.

"Is everyone here?" He spoke in a low, calm tone.

They nodded. He pursed his lips and surveyed the clearing.

They did good, he heard. *This is where it landed.*

"Send the drones out," Billy Big Game said. "Scan a square mile from the epicenter. No broadcast. I don't want to see this on the stream. I want half of the drones on continuous patrol, rotate to charge. Keep one posted in this clearing at all times."

Even though he was talking to John and Jane, the green-eyes were listening. They scattered when he was done. Blending into the forest, one of them hovered over the center of the clearing. It would record and analyze all activity. If everything went well, the footage would be streamed at a later time.

When I'm ready.

The clearing was buried in a foot of snow. Much of it, though, had been trampled. Several holes were punched into the ground, frozen clods of soil scattered as a result of a heavy impact. Distinct prints were all around.

"My God," he whispered.

A chill hummed in his stomach and raised gooseflesh. Tracks such as these were typically several inches across. These were twice that.

It's him.

Branches had been sheared. Debris was tossed and spread across the snow. It was hard to estimate the size of the rack that had done this damage—trees were stripped all around the clearing—but it was large enough and strong enough to tear through major branches like dry kindling, powered by rage and the instinct to protect.

He won't leave. At least not until Christmas.

"No one enters the clearing until the analysis is complete." He looked at Figgy. When the big furry Newfoundland didn't look back, he checked the phone in his pocket. The battery was low. He opened an app and repeated what he said. Figgy stared back. "Circle around and find a scent. Come back once you have it."

Figgy trotted off with her nose sweeping the ground. She would not enter the clearing. No one had. That was why they were waiting on the perimeter. They were made for this very moment.

They were good boys and girls.

Fifteen years of planning had led to this. Game this size couldn't walk through the forest. The trees grew too close together, the branches too low. But a creature like this didn't need to walk in order to escape.

Billy Big Game looked up.

A weepy sensation quivered beneath his beard. His eyes were steamy and wet. They called him crazy, all these years. No one would believe him. He told the world that all the Christmas legends were true and they laughed.

The irrefutable proof is here.

He walked away and wiped his eyes. The nicies followed him silently. He found Kraig kneeling on his four-wheeler and squeezed the boy's shoulder.

"Well done."

Kraig was steely-eyed and grim. He'd played his part. They all had. Billy Big Game didn't want to harm the boy, just wanted to put him in danger. The boy didn't realize an imminent threat to his well-being was like shooting a flare for help. A flare someone would answer.

And we're ready.

"We have three weeks," Billy Big Game announced. "Go about

your day as usual; be ready for further instructions. And boys and girls, thank you. The day of discovery is near."

He was all weepy again.

It was embarrassing, but sometimes he couldn't control his emotions. They seemed to flow from somewhere deep inside, from the same place his thoughts were born.

We're almost there, my boy.

"It's time to open the game room," he said.

The good boys and girls nodded. They understood what that meant. Time was short. They needed everyone to be on board before Christmas.

No more naughties.

The nicies rode back to the resort, allowing him to process his feelings. John and Jane stayed by his side. They had plenty of time, but this might be their only chance. The trap he'd set fifteen years ago was finally home, a carrot that was finally old enough to dangle. The hook was ready. The game he would capture—the biggest game of all—would not be mounted on the wall. Not this time.

"We'll find him, Father," John said.

Billy Big Game hugged his two favorites of all the favorites then ordered them to return. He would savor this moment alone. The biggest and baddest creature was near. They had three weeks.

It will be the merriest Christmas of all.

6

Don't be nice.

Ryder stared at the bottom of the bunk. His teeth were still loose. Arf was sound asleep—the entire naughty wing was still asleep—but Ryder wasn't hearing snores.

Why was the howl so familiar?

He'd heard it before but thought he'd only imagined it. It was during those times when living was too much—it was bad people and bad situations. He was alone and helpless.

And then I heard it.

BG had heard it before too. Or had he been expecting it? They'd raced after it like a dinner bell. The game had been cancelled for the first time ever. Even the naughties had been surprised it was over. The game was a stream favorite.

Bradley Cooper clicked off the ceiling. The green eye watched him sit on the edge of his bed. It was still dark outside. It was almost five o'clock. He was waking earlier and earlier.

The green eye winked off as he got dressed. He stood in the middle of the room, rubbing his cheek. He didn't like lying in bed. That was when his thoughts took control. Inevitably, they would carry him down rabbit holes with troubling stories at the bottom. It was better to get up, do something. Even if it was just walking around. He grabbed things for a shower.

Somebody was outside.

Cloaked in darkness, he pried the blinds open. Bradley Cooper washed his face in green light. The floodlight on the barn lit the figure from behind. At this time, it was usually someone wearing a cowboy hat and walking with a limp. This wasn't him. This person was smaller than that. Quicker, leaner.

And coming toward the naughty wing.

Ryder threw a towel over Bradley Cooper. There was no doubt he'd get in trouble for that, but the snitch was blowing his cover. And he didn't want to see himself on the stream spying on someone, or someone seeing him spying on them. While his drone struggled to free itself, Ryder threw a blanket over his head.

A light appeared in the person's hands.

It was a quick splash of white light, a square of illumination that was unmistakable. *A phone.* Someone out there had a phone. And something else. *There's no green eye!* Whoever it was didn't have a drone. Even BG had an eye on him. Everybody belonged to the stream. Except for the old man with the cowboy hat.

And whoever that is.

Bradley Cooper dropped on the floor and slid out from the towel. The green eye was flashing in his face. Ryder dropped the blanket and watched the figure sneak around the end of the building. He threw the blanket, but Bradley Cooper was ready for it this time and followed Ryder into the hall.

It was silent and dark.

There was no music whispering behind doors, not a creature stirring. The job board was illuminated with the day's schedule. Soup and Arf were on snow shovels in the morning and study hours in the afternoon. Ryder's name was near the bottom.

Introspection.

The hallway suddenly felt cold, the hard floor beneath his feet falling away. His stomach dropped. He didn't know what introspection was, just how Arf had looked. It felt like those moments in the doctor's waiting room.

Something metallic snapped.

It was in Cherry's room. Objects shuffled around and slid across the floor. It was quiet for a few minutes; then music began. It didn't sound like she was crawling out of bed. More like she was rearranging the room.

The door handle turned. Ryder jumped back, heart hammering. Spicy incense wafted out of the widening crack, music spilling out. He was staring.

They were both startled.

Cherry leaped back. She was fully dressed—jeans and a sweatshirt and stocking cap with a towel over her shoulder. Her socks wagged on the ends of her feet, with icy snow crystals stuck to them.

It was her. And she has a phone!

Ryder peeked inside her room. The window was closed. Her coat was on the floor along with rubber boots. Snow was packed on the soles.

"What are you doing?" Ryder whispered.

Momentary panic transformed into irritability. "Meditating."

She was lying, it was obvious. Her drone dipped through the doorway and floated next to Bradley Cooper. Hers was identical—the eye green and body round—except for the stain on the belly. It was an ink blot. She crossed her arms and shifted her weight.

"Why?" he said.

"Clarity."

He shook his head. That wasn't what he was asking and she knew it.

"I *meditate* to clear my mind." She widened her eyes. *Get it?*

She knew he knew. He couldn't flat out ask why she was outside or why she had a phone or why her drone wasn't with her. They were on the stream now. He wasn't going to ruin whatever she was doing, so all he could ask was why. She answered him with her eyes and flicked a glance at the job board.

"Good luck."

Ryder watched her walk to the bathroom with her drone in tow. It waited for her in the hall while she showered. Cold panic collared him again.

Introspection.

❄

ARF WAS AWAKE.

Ryder returned from the shower to find his oversized roommate slumped on his bed. His hair—spread in a bedhead cowlick—brushed the underside of the top bunk, where Soup was curled up. His thick lips hung loose and open.

"You're too small to fight," he said.

Ryder finished putting on socks and boots, drying his hair with a towel before covering his head with a stocking cap. Arf's eyes were heavy and slow, his cheeks splotchy.

"You all right?" Ryder asked.

They sat across from each other. Ryder was trying to decide if he'd looked that sullen and spacy before introspection.

"What'd they do to you?" Ryder asked.

He shrugged and looked off. He wasn't focusing on anything, wandering through the fog of sleep, where thoughts weaved a comforting spell. If Ryder nudged him, he would probably fall over and begin snoring. Arf never woke up before the sun.

"I had a dog," he muttered distantly.

He drifted into his thoughts again. Maybe he was sleeptalking, had been ever since Ryder got back from the showers. Their drones hovered off to the side. He never should've dressed. It was easier to be half naked with the guarantee of not being on the stream.

"Arf—"

"Her name was Happy. She would chase us around the backyard and sometimes bite. It didn't hurt, though. It was just… what she did. It was how we played."

He smacked his lips. They were dry and gummy. He swallowed a couple of times, breathing through his mouth.

"The mom had one bike for all of us. We would take turns riding around the block. That was all we could do, ride around the block and switch off. Happy would follow and nip at my shoe when I got too close to the road."

He wiped his face and sniffed.

"I didn't mean it. It was an accident. I-I-I…"

"It's all right." Ryder stood up. The drones swerved around him, so he threw the blanket over them and twisted the bottom. They began beeping. Soup rolled over.

"What are you doing?" he said. "I'm sleeping."

"Can we turn these things off?"

"What? No. Take your clothes off before they explode."

"Turn off your ears."

Soup slammed the pillow over his head and sighed. Ryder let the drones loose. They fired out like hornets, eyes blinking red. They spun around until they were green and aimed at Arf. He was still sitting up but wilting.

The sun was coming up. The morning light was bleached and dim, casting gray bars through the blinds.

Ryder lay down and closed his eyes.

He wasn't tired, but he stayed like that until the room began to quake. Arf had dripped onto his mattress and was ripping air. Whatever he was talking about had come from introspection. Something had happened to the dog. Whatever it was, he didn't want it on the stream.

Neither did Ryder.

He threw on his winter gear and looked through the blinds. No one was outside. It would be hours before they were awake, and he didn't want to spend that much time with his thoughts. The bedroom was too small for that.

He stopped outside Cherry's room and listened. It smelled like incense, but there was no music. If he knocked, she wouldn't answer.

He went outside.

Bradley Cooper felt less oppressive with the big sky over him. There were no planes streaking overhead. There wasn't supposed to be. His footsteps broke through a thin crust of snow. Soft powder fell in his boots. There were a few lights in the nicy wing. Vague shadows moved inside.

Tiny green lights were in the distance.

They looked out from the trees like one-eyed creatures, hovering in and out of the forest. They were never out this early or that far from Kringletown.

There were still fresh footsteps in the field. The prints left behind zigzagging bars from the bottoms of rubber boots that went around the naughty wing. Ryder kept walking, not paying any attention to them. If he followed them, they would end at Cherry's window. And Bradley Cooper would see them.

Then the rest of the world.

Instead, he followed them to the barn. The horses were in the paddock. A few were lingering at the fence, snorting humid breath through flared nostrils, bobbing their heads as Ryder neared. Cherry's tracks puddled next to the fence, where she must have pet them.

All-terrain vehicle tracks lined the snow. They had emerged from the side of the barn when the game was interrupted. Their knobby tires had beaten down the snow. None of them were fresh, though. This was yesterday's marauding.

He stopped in the breezeway.

The concrete was slick. He almost went down, waving his arms to keep his balance. Horses were in the stalls to his right, heads out and staring. They looked expectant, hungry. There were no horses on the left side of the breezeway. Those doors were closed. One set was big enough to accommodate a big rig truck. It wasn't secured with a padlock. There wasn't even a handle.

He didn't know how it opened.

Light flooded out of the last door down the breezeway. The room was open. The horses whinnied as Ryder peeked inside. Barrels of feed were open. Shelves were full of spray bottles and books. Saddles and tack hung next to an empty rack. It looked like a gun cabinet.

One weapon was inside it.

The stock was short and the barrel wide. Ryder had never seen a shotgun before, but he'd played enough video games to identify every weapon used in warfare.

That was not one of them.

It looked more like something from the future than it did from modern warfare, the kind that shot lasers and went *pew-pew*.

"What're you doing?"

Ryder spun around with his heart in his throat. A silhouette was in the breezeway. Ryder shaded his eyes from the tack room's light. The figure started toward him. Ryder couldn't make out the details, but he recognized the gait.

Kraig with a K was wearing sweatpants under his coat.

"You got permission to be out here?" he said.

Bradley Cooper hovered over Ryder's shoulder. They both watched the stout nicy. There was no drone behind him. Ryder, for once, was grateful Bradley Cooper was there. He balled a fist at his side.

"What are *you* doing out here?" he said.

"Checking on the horses." Kraig stopped short of the tack room and held out his hand. "And to apologize. Yesterday got out of hand. No one likes to lose. We all get a little jacked up during the big game. You're new, so now you know. Just want to say sorry."

Ryder hesitated. It seemed like a bad idea to shake his hand, but the drone was watching. He reached out and immediately regretted it. Kraig's grip ground his knuckles like marbles. His smile grew as his grip tightened. When Ryder tried to let go, he yanked him closer. A white film was in the corners of his mouth.

"I don't care how fast you can run," he whispered, "you're still one of them."

Still grinning, he flicked a glance over Ryder's shoulder. Bradley Cooper was hovering near his ear, but something was missing.

The green light is off.

"You're a misfit," Kraig said.

His white smile opened up. The white film stretched between his lips.

The horses were getting noisy, stamping their hooves. Ryder

grabbed his wrist and tried to pry it out of the bear trap. Pain knifed across his hand. Instinctively, he reached back to throw a punch at Kraig's square jaw—

"Pops!" Kraig shouted. "At it early this morning?"

Ryder's hand came free, and he nearly went down on the slick concrete. The old man was in the breezeway. His coat was thick and dusted with snow. The cowboy hat was frayed on the rim. The old man's ears were as red as the knob of his nose. He sniffed hard and spit a glob of tobacco in the snow.

"Got a naughty here who would love to help shovel a stall," Kraig said. "Nothing like the smell of horse crap in the morning."

He swatted Ryder between the shoulder blades and laughed. Pops carried two empty buckets into the tack room without even a grunt. He smelled like old leather, his eyes as gray as the sky.

Kraig winked before hustling back the way he had come. The snow was packed around his slippers.

The old man came out of the tack room with four stainless steel buckets hooked over his arms. The horses whinnied. Without looking at Ryder, he took them out to the paddock, where the rest of the herd was waiting. A squirt of dark spit shot out from beneath his hat.

Ryder decided not to hang around.

His hand was throbbing. He followed the smooth prints of Kraig's slippers out of the breezeway. Head down, he slowed as he passed the giant hangar doors that didn't have handles. Kraig had stomped through another set of tracks. It was two prints aimed at the locked doors. One was going inside, the other was coming out. He'd seen the prints of these soles already.

And the boots they belonged to.

7

Cherry was assigned to kitchen chores. At least, that was what was on the board. She wasn't in the kitchen, though. Ryder went to her room and knocked.

She didn't answer.

What was she doing in the breezeway? How did she get a phone? Why was her drone turned off? Ryder had so many questions, but oddly enough wondered, *Why doesn't she have roommates?*

Ryder went back to his bedroom and stared at the ceiling. There wasn't a time scheduled for the introspection. *They come for you,* was all Soup said. Butterflies nibbled holes in his stomach. It was almost lunch, but he wasn't going to eat until this was over.

Music bumped from down the hall, and engines roared in the horseshoe. The doors on the barn were open. Four-wheelers filed out one after another. The nicies, dressed in matching winter gear, started for the mountains, snow rooster-tailing off the back tires.

He flipped open his laptop and clicked the stream. He had been avoiding it, but felt himself more entangled with the drama. *I am the drama.* The stream started with a close-up on the trophy and all the hype. The nicies were practicing, and the naughties were throwing snowballs. Cut to Soup leading them in a chorus line with leg kicks.

Nicies mugged for the camera. "We're going to hurt them."

A few minutes later, Ryder scored a touchdown. He only wished there was a close-up of Kraig's face.

"You were intense." Cut to John and Jane.

"I don't like to lose," Jane said. "Neither do you."

"Because I don't lose."

The two debated the following plays then went silent when the flea-flicker happened. Ryder was too fast.

"He's a ringer," John said. "We weren't ready."

"You think that's why BG came back?" Jane asked.

"Nothing he does is an accident."

The stream focused on Soup crying tears of hysterical joy. The shoving started in the background. The nicies surrounded Arf, and Ryder was running toward them. Kraig pushed Arf with two hands just as Ryder leaped.

"We shouldn't have cancelled the game," Jane said.

"Little man gave us no choice. If he hadn't attacked Kraig, we would've won. How many times were they going to run the same play?"

Ryder rubbed his jaw as Kraig's elbow slammed into him.

"That's what you get," John added.

He paused the stream. It didn't look as bad as it felt, but that wasn't what caught his attention. He bounced the stream back several seconds and played it again. All the attention was on Kraig leaning into Arf. The other nicies were egging him on. Except John.

He had been watching Ryder approach.

His lips were moving as he got closer. Ryder played that snippet over ten times before he figured out what he was saying.

Here he comes.

He wasn't warning Kraig. He was updating him. Kraig turned at the last second and drove his elbow into the side of Ryder's face.

It was a setup.

"We're sore losers," Jane said.

"We're competitive. That's why we play the game. There are

consequences. Hurt one of us and we hurt you back. And if you jump on Kraig, there's a lesson in that too."

Ryder went over Kraig's back, catching the elbow and bouncing in a puff of snow. And then the four-wheelers were crossing the yard. An earlier cut of the naughties' snowball fight was followed by nicies walking through the woods.

"When's the last time we hiked like that?" Jane said.

The last time we hiked?

Scenic shots panned across the valley and down through the trees, the breathtaking visuals that made the stream so popular. There was no roar of an animal or the obsessive pursuit. It looked like a wonderful day in the trees. No mention of anything that had happened after Ryder was body slammed.

Like the game was cancelled for a hike.

Ryder replayed the incident three more times. He stopped just as the four-wheelers roared out of the barn. The final frame captured a blurry figure standing in the breezeway. His cowboy hat was turned toward the mountains.

This wasn't about football.

They had been ready to roll. The four-wheelers had been lined up and waiting. BG had smiled and nodded when the animal roared.

He shut the laptop and leaned back. It was hard to remember much of his life. No one remembered anything when they were little, but Ryder couldn't remember most things.

He was trying to forget his life.

A torn edge of paper curled from beneath the laptop. He hadn't seen that before sitting down. He laced his fingers behind his head and looked up.

Bradley Cooper was watching.

Ryder sat forward and opened the laptop again, sweeping the note into his palm. He waited a few minutes before holding it against his chest. The drone didn't move. He didn't bother taking off his shirt, simply glanced down. The note was written on the back of the same red wrapping paper with golden bells and green holly leaves. He cupped it like a poker player.

WHAT ARE YOU HIDING?

He had to read it again, pulling it closer to make sure he was seeing it correctly. There was some mistake. The first note was slightly cryptic, mostly threatening. This one was stupid. Ryder wasn't hiding anything. If anyone was hiding something, it was everyone at Kringletown.

"Ready?"

Ryder actually yipped. He spun around and crumpled the note in his palm. Jane was in the doorway.

"Impressive day yesterday," she said. "I didn't know you were that fast."

He tried to say something. Sweat was on his forehead.

"You ready to talk?" she said.

"About what?"

Her smile grew wider. "Introspection? You were supposed to meet us ten minutes ago. Come on."

She waited for him to put on a sweatshirt. He pretended to check his pockets, shoving the note to the bottom. Later, he would tear it into tiny pieces and throw them in three different trash cans.

❄

"Merry Christmas!" Jane waved at naughties looking out from their rooms. "Remember the door contest, everyone! Supplies are in the craft room. The winner with the most festive door gets to draw twice from the tree."

The naughties watched him follow her off the wing like the prisoner of a county fair beauty queen. The music changed as they turned the corner. Old-fashioned Christmas music filled the halls. Garland hung from the ceiling along with ornaments and endless strands of lights. Jane sang along as her sharp shoes tapped the hard floor.

"So you've never played football?" She hooked her arm around his elbow. "Amazing what talents we hide."

"Where we going?"

"A chat, that's all. I don't know what the others told you, but it's not going to hurt, I promise. You look nervous."

She squeezed his arm and pulled him closer. Their drones floated ahead, green eyes aimed back. This charming shot would make tomorrow's stream, and he didn't want to see it. Everything they did went through the filter of how it was going to look. All this space and he felt more trapped than any house he'd ever lived in.

What are you hiding?

They made several turns down halls Ryder had yet to see, doors that were closed and probably locked. He wasn't sure he could find his way back. They ended up somewhere near the front of Kringletown. He recognized the foyer. Jane opened the office door, where he'd arrived on the first day.

It looked the same—the pictures of BG, the glassy-eyed looks from stuffed heads—with the addition of blinking lights and a fully dressed Christmas tree.

"BG is camping." Jane pointed at the empty desk. "We'll see him at fireside tomorrow."

"You mean hunting?"

"Not like that." She glanced at the drones, a discussion that wouldn't make the stream because no one heard the howl. The viewers thought they went on a hike. "We like to know what's out there. Don't you?"

Jane went to a door on the right side of the office. Despite the festive decorations, this one was plain and empty. She stepped aside and gestured. There was a large fireplace with a roaring fire. Shelves lined the walls with old books. In the center, there were three fat chairs.

John in one of them.

Jane took his hand. The drones didn't follow. She stood behind one of the empty chairs. Ryder didn't move. The lighting was as warm as the room, contrasting with Arctic-themed paintings on the walls.

"BG is a little obsessed with the Pole," John said. "You'll understand soon enough."

Ryder was looking at the books, not the paintings. There were so many of them. He wondered if any of them had been opened since they were put there.

"Please, sit." She patted the chair. "I promise, we're just going to talk. Maybe not even that."

"What are we doing?" Ryder asked.

"This is an opportunity to know yourself," John said. "We all have physical needs, which BG provides. But we also have emotional and spiritual needs that can only be fulfilled by our own selves. The world is changed one person at a time. Introspection starts with you."

"Then why do I need you?"

"We're guides, that's all," Jane said. "Please, sit."

Ryder eventually sank into the soft cushion. The arms hugged him from both sides. The fire popped an ember against the steel curtain.

"Water?" Jane got up before he answered and put a bottle on the table. Then she opened a small container that looked like it might hold an engagement ring. "These are readers. They'll record your brain waves. We find it useful to see how you experience emotions."

They were white discs the size of dimes. Jane stuck one on each of her temples.

"See?" she said.

"No."

"Trust us, Ryder. We're here to help."

"Like during the game?"

"Sometimes help means to challenge," John said. "Growth requires pushing you into places you don't want to go. This isn't a vacation, Ryder."

"You mean like slamming my head on the ground."

"You charged Kraig. You can't put your hand in fire and not expect to get burned."

They were hiding something, not Ryder. *And they want me to trust them?*

"It's all right." Jane put the readers away. "We don't have to use these."

Ryder watched her slowly sink into the chair, realizing his chair had slowly formed around him. He wiggled about and the cushion adjusted to a new position. It was the most comfortable thing he'd ever been on.

Jane and John rested their hands on their laps in a funny way. The backs of their left hands lay flat and their right hands on top. The ends of their thumbs were touching. They looked at Ryder, not smiling. Not blinking. Very relaxed, very patient.

"What are you doing?" Ryder said.

"Just being here, that's all. Take a deep breath, draw deeply through your nose." Jane demonstrated an inhale and let it leak out. "Try it, Ryder. You can keep your eyes open if you want."

They continued deep breathing. Ryder looked around for drones or any sign of a recording device. He did not want this on the stream. Jane pursed her lips on the exhale.

"Don't be anywhere but here," she said. "Sink into who you are."

They took two more deep breaths, and Ryder went along with them. If this was all there was, it was no big deal. He could breathe.

"If a memory presents itself, let it be there," she said. "The self has amazing wisdom. You don't need us."

In.

"Let your own self move you. You don't have to speak. Just be here."

Out.

"Be with it."

Ryder felt himself sinking into the chair while they continued. The fire popped a little louder. It felt like he was sitting closer to the heat. Their eyes were closed. He was feeling a little sleepy. If he closed his eyes, he might catch a nap.

How would they know I was sleeping?

"I'm seven, I think," John said.

The words jolted Ryder. The chair adjusted to the tension rippling through him.

"I'm wearing... footy pajamas," he continued. "I think I'm too old for them, but I like them. They're red and fuzzy and my big toes stick through holes. My throat is sore."

He swallowed.

"My sheets... they're too thin for winter. I can hear a pot stirring and go into the kitchen. My nana is making spaghetti. My papa is at a small table. He's eating tamales. I sit in the chair across from him. It's hard against my back. He shares a tamale with me. The sauce is..." He licked his lips. "It's tangy. I eat with him and count pennies and help him wrap them."

John's voice was shrinking. It was small and frail. A twitch pulled the corner of his mouth.

"Mom's at the door. Papa talks to her, and I stand behind Nana. She holds a big spoon, sauce dripping on the floor. They start yelling, and I'm holding onto her muumuu..."

He clawed at the armchair fabric. Shoulders tensing. Legs shaking. His breathing was shallow. Minutes passed before he took a deep breath, letting it flow through pursed lips.

"Thank you, John," Jane said quietly. "Do you need anything?"

He shook his head. Their eyes were closed. They didn't turn to Ryder or ask him to share or come up with something. Ryder was buzzing with comfort. John's relaxation invaded the room. They took several more breaths.

Ryder was dripping into the cushions.

The chair held him. The fire rocked him. The breathing soothed him. He remembered how good it felt to be buried in blankets on a winter night. There was the time he stayed at Aunt Fran's house. She wasn't his aunt, but she didn't want to be called foster mom.

Aunt Fran kept the house cold at night. A glass of water would have ice crystals near the window. Ryder loved it, though. He would climb under the couch cushions and breathe through a little opening. Sometimes Aunt Fran didn't know he was there and sit on him. She'd let out a laugh and he would too.

Everyone laughed when Aunt Fran laughed.

On Wednesday nights, she would go bowling. Jesse was queen of the house on Wednesday nights. She would put Ryder to bed and talk on the phone. She was too old to be living at home, Aunt Fran would say.

One night, Ryder snuck out of his bedroom while she was in the shower and snuggled into the couch cushions. She came out wearing a robe and almost sat on him. He was going to scare her, when someone knocked on the door.

Aunt Fran didn't like David.

He wore T-shirts and ripped jeans and wouldn't amount to anything. Ryder could smell smoke and saw them on the back porch. He was going to run for his bedroom when they came back in. He could hear them breathing heavily.

He curled up and hugged himself.

He was almost asleep when Jesse started crying, and David was yelling. Something broke. He got louder and another thing broke. Then Jesse fell.

Ryder jumped out.

There was weird stuff on the table that smelled funny and pieces of a glass on the floor. David was sweaty and his eyes were big. The white parts went all the way around them. His mustache twitched. Ryder was in trouble.

So he ran.

"Get back here," David yelled.

Ryder ran into the backyard and crawled under the bushes. There were footsteps behind him and bad words. The streetlight wasn't working. It was dark behind the bushes. Ryder ran around the barn and squatted behind a stack of hay bales. The moonlight cast his shadow on the ground.

The woods weren't far away. The trees reached for him with crooked arms and dark faces. There was a fort in there, but he'd never gone to it at night. It was better if he stayed there until Aunt Fran was home.

"Ryder," David sang, "come out, buddy."

A phone light swept from side to side and stopped before coming around the corner. David was looking through the window. If he went inside the barn, Ryder would run for the fort.

Then a tree suddenly broke.

It sounded like a branch exploding or a tree falling. The light swung toward the forest.

"Ryder?"

There was nowhere to go. David would see him if he ran now. He felt frozen, trapped. Helplessly, he watched the light come around the corner. At the same time, a warm breeze blew down on him. It was humid and grassy.

A shadow blotted out the moonlight.

David came around the corner. The phone tumbled out of his hand, light flickering up his body, and the look on his face—

"No!" Ryder jerked out of the chair's embrace.

Panting, sweat trickled down his cheek. His eyes were wide open. He was seeing books and paintings and walls, not the barn or the trees or David.

"It's all right." Jane leaned forward. "You're safe, Ryder."

He couldn't get enough air. The room was too small, too constricted. He wanted to run and hide.

"Whatever happened," she said softly, "let it go. It doesn't own you. The memory has presented itself. It's in the light." She brushed his hair. "Let it go."

Ryder didn't know if it was a memory. It seemed so real, but how could he forget something like that? He remembered Aunt Fran and Jesse and even David. And the reason why he had to leave the house. It had something to do with that night. They'd found David with all those broken bones.

What happened?

Jane gave him a bottle of water. He drank half of it. She sat down and watched him settle. They didn't ask him to breathe deep or close his eyes. They just sat in the room until all was normal.

"Time's almost up," she said. "You've recovered a part of yourself. You know more about your true nature and your purpose."

Purpose?

They held out their hands. Ryder allowed them to pull him up. His legs were weak. He wanted a hug but wouldn't admit it.

"Do you want me to walk you back?" Jane asked.

He shook his head. It would be better if no one was with him. Besides, he could take his time and get to a bathroom. He didn't want to cry in front of anyone.

Especially the drones.

They said goodbye and thanked him. He left without a word and got lost. Bradley Cooper showed him the way back. The perspiration on his brow had cooled. He wiped his forehead to put his stocking cap on and felt something strange. His temples were sticky and tender. He felt a spot on each one.

They were about the size of a dime.

8

The sun hangs like an ornament.

The rays sparkle on the thinning ice shelf where frisky reindeer prance. The youngsters duck their heads, budding antlers clattering as they fight for a broken strap. Bells ring as Dancer and Cupid tug until Dunder crashes between them.

They give chase.

Dunder's belly swells up. His stomach gurgles like a coffee machine, gathering helium in a specialized bladder. He leaps over the herd, clearing them by ten feet or more.

Gallivanter watches from an open lead.

He sits on an icy ledge, swishing his feet like paddles in the frigid ocean, chunks of ice swirling in the eddies. He strokes long braids dangling from his chin. Thick brows shade his eyes as the littlest of the herd picks himself up and shakes off the snow.

When the herd gathers in a scrum, there's no space for the little one. Once he slips between Comet's back legs only to catch a hoof between the eyes. He rolls like a snowball, head over hooves, shakes off and tries again. While the others sport juvenile antlers, his are nubs. Still, he lowers his head.

Blixem tosses him aside.

A group of elven watches from the other side of the reindeer game. Gallivanter wonders if they've ever determined an official word for that. Would it be a web of elven? A meld? A collective mind hive?

There's a synergy that develops when elven gather. Gallivanter has experienced it many times, but being one of the elders bestows a certain predilection toward independence. He likes solitude more than the rest.

Gallivanter the Wanderer.

Each time the little one is thrown, Gallivanter feels the glances slide his way. They grunt and stew in judging silence. Gallivanter kicks the water. Even when Prancer romps over the runt, eliciting a yelp, he doesn't react. The little one never stops when they play, even when his lips bleed or his hide is torn.

He goes harder.

Gallivanter pretends not to notice one of the elven split from the others. Belle slides on one foot with her hands laced on her belly. Long blond braids drag the snow behind her. She drops on the ice shelf next to him and dips her toes.

"This is a mistake," Belle says. "He's not developing, Gallivanter. They're not accepting him."

It's Gallivanter's turn to grunt.

"Your intentions are good, but we need to consider reverting him back to nature. It's not too late to reintroduce him to a herd."

Reverting him.

He'd been questioned when he brought the runt back to the colony. He had intervened with the course of nature. When he suggested genetically modifying him to fold him into the herd, there was almost a revolt.

Creating the herd had sent a ripple of controversy through the colony. If they were to remain neutral in nature, modifying their DNA seemed to oppose that oath. But the world had changed, some argued. The herd would give them the advantage of flight. It wouldn't be long before humans learned to fly. The invention of flight wasn't far away, and these reindeer had been rejected or abandoned by their herds.

There were only supposed to be eight.

Gallivanter's long-standing status allowed the unusual request of *adding a ninth reindeer on a trial basis. Perhaps his emotions were getting the best of him. After all, Belle is right.*

The runt isn't keeping up.

She returns to the group of handlers and their evaluating glares, leaning together to pass along their judgments. But they don't see what he sees. It's not that the herd knocks the little one about until he's bloody and bruised, or that he can't quite leap or his antlers are still so small. None of that is what makes him special.

It's that he keeps getting up.

The bedroom was different.

Blinding stripes of light fell over Ryder's face. It was morning. And the sun was up. It was the longest he'd slept. And something else. The room was silent.

Soup and Arf were gone.

Their beds were made. A note was on the floor. It was torn from a spiral-bound notebook. He looked around and quickly snatched it up but not before Bradley Cooper fell off the ceiling. There was no use hiding it.

Get your beauty sleep.

Soup's handwriting. They were already off for chores. Ryder's name must not be on the board or they would've woken him. Or maybe they tried. His head was a concrete block. He dropped back on the pillow and closed his eyes. Something spoiled and ugly was sitting in his stomach.

That memory.

It was so far away. They'd tricked him into remembering it. He was even doubting it, but Aunt Fran was real. So was David. *How did I forget that?*

But there was more. It was the way John and Jane were acting. Like they'd pried open his head and peeked inside. *No, it was what she said. You have a purpose. A purpose. What did that mean?*

He took a shower to wash off the feelings. He didn't sit down when he was done, kept moving to keep ahead of the thoughts. He went outside and walked until he was in the trees. Bradley Cooper was joined by a drone patrolling the woods.

Ryder kept moving.

He stayed out of sight, stayed boring. There was no reason this would be on the feed. He focused on the dream, occupying his mind with the vivid details that were so clear and familiar. He dreamed of elven, knew their names.

And reindeer.

Dreams were strange, but this played like a movie. *Not a movie. A memory.* Everyone knew the reindeer and the games they played. But the dream kept getting wrestled out of the spotlight by what had happened in *introspection*—the dark trees, the sound of David's bones, the smell damp and furry. Because that wasn't a dream.

That was a memory.

❄

"Where you been?" Bits of sugar cookie shot from Soup's lips. "Arf's worried."

It was a big room with a high ceiling. A flock of drones floated through an elaborate chandelier. Skylights were illuminated on the domed ceiling, but that wasn't sunlight filling the room. Ryder had taken the elevator down three stories.

A fireplace warmed the room. The naughties were sitting on the floor or lying on sofas with cups of soda and cookies. The nicies were on the other side of the room, wearing matching uniforms—the boys in ties and girls in skirts—with the Kringletown logo on the front. They sat on chairs and divans with little plates of cookies.

"Your bestie saved you a seat." Soup waved at Kraig. He didn't wave back. "I think he wants to eat you."

"You okay?" Arf asked.

Ryder rubbed his temples. They were sensitive, like he was scratching his brain with a wool pad. Ryder scanned the crowd. Cherry was tucked in the corner, sitting behind a lamp. She was cross-legged on the floor.

"This thing isn't going to start for a while," Soup said. "I got to whiz."

The hall was cool and humid, the kind of cold that bypassed a sweatshirt and sank directly into bone. Their drones tagged along. They didn't drift inside the bathroom, the only place they were guaranteed not to make the stream. *It doesn't mean they aren't listening.*

"Sorry," Soup said, "I got a number two."

He locked himself in a stall. His belt hit the floor. The drones would hear the noises outside the door. Ryder splashed his face with water and examined the sides of his head. He felt different. There were no visible marks, no proof Jane had put those disks on him.

But she did.

"It feels weird," Arf said, "doesn't it?"

"She put them on you?" Ryder said. "I told her not to…"

"Ha-ha-ha!" Soup barked. "You really thought because you asked them not to do something they wouldn't do it. You're funny."

Ryder paced the length of the bathroom. He was infected with restlessness and anxiety. Arf had just looked gutted when he got back. Ryder wanted to rip something off the wall.

"What do they do?" Ryder said. "The disks."

The toilet flushed. Soup pulled the door open and looked at Ryder's reflection. "They suck out your thoughts. They're making copies of all the things you forgot. That's why you remember."

"That's impossible."

"Open your eyes, man. This is Kringletown. Billy goes big or goes home. He's got things in the hizzy no one in the world has seen. You don't think he can pull a few thoughts out of your head? Please. That's not even a secret. You can see him do that on the stream, how he networks brain waves with a computer. He already did it when he worked at the one place. Right, Arf? How do you think he affords this crazy town?"

Arf nodded along, mouth open. Eyes liquid.

"He patented the brain-to-computer interface. Yeah, wrap your noodle around that. Your brain, your computer." He laced his fingers. "Linked. The new age is here, and Big Billy is leading the charge. You're standing in the middle of it. Awesome, right?"

"Why?"

"Because I won't let them." He got quiet and scrubbed his hands. "You watch what happens when they put my name on introspection. Sweet Jane and Jocko Johnny will have to rope me like a steer."

There were things in his past he didn't want to remember. Things that had to do with his name. *Your name is Campbell.*

"No, I mean why are they doing it?"

"Who knows why he does anything. Seriously." Soup shot a wadded paper towel at the trash and missed. "All I know is that introspection turns you nice. That's how all them got over there; they went to intro and came out moonbeaming. Not us, though. Naughty for life."

Arf and Soup slapped hands. It was complicated and ended with *weeeeeee.*

"Good girls and boys do what I tell them," Ryder muttered.

"That's what I'm talking about." Soup raised his hand. Ryder left him hanging. "That's all the Big Game wants is a bunch of robot yes-boys and girls who do what he tells them. That's what he calls nice, bo. That's what he calls 'good.'" He added air quotes.

"That's what Cherry said," Ryder said. "Good girls and boys do what I tell them."

"Well, she should know—wait, you talked to her?"

"No, she just, uh, I heard her say it."

Soup and Arf wanted more details.

"It doesn't make sense," Ryder said.

"Her not talking to you?" Soup said. "Makes total sense."

"No, why the stream? I mean, if he's up to something, why so public, you know? He's putting everything out there. Everyone's going to see it. Doesn't make sense, you know?"

"Because he's a genius. I am not a genius, so I don't know why he does any of this. He's also crazy. He believes in Santa Claus, you know that, right? Enough said, but there's more. He thinks they're related."

Ryder stopped pacing.

"For reals," Soup said. "Billy Sinterklaas? It's Belgian or something, supposed to be where Santa Claus is from. He thinks he's a great-great-uncle or something. Get that. And he wants the whole world to believe it."

Something started beeping outside the door followed by tapping. The drones were banging on it. They were being called.

"Tell him not to worry his pretty little head, Arf."

The big guy started for the door without a response.

"None of this makes sense," Soup continued. "That stupid football game, you think that's normal? The wookie screaming in the woods and the way all the nicies wet their pants on four-wheelers? The way Billy looks at you?"

Ryder frowned. "You saw that?"

"The way he looked at you? Bo, I told you. He loves you. You're some kind of golden child. He almost giggles when he looks at you. Serious, it's weird, bo. Like Kringletown weird."

What does this have to do with me?

Arf waited with his hand on the door. Soup took one more shot at the trash can and pretended like he made it.

"And wait till you hear what's next," he said. "You'll see."

"What are we doing?"

"The chat? Oh, right. You don't watch. Let me tell you a secret: it's for the stream." Soup threw his arm over Ryder's shoulders and whispered, "It's all for the stream."

Arf opened the door and Soup screamed he wasn't decent. The drones stared with unblinking green eyes as he pretended to cover up. The beeping grew louder. Producers were calling.

"He really believes in Santa?" Ryder said.

Another shot and another miss. "What do you think?"

❄

Jane and John were at the fireplace with three producers fussing over a rocking chair. A polar bear was spread on the floor, including claws and a snarling head. Ryder hid behind Arf while Soup pillaged the cookie trays.

"Put these in your pockets."

Ryder ignored him. He wasn't hungry. More importantly, no one had noticed him.

"Here's the deal." Soup leaned in with a mouthful of crumbs. "Once big daddy gets the crazy train going, don't laugh or roll your eyes. It won't make the stream if you do, but I guarantee we'll end up shoveling the stalls for a month. Maybe not you, the golden child. But me, the deaf runt. Def."

"Ho-ho!" BG raised his arms. "Merry Christmas, children!"

"All aboard." Soup immediately rolled his eyes.

Everyone else cheered as he made his way around the room, hugging and shaking hands and high-fiving, stopping to ask someone how homework was going or how a toothache was feeling. He seemed to know specifics, too. With the reddish beard and bold stature, he looked plenty jolly.

Maybe he is related.

Cherry was sitting on the floor. She had moved behind a lamp so that most of the room couldn't see her. Her ink-spotted drone hovered over her like a rain cloud.

"Hey, speedy." He rubbed Ryder's head. "Who knew he was a football star, huh? Who knew?"

Soup raised his hand.

The producers moved the rocking chair as BG neared, moving it a little farther from the fire. Thirty-one stockings hung from the mantel, each with a name written with sparkly letters. They were all the same size, same color.

"Where you going?" Soup said.

Ryder was moving across the back of the room, stepping over people and squeezing between chairs until he made it to the corner. All the attention was on BG plopping into the rocking chair as Ryder sat on the floor. Cherry pulled her legs into a pretzel.

She looked annoyed.

Jane presented BG with a gift bag. "Look at that!" He raised a plastic pipe. "How'd you know?"

Everyone clapped. He leaned back in the rocker and planted the pipe between his lips, pretending to blow rings toward circling drones. Jane and John stood at his sides like helpers.

"I know what you're doing," Ryder whispered.

Cherry shot him a look. He didn't know what she was doing, but she had a phone, and her drone wasn't always awake. And she had gone through the locked door on the barn that morning when everyone else was asleep.

He knew enough.

Soup had conspiracy theories—robots and mind-reading computers. He knew there were secrets, but they all knew that. Cherry was the longest naughty on the wing.

She knows something.

"You're sending me notes," he whispered.

Her annoyance momentarily passed. She turned inquisitively. Her lips parted then promptly closed.

"Well, well," BG said, rocking thoughtfully, "another year has passed. We're another year older, another year wiser. And our family has grown. Would our new brothers and sisters stand up?"

He looked to the naughty side of the room.

"Come on now," he said. "Bashful was a dwarf, not a naughty."

A funny one for the stream.

Jennifer with braids waved her hand but wouldn't stand. She hid her face when he pointed at her. It was easy to forget the drones were the eyes of the world, but when everyone in the room was looking, it was a hot reminder.

"Johnny Football? Where'd you go?"

Ryder stood up before it got worse and sat down so hard that a jolt shot up his back. BG led the room in laughter. It was awkward and painful, but it got the job done.

"We're more than family," he said. "We have purpose."

A tingle ran across Ryder. *A purpose.* Jane had said that to him, that he had a purpose. Viewers would think he was talking about a higher calling. Ryder thought it sounded like training.

"I'm very proud of how hard all of you have worked to find your own truth. Even Campbell."

Soup's expression didn't change. He was caught with a cookie in one hand and crumbs on his lips. Kraig's laughter erupted from the nicy side of the room, but BG laughed the loudest, a very distinct and very weird ho-ho-ho.

Weird because he meant it.

"We are the lucky ones," he continued. "There is so much work to do because there are still so many in need. I'm proud to call each and every one of you my children." He popped the plastic pipe between his lips and rocked back. "That's all I got."

The protests started from the nicies. They wanted more. It was like a band walking offstage before the final encore, the expectant cheers to bring them back. It was all part of the show.

"Story! Story! Story!"

Fists pumping, fingers pointing, teacups spilling and cookies crumbling, everyone was on their feet. Even the naughties got up because until they did, BG was just going to rock that chair. The stream would show everyone standing up and wanting more.

BG raised his eyebrows. His *ho-ho-ho* was drowned out by excitement. He lifted his hands and smiled with a sparkle. In a couple of seconds, the chaos went from celebration to silence and caught Cherry by surprise as she turned to Ryder.

"Leave me—"

Heads turned and smiles turned up. She flushed the color of her name. BG aimed the pipe. "Do we need to separate you two?"

"Get a room!" Soup shouted.

"That's enough." An edge sharpened his words. He was glaring at Soup, but he wasn't the only one fuming. Cherry's head was smoking.

"Yes, a story, then," BG said. "Every year I tell a story, a true story, make no mistake. A story about a fat man who lives in one of the coldest places on earth. A place where there's no soil. He's not alone."

BG stood with a groan and stepped over the polar bear.

"The elven were on this planet long before humans existed. They were the very first to establish colonies, and thrived during the Ice Age. Their bodies short and fat with blubber to withstand the cold.

Their feet long and wide to walk upon the snow. But sliding is their style."

He pretended to ice skate, doing a pirouette to giggles and smiles.

"Their soles are scaly, lying down to slide forward but pointing toward their heels to grab the ice. They shove forward as graceful as a figure skater, as quick as a hockey player. Playful and joyful, they live thousands of years. But don't mistake their youthful demeanor as immature. Their long lives have brought them wisdom and technological genius... yes, technological."

He raised a finger.

"They are light-years ahead of the human race in biology and communication and data storage—all the things we think we have mastered. They know when we are naughty—" He pointed toward one side of the room. "And when we're nice."

"How?" Jane asked, on cue.

"Microscopic drones the size of ice crystals that float on the wind, that settle on your windowsill at night. But that's not the greatest of their achievements. Every year, the fat man flies around the world in a single night to deliver presents to all the good girls and boys. A *single... night.*"

He held up a finger once more.

"How, you wonder? Because the sleigh upon which he flies can freeze time inside a bubble. For the fat man, nothing changes. Time crawls. But for the outside world, it continues. He visits each and every house inside this bubble, spanning the world to deliver presents."

"But—"

"How does he carry that many presents? Another excellent question, Jane. He has a magic bag, only it's not magic. It's science, children. Magic are those things we do not understand and the elven understand quite well. The fat man wears a special glove. His bag of goodies is empty until he reaches inside. With a thought, the glove assembles matter to form whatever object he wishes. Gift-wrapped or not, he places it under the tree. And in his time-warping bubble, he has time for a swig of milk and a bite of cookie."

He sat back down and sipped his hot chocolate, sighing with satisfaction. The rails creaked back and forth.

"How does he get down the chimney?" John asked.

"Does he read all the letters?" Eric the long-haired nicy asked.

"Does he have a talking snowman?" someone else shouted.

The questions continued with more and more enthusiasm. BG put his hand to his ear, waiting for the right one.

"How do the reindeer fly?"

"That!" He pointed at Sally with a yellow bow in her hair. "I don't know all the answers, but that... *how do the reindeer fly?*" BG crept toward Sally with his pipe in hand. "How does a balloon fly?"

After several moments, she said, "Helium."

"Precisely." A large and cherubic smile rounded his cheeks. "Nine special reindeer are harnessed to this time-stopping sleigh. Nine special reindeer, each with a bladder in their belly that inflates with helium. Nine special reindeer that can run across the sky."

Laughter accompanied BG as he pranced around the bear rug. Ryder wasn't rolling his eyes. He was caught up in the story. It was a fantastic fantasy tied together with flimsy threads of logic that was entertaining and hysterical. A story the bearded man believed. Soup caught Ryder's attention and rolled his eyes.

A story I dreamed about.

"And what's their names?" BG asked.

And the room called them out in no particular order. Everyone knew the song.

"Donder and Blitzen, Vixen, Prancer... Dasher, Cupid, Comet... Dancer..."

"And?" BG put his hand to his ear. "And?"

The room descended into chaotic giddiness, guessing the same names over and over. BG lifted his arms for quiet.

"Urban legends have taught us all we know, but they haven't taught us everything. Some things remain a mystery. The name of the last reindeer, the biggest of them all, who is tethered to the front, the one who leads them through snow and sleet, wind and rain. Whose nose does not glow, who is not ignored in any reindeer games."

He spread his arms and looked over the expectant faces. Perhaps this was a new story. Most of them had heard this fireside chat before, but now a snowflake could be heard if it landed on the floor. Even the naughties were rapt.

"Ronin." It was Jane who answered.

BG began to smile and nod. "You've never heard of him," he said, "because some things on the Pole remain a secret."

He began pacing and sucking on the pipe, meeting each and every one of his children's hopeful looks. Even Soup was listening, cookie in hand.

"Elven technology would be dangerous in human hands, so they hide in the ice to keep us in the dark. But the human race is not an infant. We're not children to be ignored. Truth dies in the dark. It's why we stream everything we do, to show the world what we're capable of doing, to set an example of our human potential. We will lead the human race into the age of enlightenment."

He pointed across the room, making sure he gestured to every single one of them.

"This year, we're all going..." he said carefully, slowly, "to the Pole."

The nicies lost their minds. They stood and cheered, high-fiving and hugging and leaping. Some of the naughties did too, but most were stunned and confused. Ryder wasn't sure what he meant by that.

"You are my family," BG shouted. "I will not leave you behind in this moment of truth. Together we will find the fat man. We will find my brother! We will find Claus!"

Find my brother? Ryder looked toward Soup, who was nodding at him with wide eyes. *Told you.*

BG's voice continued to rise. It carried the excitement to a fevered pitch, sweeping the naughties into celebration. They were caught by surprise. This year, the fireside chat was more than just story time.

It was a gift.

BG just stood and watched, a smile parked on his face, plastic pipe in his mouth. It would be an iconic shot to stream—his children in frenzied adulation with his two trusty sidekicks at his sides.

"Conditions are harsh on top of the world..." he started.

Jane and John helped restore order. When the room calmed to a bubbly jitter, he started again.

"Conditions are harsh. We won't be the first ones to trek to the top of the planet, but we'll be the first ones to discover that ancient race that hides inside the ice. We'll have to train. We'll take advantage of the mountains here at Kringletown. We'll hike; we'll camp. We'll learn to survive in the cold."

A hush filled the room like a blanket of Christmas snow. He was leading up to something that sounded miserable. It dampened the excitement like a wet towel over glowing embers. BG drew the anticipation out with a twinkle in his eye.

"Until then, I've suspended chores."

A murmur crawled through the room. The naughties were holding their excitement in check because there was more good news.

He worked the pipe between his lips. "And opened the game room."

The cork had popped, and the naughties matched the nicies' enthusiasm then shot past it. Arf was swinging his arms. Soup climbed onto his back. Napkins and plates hit the floor; cups bounced off hovering drones. BG blew on the pipe, and soapy bubbles boiled out. He laughed a hearty *ho-ho-ho*.

"Merry Christmas!"

Cherry melted into the stir. Her drone navigated the melee and dipped out behind her. Nicies were hugging BG while Jane and John attempted to keep control. Producers entered the room.

The chat was over.

BG was going to drag them all to the North Pole to find Santa Claus. And they were celebrating. This was madness. The truth Ryder wanted to know wasn't in that icy polar cap. The truth he wanted to know was somewhere at Kringletown.

What's our purpose?

9

The naughty wing was quiet.

Doors were closed, a few of them decorated. Arf had wrapped their door to look like a giant present with a bow and curly streamers. Glitter dusted the floor. It was enough to win the door-decorating contest.

No one else had made an effort.

The board was mostly empty. No chores, like BG had promised. And no introspections. There was just one activity. It hadn't changed in days.

Game room.

Cherry's door was a blank slate of wood. Not a glitter of Christmas spirit. Ryder tapped three times and leaned closer, listening for music and smelling for a whiff of incense.

When she didn't answer, he squatted down to tie his boot. Then he tied the other boot, turned away from Bradley Cooper, and quickly shoved a folded piece of paper under the door. Knocking on her door wasn't going to make the stream.

Sliding a note would.

Because that was what third graders did before cell phones and laptops, when you couldn't text someone your feelings but had to write them out on paper and pass them across the room.

Or shove them under a door.

Outside, the horseshoe was blanketed with fresh snow. Several tracks led to the barn. A few people were riding horses. They were too far away to see who they were, but they weren't wearing cowboy hats.

The big mysterious doors were still locked. Carefully, he walked through the breezeway to avoid slipping. The tack room was empty. The drones were still in the woods, as far as he could tell, but the four-wheelers hadn't left the barn since the game.

Ryder looked up. "To the game room."

Bradley Cooper led him back inside. Ryder tracked snow into the main corridor. The elevator dropped into the ground a few stories and paused. Ryder braced for the sideways track. Several seconds later, he could hear the party.

Ryder zipped up his coat.

It was hardly a room. The floor was ice and snow. Literally, ice and snow. And the size of the place was impossible to determine. The walls and ceiling were limitless projections of a night sky. Colorful ribbons mimicked the Northern Lights. Ice floes appeared to reach a dark horizon. Gusts of sleet actually stung his cheeks.

Everyone was bundled in winter gear with red cheeks and runny noses. A full-scale helicopter was suspended ten feet off the floor. Eric was dropping snowballs on bearded elven popping out of the ice. It was cold and dark, but no one was going to die of frostbite or get chased by a polar bear.

He's training us.

There were several other games in action—snowball fights with giant snowmen, sleigh rides, and dogsleds. He leaned into the wind and raised his arm to fend off the sleet. Soup was shouting through his hands. The wind died as Ryder approached.

Arf was inside an icy dome.

He was wearing a black skin suit that stretched over his head. The ice below him moved like an icy treadmill. He leaped over open leads. Elven popped out of holes to throw ice balls, and polar bears roared.

A red and white striped pole wasn't far away.

"Left!" Soup shouted. "Left, left, left!"

Arf picked up a pair of snowshoes. He was lacing up for a trek over soft snow when a crack appeared. He plunged into black water and emerged shivering. A scoreboard hovered over him. He ranked third.

"Seen Cherry?" Ryder asked.

Soup stared for a moment, recalibrating reality. They weren't on the North Pole. Arf shuffled to the exit and stripped off the skin suit. Somehow, his clothes were dry, but he was still quivering. They talked strategy while Soup dressed. The suit auto-adjusted to his size like a vacuum seal. The scene inside the dome shifted.

The North Pole appeared in the distance.

"You *want* to go to the Pole?" Ryder said.

"Not in a million," Soup said. "I want a warm bed. I'm going to flunk the training and stay home."

"Soup, this *is* the training. Look around."

"I know. But I can't stop; it's straight up Christmas in here, bo. That's why Cherry is nowhere. She's the opposite of fun, probably digging a hole somewhere." Arf pulled the hood over Soup's head. It wriggled around then seemed to vacuum seal around his face. "Go for a helo ride. You'll see."

He looked like a human seal. Circuit ridges raced along the suit's surface. Ryder noticed the subtle bumps near his temples.

"Those are discs." Ryder tapped his head.

"It's a neurofeedback suit, simulates the environment. It's not real in there, Ryder. It's fake, but my body doesn't know it."

"They're sucking out your thoughts is what they're doing. That's why there's no introspections. You're in the brain drain."

"Bill can have them; what do I care? This is awesome."

He knocked on the dome. The surface rang like a gong. He stepped through the entrance and was knocked down by a sudden gust. Crawling to his feet, he ran to a pair of skis and locked in.

The illusion began.

"She was here," Arf said.

"Cherry?"

"Didn't stay long. Saw her at the snowman game. Didn't play, though."

There were half a dozen people at that dome, but no one with red hair. He didn't expect to find her. They weren't being forced to play. She was probably hiding in her room. Ryder could knock all day, but she wasn't going to answer. Maybe if she read the note.

"He's not a bad guy," Arf said. "He means well."

"Who?"

"Billy."

"You trust him?" Ryder said.

Arf shrugged. "It's better than it was."

It was hard to argue that. He didn't know what Arf had been through. Judging by the scars on the side of his face and the misshapen ear, it probably wasn't good. They had everything they needed, everything they could want.

Except privacy.

Soup was walking over an ice bridge. A polar bear was charging and the bridge started to crumble. He crossed just in time.

"His name is Campbell," Arf said. "He don't like that name much."

"Why?"

Arf shrugged. Everyone had bad things. Arf had a dog. Whatever they had, introspection was pulling the curtain back. Soup didn't need thought suckers to remember.

Just his real name.

A howl filled the game room. Angst trickled down Ryder's knees. Across the room, an enormous rack of antlers had risen up. A snout was aimed at the colorful night sky; the lips let out a worried and angry howl. The one at the game. The same one behind the garage when the flashlight was on David's face.

Did I hear a howl?

"You okay?" Arf said.

Ryder had closed his eyes. He stepped away from the dome and met a blustery alleyway. A reindeer was inside a dome surrounded by nicies in matching white coats and wool caps. Hands raised in fur-lined mittens, they cheered the rider on.

Inside the dome, Jane hung onto the harness, leaning into the turns, steering the reindeer around random birds. Her hair whipped off her face, tears streaming. The ice gave way to rocky ground. A village sparkled in a valley.

"The light!" John shouted. "The red light!"

Warm lights lined the streets; windows were brightly lit where chimneys exhaled smoke. But one house was illuminated by a swinging red light.

Santa Claus was waving.

The reindeer's legs pedaled the air. Ryder could smell the musk behind the garage, could feel the warm breath on his neck. He shook his head, the memory flashing in vivid detail as the reindeer hit the roof too hard. His backside slapped Santa off the shingles.

Jane went flying.

It looked like a long fall where Santa had landed, but the floor was only a few feet below her. She hit a cushioned pad, laughing as she rolled to her knees. Words floated above her.

No presents for the children!

The nicies clapped their padded mittens. She exited with her arms over her head. Ryder blocked the exit.

"What did you do to me?"

She stepped back into the dome and appeared to levitate over the village.

"I told you not to put those things on me." He touched his temples.

Kraig grabbed him. Drones smelled blood and swooped in to capture the gold. Ryder spun quickly and ripped out of his grip. John stepped between them before Kraig tried again.

"Hey, hey," John said, "we're having fun here, that's all. If you want to talk about this, let's do it later."

The reindeer was staring at Ryder now, blinking big black eyes.

"How'd you do that?"

"It's a game," Jane said. "That's all this is."

That wasn't just a reindeer. That was behind the garage. It was the one that had attacked David. Ryder never saw him, but he knew that smell.

They made it real.

"There you are!" Soup grabbed him. "We're over here. He got lost. Sorry, he was looking for us. Wrong crowd. We look just alike, all of us. So easy to get confused. Merry Christmas, everyone."

Soup was still suited up, the black hood tightly vacuumed to his head. Arf and other naughties were behind him.

"No." Ryder balled his fists. "They made a game out of my memory, Soup. They're stealing thoughts!" He tapped his temple too aggressively. Pain lanced through his brain. He felt it in his legs. "That's what they're doing to us."

Ryder aimed a finger at the growing circle of naughties. The game room was quiet. Snow fell.

"What if your dog was in the dome?"

Arf twitched. He looked more hurt than angry. Ryder was hurt, but he transformed it into rage. All the complaining the naughties did and all BG had to do was wave a few shiny games in their faces and they dived in like penguins into a den of sea lions.

"Back up." Kraig pushed forward. "She didn't do anything wrong."

"What she take from you, Kraig? Huh? They steal your only memory of playing with dolls? Do they tell you when to bark?"

Kraig made a serious charge this time. It took John and a few others to hold him back. Ryder stood alone, tense and ready. He'd done this before, baited the bully into a fight. He didn't win many of them. But every once in a while he got lucky.

"He won't protect you this time," Kraig said, spit flying.

"What'd you say?" Ryder said.

"You're alone!"

Arf grabbed Ryder. Kraig sounded like a wild animal. John whispered in his ear. Kraig's crazy eyes—unblinking and all white—slowly relaxed. His breath eased to an occasional snort.

He lifted his arms.

"Listen, we're family." Jane stayed in the middle. "If we're going to trek the Pole, we have to act like it. We need to work together."

She looked around and let her voice carry then stepped aside. Kraig sniffed, his jaws clenched. He held out his hand.

"Apologies," he said. "I'm sorry."

Ryder stared at it. The silence was uncomfortable. Ryder braced for a bone-crushing grip, but it didn't come. They shook once and let go.

"We've all been through the same thing." Jane put her arms around them. "We've all been there, trust me, Ryder. And now we're here. We're better people. I promise we did what was best for you."

She hugged him. John did, too. They both clung to him and he stood there. They weren't letting go. Soup put Ryder's arms around them.

The nicies applauded.

The tension drained away. The drones soaked up the footage and the storybook ending. *This episode brought to you by healthy conflict resolution.*

"Goodbye." Soup waved as Arf led them away. "Love you."

The game room slowly began grinding into action. Frigid gusts of Arctic wind blasted down the aisle as everyone grabbed a place in line. Soup and Arf walked at his sides like armed guards.

"Merry Christmas!" Soup waved like a beauty queen. "Happy holidays, nothing to see here. We're just going for a walk—holy crap!"

They ducked behind an empty dome.

"You are bonk. Woooooo!" Soup blew a steam cloud at the drones. "You're a guaranteed star. That's not even close to lying low, bo. I mean, getting lippy with sweet Jane is one thing, but bowing up on Kraig takes jingle bells—great big, giant ones. He's a nicy and all, and he's also fifty-one cards short of a full deck. He'll eat your face, you know that, right?"

"You all right?" Arf asked.

Ryder leaned against the dome. The adrenaline crash left his legs empty. His hands finally unclenched, the joints aching.

"Sorry I said that," Ryder said, "about your dog."

Arf rubbed the side of his face and nodded. The scar was brighter in the cold.

"What dog?" Soup said.

Maybe the dog and the scar were related, maybe not. It didn't matter. Ryder shouldn't have dragged it out.

"That game they were playing," Ryder said, "the reindeer Jane was riding, that came from my memory. That's what I was trying to say. They pulled that out of me during introspection, and now it's in the game room."

"You have a memory of reindeer?"

"No, it was a—look, what are you guys doing in here? You're going along with everything. BG is training you for something and it isn't the Pole. There's something in the—"

"Stress, folks." Soup waved at the drones. The area washed in their green eyes. "He doesn't sleep much, still new to Kringletown, so if we can just... we'll be all right."

Soup pulled him close and whispered, "We're not in the bathroom, bo. So save the hate."

"And pretend this is normal?"

Soup was a little stunned. He frowned and, maybe for the first time, looked serious and more than a little hurt. "What're we going to do, Ryder? Get an apartment somewhere? Go get jobs and live in the city or on a farm or in the suburbs or pick your destination? We don't have a choice. I say things about Billy, okay. I get it. But what else are we going to do? Every kid in the universe would beg to play these games, so I don't care if he's training us to take over the world. I'm going to have some fun, so relax a second and melt your brain."

Ryder looked around. Soup wasn't the only one going along with the madness. They all were, naughty and nice. No one cared. Or knew there was nothing they could do about it.

At least they would have some fun doing it.

Bradley Cooper illuminated the path and Ryder turned to leave. The wind picked up.

10

Cherry wasn't at dinner.

Her door was closed. Everyone was hanging out, doors open, music up. A sense of exhaustion haunted the naughty wing, a game room hangover of spent muscles and tired ambition. Soup and Arf were the last ones to come back. Their hands were pale from too many plunges.

"We beat it," Arf said. "Finally."

Ryder was on his bed, staring at the sage advice carved into the bottom of the top bunk. He wondered if he had a choice to be naughty or nice.

"Look." Soup held a folded square of paper. A message was written in green ink. "Watch the light," he read. "Worst love letter ever."

He flung it on Ryder's bed and climbed onto his bunk. It was exactly as he read it, written in thin green lines. The back of it, though, had a different message scribbled in blue ink.

Why am I here?

This was the note he'd slid under Cherry's door. The blue ink was his handwriting.

"Where'd you find this?" Ryder said.

"On the floor."

He went down the hall. Her door was still closed. It was still quiet inside. He went back three more times. Arf was chainsawing his way through sleep. He'd never changed out of his clothes. Soup was crashed in front of his laptop, the stream flashing across the room. Ryder was awake until midnight. He decided to send a note back in the morning.

What light?

It was one o'clock before he fell asleep. He dreamed of trees and snow and the ragged edges of mountain paths and wondering what the note meant.

At three thirty, the answer woke him.

Every morning, there was a spotlight mounted on the barn. Ryder opened his eyes to see bars of light streaming through the blinds.

He rolled off the bed. Bradley Cooper followed him to the window, casting eerie shadows across the desk. The spotlight was just above the breezeway. It blazed with starry brilliance, aimed right at him.

He sat back and waited.

He was relaxed but wide-awake, resting in the ebb and flow of Arf's snoring. At four o'clock, the spotlight hadn't changed, but the bedroom began to twinkle. Bradley Cooper was camped over him, casting his shadow. The green eye flickered.

And then died.

Bradley Cooper hung in midair as if weightless. Ryder waited for it to wake up. He hadn't moved much in the chair, but that had never put it to sleep before. He stood up without a response, put a finger on it and pushed. It floated like a rudderless balloon.

Watch the light. The message was in green ink. *Watch the "green" light.*

Ryder went into the hallway and left the door open. When he looked back, Bradley Cooper was still gliding like an object without gravity or direction.

Arf's snoring followed him down the hall. He snuck to the chore board and listened at Cherry's door. There was no music, but incense leaked from beneath it. He tapped. When she didn't answer, he went back to his bedroom—Bradley Cooper now in timeout corner—and grabbed the note. He pushed it under Cherry's door and waited. The corner was just visible.

Then disappeared.

Several moments later, the doorknob turned. She peeked out from the dimly lit room, warm candlelight behind her. She looked over his shoulder then pulled the door open and searched the hall.

She yanked him inside.

Pillows were stacked in the center of the room. She blew out the candle, plunging the room into darkness. Her drone was a cold lump near the ceiling. Cherry was a dark form. Hands on her hips, she was waiting. When no one came to her room and no drone came tapping, she lit the candle and whispered, "Where'd you get this?" She flashed the note.

"I put it under your door two days ago." He flipped it over. "I found this under my door."

She made a lap around the room while he explained the notes he'd found on wrapping paper, the ones asking who he was and why he was here. He thought that maybe she was the one sending them.

"Bradley Cooper is off," he said.

"Who?"

"I'm sorry, it's, uh, my drone." He shook his head. "What's happening?"

She picked up the candle. It threw shadows across the room, her face dark and mysterious. Three of the four beds were perfectly made. Ryder sat on the one with the covers thrown back. No one on the naughty wing had a room to themselves. She inserted her hand in a slit cut in the mattress. A panel of electric light beamed from her hand. She swiped her thumb across the phone.

"When did you get the first note?"

"The first day." He told her what it said. "You get one, too?"

She rubbed her face, starting and stopping a few times. "I don't know what's going on. I got here a few years ago. I had a roommate. She'd already been here a year. She was, uh, pretty smart, kind of knew how things worked, not just at Kringletown but other things too."

She pointed at the stack of pillows.

"She taught me how to keep off the stream by staying out of drama, keeping to myself. What you did at the fireside is the first time I've been on it in months. Don't do that again."

"What happened to her?"

"Turned into one of them." Cherry shook her head. "She's not bad, but she's... *different*. She had this scar on her chin that's not there anymore. She also had a missing molar from when she fell off her bike before she got here. That's fixed too. She had some other things, but I'll bet they're fixed. It's her, but not really."

"Who?"

"Jane."

Ryder didn't expect that. Jane seemed like she'd been here longer than any of them. She was so comforting, so in charge. *On the naughty wing?*

"After she left, I got this." Cherry retrieved a stack of notes in a notebook. One was torn from a roll of wrapping paper.

Who are you?

"The others kept coming, but I didn't know why or who was sending them. I still don't. Then this showed up." She tossed the phone to him. "He takes away our phones and gives us a laptop so he can see everything we're doing. He controls what we access, knows what we're looking for. If you do a search for his past, you won't find anything." She shook her head. "Everything is on lockdown."

"You searched for him?"

"Jane did."

The phone was an old model. The screen was cracked. There wasn't much on it.

"My drone started turning off when you arrived. There was no note, I just noticed one morning that the green eye was out. It happened at four in the morning and turned back on at five. It took a while before I realized it wasn't watching me."

"That's why you went out to the barn."

She pierced him with suspicion.

"I saw you," he said. "The phone lit up your face. That's why I was pretending to read the board that morning. I heard you climb through your window."

A wave of panic passed over her.

"You need to be more careful," Ryder said.

"It has a map." She sat next to him and touched the phone. A map of the property appeared. Their shoulders were touching. She tapped the barn. "The door wasn't locked. I looked inside and came back."

"What was in there?"

She shook her head. "I'm not sure; I was nervous. There were a lot of... cages."

"Cages? Like cells?"

She got up. He knew the feeling, the urge to keep moving ahead of difficult feelings and thoughts, when there just wasn't enough room for what he was feeling.

"Someone wants us to know. You're in it now." She sounded relieved. She wasn't alone. "He's up to something. So is JJ."

"JJ?"

"Jane and John."

Her smell was more earthy than fragrant. When she leaned over, her hair fell across her face and their shoulders touched again. His chest was melty. She touched the phone he was still holding, pulling up her last searches.

There were pages on BG's family, how William grew up on a ranch but grew wealthy with investments and patents in the technology industry.

"Who's the old man with the cowboy hat?" Ryder asked.

"BG's brother, I think."

"Not his dad?"

"I don't know. Listen, you should go back." She took the phone. "Be in bed when the drone wakes up. Go back and do whatever you were doing when it turned off. You know, just in case."

It made sense. If there was any indication that the drone was malfunctioning, someone would come check it. *Thou shalt not interrupt the stream.*

Cherry peeked into the hall before stepping aside. Ryder forced himself to leave. It was the first time he didn't feel like running away.

"Hey." She grabbed his arm. "Don't talk to me, all right? I need to stay off the stream. It'll be impossible for you, I think. Especially after the game room."

"You saw that?"

She pushed him out the door and watched through the crack. "Be careful."

He turned around to tell her the same, but the door clicked shut. He lingered at the board for a few minutes, debating on knocking and telling her thanks or he was glad to meet her or something equally stupid, but he rushed back to the bedroom.

Bradley Cooper was still drifting near the ceiling.

He sat at his desk and stared out the window like he had been doing at four o'clock, trying to remember if he'd had his hands behind his head. The spotlight was still beaming across the empty yard. At five o'clock, Bradley Cooper spun around.

The green eye on.

11

Four o'clock. It took a few moments to climb out of the fog. Ryder threw his feet on the floor and rubbed his face. Bradley Cooper didn't fall off the ceiling. He quickly went to Cherry's door. She peeked one eye through a growing crack.

"Your drone's asleep?" she said. "You sure?"

Perhaps she'd been doing this alone too long. Her pillows were stacked in the middle of the room. The incense was burning. The calm sounds of a stream babbled from her laptop.

She lit another stick of incense. It smelled more like cinnamon. She searched her laptop for another track, this one wind chimes and a flute. Ryder watched her pull her legs into a pretzel.

"What do you do, just sit there?"

"Breathe."

He was breathing, too, and was pretty sure it wasn't hard to do. She placed her hands on her knees and drew several easy breaths.

"It's just being present," she said. "Letting thoughts rise and fall, experiencing this moment. Listening, seeing, smelling, fully engaging the senses... being here."

"Sounds boring."

"What is boredom?"

"It's boring."

"What's the *experience* of boredom?"

He cleared his throat. "That."

She returned to breathing; then a smile cracked her face. It was the first time he'd actually seen her smile, but it didn't look happy.

"Should I leave?" he said.

"Here." She tossed the phone on the bed. "Do a search for Billy Sinterklaas."

"You mean like Google him?"

"Yeah. It's all out there; it's nothing secret. I think BG just doesn't want us Googling him once we're here. How many of us did it before we got here? Even if you did, you wouldn't think anything of it. But once you've been here a while, it reads a little different. Go ahead, hit up his Wikipedia."

She resumed her posture—back straight, legs folded. Ryder opened a browser. The most recent stream came up followed by Wikipedia.

Son of William Tomlin Sinterklaas Sr. and Melinda Ann Sinterklaas, Billy was born in Casper, Wyoming, where he grew up on the family ranch raising livestock. He was known for his adventurous nature as well as his penchant to hunt large game.

He graduated high school early, studied biology at the University of Wyoming, and played football. He later attended graduate school at MIT to study biological engineering. Recruited by industry before finishing his doctorate, he was instrumental in starting the biotechnical division at Avocado, Inc.

After several productive years, he left following the tragedy of a facility meltdown that took the life of his estranged wife, Heather Miser. He was suspected in the development of a rogue artificial intelligence program that named itself Humbug, but was never directly implicated by the company.

A successful investor and entrepreneur, he became one of the nation's largest private landowners. He went back to ranching while building a private bioengineering research facility to continue the work he started at Avocado, Inc. His research had advanced synthetic medicine around the world. His company annually donated supplies to Third World countries.

His real work began when he established the Home for Children, Kringletown, developing a model for helping children in need. Adopting children throughout the country, Billy had provided a home to forty children to date, who remain on the ranch.

"Where's the rest of them?" he said.

She nodded then shrugged. "See what I mean?"

It wasn't adding up. None of this was alarming unless you were looking at it from the inside. There were thirty-one stockings hung on the mantel and forty children to date? Where did they go? Kringletown ranch was huge, but he hadn't seen anyone besides BG and the old man.

And what about the football game? The trophy had fifteen years on it, but no one was that old.

"What's over the mountain?" he said.

"Keep reading."

Touting himself as an adventurous philanthropist, he had been criticized for monetizing his altruism when he began streaming daily life at Kringletown. To date, it was the most downloaded reality program. His supporters claimed his selflessness was on full display, demonstrating how structure, love and support could change lives and mold anyone into a model citizen.

He had also been criticized for hunting animals and avidly displaying them as trophies. Billy claimed to no longer hunt for sport but insisted that displaying his past behavior was a reminder of his past and who he had become. He channeled his adventurous nature into exploring harsh climates, in particular his love for the North Pole.

Billy had fifty-five documented excursions to the North Pole. He had garnered national attention when he announced the existence of an ancient race of elven living in the Arctic ice as well as a man named Nicholas Santa.

Better known as Santa Claus.

While he had travel records of a man named Nicholas Santa in 1904 destined for the North Pole, he had not provided any evidence beyond this and insisted there was a link to his family name. Skeptics doubted his sanity and asked for an investigation into his fitness as a foster parent.

Billy, however, claimed he would provide the world all the proof in a live documentary called *Finding Claus*. The live stream was expected to break downloading records.

There were photos of Billy trekking the Arctic ice with icicles clinging to his beard and eyebrows. The credited date was twenty years old. Oddly, he looked exactly like BG did now.

Ryder scrolled down to a section titled "Fountain of Youth." Billy, it stated, credited his agelessness to his private research. His claims were widely criticized as misleading and fraudulent, yet his skeptics could not explain his physical appearance given his age. Ryder glanced at his birthdate and did the math.

He's seventy-five?

The man on the Wikipedia page looked fifty years old and exactly how Billy looked now. Whatever he was doing, his avid supporters said, was beyond doubt since he streamed everything to the public.

His net worth was estimated to be in the billions. If his claims to agelessness were ever patented and released, he would easily become the wealthiest man in the world. William continued to refine his aging technology, claiming it would be made available when the general public was ready.

Cherry was still sitting with her eyes cast down, hands folded over her belly. "What did you see?"

"We're test subjects."

She nodded along. "Yeah."

"Why is he streaming?" Ryder said. "If he wants all of this to be private, why put it out there?"

"Ego. Money. What else did you see?"

"That was it."

"What about his dad?"

"What about him?"

"Scroll to the top. What do you see?"

Ryder went back to the beginning and read the bio three times. He wasn't seeing something, but it was right in front of him. His dad would be ninety-five years old.

"He's dead."

"Both his parents," Cherry said, "died when he was working at Avocado. That's about the time he moved back to the ranch."

"It doesn't say anything about an older brother."

"There's ways to keep that off Wikipedia."

"That doesn't mean it's his brother."

"Have you seen the old man up close? There's a resemblance. Maybe he's a cousin, I don't know. All I know is they look like twins separated by about twenty years."

Ryder had seen him up close when Kraig caught him at the barn. He had been too nervous to notice any resemblance between the old man and BG. There was something strange about that.

"Someone brought you here for a reason," she said. "It wasn't to score touchdowns."

"They brought you here, too."

It was difficult to tell if she was smiling or if the dim light was playing tricks. Ryder lay back on the bed and stared at the bottom of the bunk, expecting some words of wisdom carved into it. There was none. He folded his hands and focused on his breath. They stayed quiet till he had to go back. She told him to be careful and not to talk to her.

The next night, he learned how to meditate.

❄

"Where you been?" Soup asked.

It was late morning when Ryder came back from wandering around the trees. Soup and Arf were still coming back after midnight and hadn't showered since the game room opened. The room smelled like a den of wolves. Soup didn't ask where he was hiking or why.

"The trek is over," he said. "Arf was the first person to the Pole, but then we went into these ice tunnels to find where the elven were hiding. It was cool but nothing like the A-bomb."

"A-bomb?"

"A giant snowman," Arf said from his pillow.

Soup had been sleeping in the same clothes for days. He stripped the blankets off Arf and bombed him with socks until he was up.

Ryder went to the showers.

When he got back, they were gone. He took a short nap then hiked out to the barn to watch the horses. Cherry would sometimes be somewhere on the fence, but they rarely came within shouting distance. He huddled against the barn overlooking the mountains. He looked bored. Bradley Cooper wouldn't know the difference.

No footage here.

A stream of smoke was coming out of the trees. He planned to hike that way and see what was out there. It wouldn't take long. Halfway across the horseshoe, he reached into his coat for a second pair of gloves.

He was missing one of them.

A horse was saddled in the barn. He saw the glove. Sweeping it up, he hustled through the breezeway—

The old man stepped out of the tack room.

They nearly collided. The old man reared back with a frown and dropped his gloves. Barehanded, he bent with a groan and snatched them off the concrete. Ryder took a step back.

The old man was missing two fingers.

"I'm sorry," Ryder said.

He wasn't sure why he was apologizing. Maybe he wasn't supposed to see his fingers, or his face. The old man pulled his gloves on and spit on the floor. He smelled like evergreen boughs that were on fire.

Ryder moved out of the way. The old man led a horse that was loaded down with packed gear out of one of the stalls. He put a boot in one of the stirrups and threw his leg over the saddle. The leather stretched and buckles rang. He clicked his tongue. The horse clopped over the hard ground.

Not a word.

Ryder stood as frozen as the ground. The old man's beard was a white shrub covering his face. His cheeks were leathery and his eyes hidden beneath bushy red eyebrows. Maybe Cherry was right, but it was hard to tell if he looked like BG. That was the thing with Kringletown.

It was hard to know what was true.

12

Ryder rolled over.

Barefoot, he hurried down the hall. It was ten minutes past four o'clock. There was so much to talk about. There was a lot of noise inside Cherry's room. The door yanked open. A frigid breeze blew past him.

"Where have you been?" she hissed.

"Sorry. I—"

She shoved the phone in his face. He flinched and squinted. *A map.*

"Get dressed," she said.

Ryder ran back to the room and came back in winter gear, his laces dancing around his boots. Cherry was at the window, the phone lighting up her face.

"Wait." He grabbed it from her. "We can't turn this on when we're out there."

He studied the map. One of the dots was Cherry's room. The other one was in the forest, north of the trees. It was labeled *HO-HO-HO.*

"What's that mean?" he said.

"We'll find out when we get there."

Snowy specks flew through the window. They left it cracked open for their return. The snow was thin outside her room. They were going to need it to snow to cover their tracks.

They took a long route into the trees, sprinting at full speed and stopping only once to check the phone. Subzero air was burning his chest. He struggled to breathe, snot running down his chin. There wasn't much snow beneath the trees, but it was still difficult to run.

She suddenly stopped. He rested his hands on his knees. Cherry held the phone inside her coat and checked the map. It was so dark that even the light leaking from her collar lit her face.

"That's it."

Ryder couldn't see the dark building at first. There was a porch and chimney. The windows were black. This wasn't the barn they were exploring. Somebody lived there.

The old man.

Maybe he was the one sending the notes and was calling them for a chat, but he wasn't on the front porch, and the lights weren't on. He'd had the horse loaded up with packing gear the other day like he was heading out.

He's not home.

Cherry was already on the porch. There was no snow leading up to it and the ground was frozen. There were plenty of tracks leading in and out, so anything they left behind wouldn't be noticed.

"Kick your boots," she whispered.

He knocked bits of snow off. She was cupping her hands to one of the windows. There was no light inside or fire.

No green eyes.

She crept to the door. Ryder's heart was beating louder than her footsteps. She slipped her boots off. He was still trying to calm his breath when she turned the doorknob. The hinges creaked.

We're doing this.

He wanted to know the truth, but doubt had nailed him down. He liked it better when they were meditating in a warm and safe room with nature music.

"Come on."

It was cold inside. The cabin was simple. There was a bed and a table and a small kitchen area. The fireplace was filled with ashes and a blackened log. An elk head was staring from above the mantel.

"What are we supposed to do?" he whispered.

She shrugged. "Look around."

They crept around in their socks. There wasn't a single item of technology in the cabin. No tiny lights, no television or laptop. No phone. A desk was in the corner with pads of paper and notes taped to the wall. Candles were on a shelf. There was a picture of an Avocado, Inc., factory. Another photo on the wall, this one a silhouette of a man on a horse.

Cherry almost kicked over a spittoon. "Gross."

There was a bathroom next to the desk, hardly big enough to be a closet. The curtain was pulled aside and a composting toilet in the corner. The kitchen had a wood-burning stove that could be used for cooking. But there was a refrigerator softly humming, so there was electricity. That, however, seemed to be it.

"Where is he?" she said.

He told her about the other day when he had taken the horse with all the packed gear.

"Why would he bring us," she said, "if he's not here?"

So she was thinking the same thing. Ryder looked closely at the floor. If they were wrong and the old man found one of their footprints, they might never find the truth. They'd have another home.

The cabin was suddenly filled with light.

"What are you doing?" Ryder said.

The phone was lit. "We need to get going."

It was only on for a second, but the woods were dark enough that a single flash would look like a lighthouse. However, that moment of light revealed a narrow door next to the refrigerator. It was a small pantry with canned goods. There was no light.

"Let me see the phone."

He stepped inside and closed the door. He lit up the phone. The shelves were dusty and so were most of the cans. The bathroom closet would be on the other side.

He opened the map again.

They were exactly where it told them to go. Maybe they were just supposed to see where the old man lived and that was it. That wasn't much.

HO-HO-HO.

Maybe it was just more Santa Claus conspiracy, but there were no candy canes in the cabin or Christmas trees or one single wreath. It could be any day of the year.

The floorboards were heavily worn, the wood a lighter color where someone had frequently walked. Who would spend this much time in a pantry? The traffic pattern went up to a blank wall. If someone came inside to get something off the shelf, they wouldn't walk against the wall.

He tapped on it.

"What are you doing?" she said.

He noticed a can of green beans. It was by itself. The label was clean, but the top of the can was covered in dust. The shelf was dusty, too. The can hadn't been moved.

So why the clean label?

A green giant was on the label. Ryder had lived with a family that ate green beans straight from the can, didn't even heat them up. Rick, the foster dad, would imitate the commercial when he opened it. *Ho-ho-ho* wasn't about Santa Claus.

Ryder reached to spin it or lift it. All it took was tipping it slightly. White light leaked from a seam along the floor. Ryder pushed the wall with his fingertip.

Light flooded the pantry.

He turned off the phone and pulled Cherry inside. A black staircase spiraled down. Electric light flickered from below.

"Ho-ho-ho," he said. "Green Giant."

Ryder peeked through the steps. The room below was larger than the cabin and fully lit. And nothing about it was woodsy. There were multiple computers and several desks surrounded by electrical cabinets and strange equipment.

A circular platform was in the center of the room. It was silver and shining, just like the one in the library where BG appeared. A hologram hovered above it, a figure with the arms out. There were no details, just a mesh outline of a human body matrix.

The wall was covered with monitors.

There were dozens of them. Most were gray images of bedrooms with bunkbeds. Some had moving images from a point of view above the ground—above Kringletown, above the barn. Above the trees.

"Drones." Ryder stepped closer. "Look."

He found the one he was looking for. Someone was curled up on the top bunk. The person below him was hanging halfway off the bed. The other bunkbed was empty, but there was someone sleeping on the bottom.

It's me.

"He's looping the feed," Cherry said. "That's how we get away with it. Once four o'clock gets here, it shows you sleeping."

"No, look." He pointed at Soup. His lips were moving. He was grinding his jaws. "The drones are supposed to be off when we're sleeping."

Cherry found her drone. The monitor showed her underneath the covers, her pillows stacked on the floor.

The phone started buzzing.

The map illuminated. "We got to go," he said.

Cherry was first up the staircase. Ryder stopped halfway up to take a picture. He took the time to make sure everything looked normal in the pantry, but there wasn't time to look for footprints. They didn't even tie their boots. Snow packed against their socks as they sprinted through the trees.

They fell through her window and crashed on the floor.

Ryder didn't check the hall before charging out. He jumped into bed fully clothed, throwing the covers over his head. He huffed beneath the blankets, his breath masked by Arf's breathing. He stayed that way until the sun was up. He was still wide awake.

The old man is watching, he thought. *Who exactly is he?*

13

The phone was still in his pocket.

Soup had jumped out of bed half an hour ago. Ryder had pretended to be asleep. When he grabbed a towel and left, Ryder ducked beneath the covers.

He swiped the photo.

The lab beneath the cabin was well lit. He zoomed in on the equipment and recognized centrifuges that looked like the ones from school, but the rest of it was rocket science. There was a cabinet with shelves and transparent doors. A dozen or more drones were inside. The computers were running foreign interfaces with strange data.

The body matrix was faded and blurred.

It was the size of a boy. The legs were apart and the arms out. It reminded him of da Vinci's *Vitruvian Man*, only there wasn't a circle or superimposed figure over it. The form was an empty matrix of contour lines, but the details were very specific.

Definitely a boy.

There were fifty monitors on the wall. Five rows of ten. The majority were monitoring bedrooms. One monitor showed someone at a bathroom mirror brushing their teeth. He hadn't noticed that when they were down there. Ryder zoomed in to see the bushy beard in the reflection.

Even BG was being watched.

The bottom row was feeds from outside—trees and buildings and horses. The drones were still scanning the woods. *Did they see us?* he wondered coldly. There was no way to know unless someone told him.

Or when the old man gets home.

The last monitor wasn't a bedroom. Ryder zoomed until it was pixelated almost beyond recognition. It looked like the lab below the cabin. If that was true, they were definitely busted. However, there were slight variations, as far as he could tell—more cabinets and no da Vinci man. This was a different lab.

And much bigger.

"Busted!" Soup shouted.

Ryder swallowed his tongue. His heart rate doubled. He slid the phone under the pillow.

"Check the board, bo."

Ryder's voice quivered. "What's it say?"

"Hey, stinky." Soup shook Arf's bunk. "Get up and shower. It smells like a dead dog in here. We're hitting the game room. Ryder's coming with us."

Arf smacked his lips and sat up limply. Soup threw a towel over his head and pushed him out the door. Arf shuffled down the hall.

Check the board. Ryder was frozen. He kicked his boots off before getting out of bed, leaving them under the covers. He was still dressed.

Soup was arguing with someone across the hall. The board was lit up. It had changed since he'd gone to Cherry's only a few hours ago. Maybe it had been like that when he ran back. There wasn't much to read, but he stood in front of it, trying to decide if he should be worried.

Everyone report to game room at nine o'clock. This is not optional.

Cherry opened her door. Her ink-spotted drone swung out behind her.

"What do you think this means?" he whispered.

"Guess we're playing a game."

He remained at the board, partially petrified. She strolled down to take a shower. He needed to meditate more.

He was anything but relaxed.

❄

"We give Evan the boot," Soup said, "and put Ryder on the team."

"I don't think that's fair," Arf said.

"He sucks. And Ryder's our boy."

They boarded the elevator, dressed for winter, wearing coveralls and boots, scarves, gloves and stocking caps. There was snow on the floor. His stomach dropped as they descended.

"Wrap up." Soup pulled a cap on.

The doors opened before Ryder could do the same. A bitter wind threw his coat open. Snow swirled inside the elevator. He hid behind Arf as they leaned into the Arctic. Soup led them up a short flight of stairs toward an observation room. A few naughties were already inside hiding from the weather.

"So stupid," Soup complained. "You get frostbite just trying to get there."

The game room had changed. There were only three game domes. The one on the left was the Arctic trek. The dome on the right was the helicopter simulation. The reindeer game was gone. It was replaced by one twice the size. The surface was opaque and frosty. A line of people was scattered around the perimeter with their hands to the sides.

"There's a twenty-minute line," Soup said. "I knew we should've skipped breakfast."

Ryder scanned the crowd. Everyone was geared up and hidden beneath coats and caps. He couldn't see if Cherry was down there.

After waiting ten minutes, they left the safe room. The Arctic howled in his ears. Ryder held the back of Arf's coat. If this was the North Pole, he didn't want to go. The wind abruptly died.

"Welcome!" Jane shouted. "I'm so glad you're here, Ryder."

"Oh, yeah, hi," Soup said. "We're invisible."

She and the other nicies wore white coats with furry trim. Their mittens were thick leather. Soup and Arf joined the others against the dome. The floor shuddered. Snow spattered the inside of the dome.

Cherry was by herself. "Hey," she said.

Jane didn't seem suspicious he was standing next to her. He wanted to ask her if she'd heard anything, tell her the phone was hidden beneath his pillow, ask if they should hike into the woods after lunch. But he kept quiet. There was nothing she could say that would make him less nervous.

Jane went to a rack where Paul and Shelly were stripping off black rubber suits dusted in snow. They were still fully dressed beneath, coats and boots and hats and all. Jane grabbed a loose suit hanging on a hook.

"An auto-feedback suit," she said, "with a neural stimulator that will track you in real time. The dome is an illusion of space. The suit simply enhances your experience."

Ryder took it from her. It was thick and heavy. The hood flopped in his hand. He felt the dime-size lumps that would be positioned over his temples when he pulled the hood on.

"What's in here?"

"It's not mind-reading, Ryder. Trust me."

"Trust you?"

"It's an experience enhancer, that's all. This is a great way to acclimate to the weather extremes that we'll all be facing in a few weeks. You felt how cold it was on the way here, right?"

Another thundering collision occurred, and everyone reacted with surprised cheers. They hammered the dome with closed fists. The dome's opacity turned transparent. He could see what was inside, but it wasn't anything special. Snow was stuck to the inside, but the floor was empty. Several suit-clad players exited in vacuum-sealed diving suits.

"Not happening. That'll strip my rank." Evan pulled a suit from Soup's grip. "I'm not starting over on another squad."

"You don't lose rank," Soup said. "Ryder's our roommate, he has to be on our squad, and you don't. Besides, you suck."

"*You* suck."

Soup grabbed the suit and they played tug-of-war until Arf interrupted. Several others took sides, including Jane.

"I'll go with her," Ryder announced. "Evan can stay on with Soup. I'll team up with her."

He was pointing at Cherry, who looked mortified. The drones were all aimed at her.

Soup screwed up an expression. "Oh, I get it."

"You know what, I don't want to be on the squad anymore," Evan said. "Find someone else."

"Good!" Soup blasted. "Ryder, come on."

"What about Cherry?"

"She hates this. Right, Cherry? You hate this. Ryder's in; Evan's out."

"I think it's a good idea," Jane said. "Everyone has to play at least once, and the newbies can work together. We'll reset the game to Beat the King and do a three-way with teams of two. How's that for compromise?"

"Whatever." Evan yanked the suit away.

"He's still fighting," Soup said.

Ryder just wanted to get this over with, but this was a chance to break the public ice with Cherry. If they were forced to be teammates, they could talk without anyone getting suspicious. The others were suiting up. Ryder stuck his hand out.

"I'm Ryder."

She shook her head. "What are you doing?"

"Introducing myself."

"Suit up, loverboy." Someone threw a suit over his head.

Cherry took one off the rack, stepping into it like the others. As cumbersome as they looked, she easily pulled it on. She left the hood dangling between her shoulders.

Ryder pulled his suit on while arguments continued. Despite being fully clothed, his skin tingled. First his legs felt itchy then his hands and arms. The suit was transmitting through his clothes. He pulled it over his shoulders, and the sensation passed through his chest.

"Now I have to destroy you." Soup pushed a pair of ski goggles at Ryder. "See what you make me do."

The glass was reflective and would cover half of his face. The other two teams entered the dome like lumpy aliens. Cherry's hood still hung loosely over her shoulders. She flipped out the inside to show him the imbedded mesh.

The lumps were just inside the seam. It was smaller than before. When she pulled the hood on, they would be snug against her temples. The entire suit was a neural-mesh interface. If they didn't know what Cherry and Ryder were doing in the early morning hours, they would after this.

That's why it's required.

There hadn't been an introspection since the game room opened. They were sucking out thoughts every time someone put on a suit. This wasn't an option.

"Players!" Jane shouted. "Inside the dome."

"I'm not feeling good," he said.

"What's wrong?"

He shook his head. "I think I'm going to puke."

"You're just nervous. The suit will tell you if there's something wrong. Just play it once, just for a minute. You don't have to stay in there long."

"Yeah, I don't want to."

"You have to." Her smile wasn't there. She reached for his hood. Cherry tugged him closer.

"Let me talk to him."

The crowd was getting antsy, jeering them to get going. If they didn't want to go, someone else would.

"Don't give them any thoughts," Cherry whispered. "Empty your mind and focus on your breath. You can do this."

It was just like meditating, keeping his attention on the breath without distraction. He'd been meditating a whole week. *Some people* meditate all their lives and can't empty their mind. *This should be no problem.*

When the hood went up, the tingling turned into pinpricks. It squeezed him like a giant hand getting the last bit of toothpaste. For a moment, he lost feeling. The barrier between him and the world dissolved. His temples began to throb.

Breathe, just breathe. One, two, three...

"Players in!" Jane called.

The spectators thumped the dome and chanted. The other teams were paired up and waiting. The floor was silver and empty, like fresh ice on a hockey rink.

"Goggles," Jane reminded him.

When he snapped them over his face, everything changed. The floor transformed into a snowy tundra; the walls vanished in a dark, endless horizon. The sun was cresting. He plunged into subzero temperatures, the frozen air stealing his breath.

The entrance closed behind him.

Cherry's suit had transformed into Arctic camouflage. Her goggles had disappeared. She pointed. "Over there."

A wall of ice was behind them. The other teams ducked behind their own icy forts, the size of their walls rapidly expanding. A giant silver orb was nestled in the middle of the dome. Symbols were etched onto the surface. Numbers floated above it, counting down from sixty.

I've seen that orb, he thought.

It looked like a Christmas ornament the size of a bowling ball. It was the heart of something, an electromagnetic field generator. *Did I dream that?*

"Just breathe," she said. "We can do this."

She held his forearm. He wanted to hold her hand. There was a snowball cannon behind the wall and a catapult lying on its side. Ryder leaned against the wall, felt the ice on his back and the breath inside his nostrils. The countdown began beeping.

The wind picked up.

It was followed by howling that rumbled the ice. This wasn't the sound of an animal. It was monstrous. Otherworldly. If this was a replication of the North Pole, then the Arctic Ocean was below them. Thoughts of plunging into icy waters broke his concentration.

One, two, three, four—

A section crumbled from the top of their fort. A giant snowball crashed through it. He peeked through the opening. The silvery orb was gone.

An enormous snowman raged in its place.

It swung giant arms at the other forts, batting away a continuous stream of snowballs. The battle tore holes in its swirling body. It stomped legs the size of tree trunks and swung wrecking-ball fists.

Flury, Ryder thought.

The head spun like a turret. The eyes bore down on Ryder like it heard its name. A snow flurry engulfed Ryder. In seconds he was lost in a whiteout. He opened his mouth to call out for Cherry, but his breath was snatched away. Then the ice flipped. The sky was below him. He flailed to grab something, to stop from falling into icy water.

Frigid air across my face. Tears don't stream. A second pair of transparent eyelids protect my eyes. I reach out and paw the clouds, soaring through them, condensation on my lips. I emerge over a valley and descend toward lights. I'm not falling.

I'm flying.

I drift down slowly, my belly deflating like a balloon. Straps around my neck and across my back. There's weight behind me. I extend strong legs covered in dark fur and aim for a snow-covered roof. Hooves gently thud behind me, and sleigh rails slide through snow. We come to a stop, and I see the yellow truck in the driveway.

I hear an infant cry.

"Ryder!"

A funny face was looking at him. A pair of goggles hung from Cherry's neck. Other faces joined her, huddling over him and blocking out the milky dome. Cold sweat beaded on his forehead.

"Back up!" The crowd parted. "Don't move him."

Jane knelt next to him. There were no forts, no snowballs. No giant snowman with a turret head.

"Clear out," John announced.

They backed up but didn't leave. Someone brought him water. They sat him up and helped him drink it. He could feel the floor again but was still partially numb. They stripped off the hood and unzipped the suit. The cold air felt good. He tried to stand.

What just happened? It was a dream again, like the ones he sometimes had about the North Pole. Only this time it wasn't about an elven or a reindeer. *I was the reindeer.* There was something about the yellow truck. It was the middle of the night and there was a baby in it. A baby who was all alone.

They would see that, he was sure. The suit would suck those thoughts from his head.

"Does that mean the game's over?" Soup asked.

Cherry guided Ryder out of the dome. Even the wind in the aisle had died. They left the game room. BG got what he wanted, he guessed. It was a dream, that was all.

But how did I know the snowman's name?

14

The sun hid behind the mountains.

The drones were returning from the mountain. A wave of freshly charged green eyes was heading out. No one from Billy Big Game's childhood would have guessed he would own mountains. He didn't dwell on the past, never ruminated on his beginnings. He had no childhood friends. No family.

You have me, my boy, he thought.

There was a time when the world was flat and the moon was made of cheese; a time when disease was cured by leeches. Silliness, really. Everyone knew better now. But there were still myths in the world. Billy Big Game would dispel the greatest of all them hiding in plain sight. It was his duty.

What I was born to do.

The office door opened. His two favorite prodigies were at their chairs along with Mindy. These were the people he trusted. They didn't believe in his mission, not completely, but they trusted him. That was all he asked. They didn't know the things he knew.

Not yet.

"Prepare for a hike," he said. "Tell everyone it's practice; we'll spend the night on the mountain. Have everyone on the nicy wing packed and ready first thing in the morning."

"Christmas is in a week." Mindy chuckled. "If you're planning for the North Pole, is this a good idea?"

He looked over his shoulder. "How's my boy holding up?"

"He's a little shook. He needs some rest. I think you're pushing a little here, Billy."

Shook. That was precisely what Billy Big Game had expected when he'd required everyone to participate in the game room. He needed to unlock Ryder's memories. The more he remembered, the more irresistible he would become.

The world needs to know.

Billy had witnessed the dream he had in the dome. It was unlike any dream they'd pulled from the children. So vivid and real. *And in first person, as if he were the reindeer.* But it wasn't the quality that surprised him the most. It was the content.

He saw the truck.

It was more than a dream. This was a memory. *But how did he have this memory? It was impossible.*

Billy Big Game was a biology engineer. There was still so much he didn't know, like how such a thing could gain flight? Even with the theory of a helium bladder, given its mass, it should still be impossible. And how did a thing that size remain so elusive?

The answers are on the mountain.

"The naughties will remain here. They'll begin final introspection after we leave. I want all of them converted in three days' time. We'll all be nice for the Pole."

"Can we talk about this?" Mindy asked.

Billy Big Game frowned. *Hear her out, my boy. We still need her.* "Continue."

"The Pole's a dangerous place, Billy. I know you know this, but it's hardly a trek for a group of children. Please reconsider. Take John and Jane, if you must. The drones can go without putting the rest of them in danger. Whatever you hope to discover, if anything happens, you'll be labelled as reckless. You'll undo everything."

Hope to discover? Hope? He sighed. She loved his outrageous claims. Ratings were her first love. John and Jane, though, were different. They trusted a bit more. Of course they did. He wanted them to believe. So they did.

Because good girls and boys do what I tell them.

Billy Big Game squatted. Figgy was curled up in the corner. He rubbed her ears. "Jane? John?" he said. "Your thoughts?"

"They'll be ready for the Pole," John said. "I have no doubts."

Jane smiled. "Absolutely."

"You're rushing this," Mindy interjected. "Go to the mountain and get what you're looking for. The Pole will still be there next year. We can use the time to promote."

He bristled. There was still so much she didn't understand. How could she? If the mountain trek was successful, he would need to get to the North Pole as soon as possible. Alarms would be sounded. They would know what he was planning.

There's no time to waste. We've waited long enough.

"We launch for the Arctic Circle in a week's time. And by tomorrow, we capture new game from my mountain."

"Don't hurt it," Mindy said. "You know that'll be bad—"

"For ratings. Don't worry."

He refused to remove his trophies from the office and dining hall. The producers had tested their audience and found it to be distasteful. But that was in the past, where he didn't look anymore. And he didn't hunt anymore.

At least not like that.

Billy Big Game wouldn't kill what was on his mountain. Oh no, not in a million. He'd been building a trap for it for almost fifteen years now. It was ready to snap. Something would get hurt, but it wouldn't make the stream.

Not until he was ready.

"Anything else?" he asked.

"Ryder's a little stressed," Jane said. "The thoughts we pulled from the game room are strange. The perspective is just... it's like nothing I've ever seen. Have you looked at them?"

He flinched. They weren't supposed to see Ryder's thoughts. His anger flared then was quickly extinguished with a thought. *Don't make a scene. We're very close now. They'll know the truth soon enough.*

"We'll understand his thoughts soon. No need to worry."

"He's also gotten close to Cherry," Jane said. "They don't talk much, but there are subtle interactions that suggest their keeping things off the stream. She's smart that way. I think we should keep a closer watch on them. Maybe bring her on the hike."

"I don't want him at ease, Jane. The greater the stress, the sweeter the bait. You understand that, don't you?"

Of course she understood. He couldn't fault her for emotional urges. It would take time for them to fully control their impulses with a thought like Billy Big Game could. He was patient exactly because he did have control.

He excused them and looked out the window.

The drones were in position. Everything was ready. He called Jane and John back. When Mindy closed the door, he gave them their last instructions. He told them why they were really going to the mountain.

It wasn't to prepare for the North Pole.

15

Yellow truck.

Ryder woke sore and achy and threw the covers over his head. It sounded like a rugby match in the hall. He hadn't heard Arf and Soup wake up. He'd spent the night swirling in dream fragments of what had happened in the game room.

What's in the yellow truck?

Someone tapped on the door and slowly opened it. Chaos bled into the room. Cherry looked around and wrinkled her nose. They could use a candle. Her drone followed her inside. She pulled a chair from his desk and sighed. He'd slept past their early morning meetup. Too bad. He wanted to talk now more than ever.

"Bad things are going to happen," he muttered. "I shouldn't be here."

She folded her hands in her lap like she was meditating. "You're not special, Ryder. We all feel like that, like something's wrong. We're misfits. But those are just thoughts, that's all."

"You don't get it. Bad things happen wherever I go. People get hurt; things get wrecked. Everywhere I go, Cherry. Everywhere. Those aren't just thoughts. They happened."

He took a deep breath, imagined exhaling all the bad feelings he couldn't shed, but the crumminess was still there. He wanted the bad feelings to go away. *That's not the point of meditation,* Cherry once told him. *Not to feel good or bad, but to be open to your experience no matter what it contains.*

He still wanted it to go away.

"I wish I could talk to you." He glanced at Bradley Cooper circling the top bunk.

"Don't."

Yeah, don't give them what they want. Not BG or the millions of people watching. Just stuff it all down. What choice did he have?

"Get out of bed," she said. "You'll feel better."

"I'm not going to the game room."

"Yeah, no one is." She pushed the chair back under the desk and nodded. "Where, by the way?"

She was asking where the phone was. It was a sort of shorthand language everyone at Kringletown spoke. He was going to bring it to her at the next early morning meetup. But just in case that didn't happen, he fluffed the pillow.

The phone's under here.

She got up and closed the door behind her. He got dressed to find out what was happening in the hall. The entire naughty wing was arguing, more than usual. Cherry was outside his room. She'd have to part the crowd to reach her room.

"There he is!" Evan shouted.

They all turned toward Ryder.

"The big hero," Evan continued. "Afraid of the snowman."

"Shut up." Soup was somewhere in the crowd.

There was a scramble near Cherry's door. Arf parted the crowd and separated Evan and Soup, but the insults kept coming. At least it pulled their attention away from Ryder. He got a glimpse of the board.

Game room closed.

It didn't say broke or until further notice. It was closed. Worse, there was a list of names on the board. *Introspections.*

Everybody's name was on it.

"This is his fault!" Evan shouted.

Hands began to fly. A chant started. "Fight! Fight!"

"You're making friends." Cherry laughed.

"Still have more than you," Ryder said.

"You sure?"

Arf pushed back the crowd and threw Soup over his shoulder like a sack of road salt. Soup kicked and punched, but no one got hurt or stopped laughing, and Arf didn't put him down.

"Any time," Evan taunted.

"You suuuuuuuck!" Soup screamed.

Balled-up socks rifled out of rooms as they passed, bouncing harmlessly off his red face and spastic legs. Arf lugged him into the bedroom, kicking and screaming.

"I'll be hiding in the bathroom." Cherry started in the other direction but stopped outside Ryder's bedroom. His roommates were strangely quiet. They were next to their bunks. John was in the middle of the room and Jane was on his bed. They'd slipped inside during the distraction.

There was a backpack at John's feet.

"What's going on?" Ryder said.

"We're here to invite you on a hike," Jane said. "We're climbing up the hill for a couple of nights in preparation for the Arctic expedition. I thought you'd like to join us."

She leaned back on his bed. Her hand slid near the pillow, her fingertips just under the pillowcase. She smiled and winked. A cold sliver of panic impaled his stomach.

"No, thanks. I'm good."

"It's not an invitation, bo."

"Don't be a crabby, Soup," Jane said. "Of course it's an invitation."

"A crabby? Take my name off introspection and I'll be a happy and a…" He stopped before he said the word. Calling yourself a nicy was not a joke.

"You'd rather go hiking with us?" John asked.

"Billy gives us this awesome game room and now he just shuts it down like that," Soup said. "I mean, what kind of sicko does that?"

"The man who feeds you and clothes you and houses you and educates—"

"Okay, all right. I get it, *Dad*."

"Listen, the game room was there to condition you for the expedition," John said. "That's all it was. I think you're ready."

"Yeah, well, I'm not going to the Pole. Neither is Arf."

Jane laughed. "We're done with games. This is real life. The trip is in one week. You'll spend the rest of your time learning about the Arctic and getting mentally prepared. That's what the introspections are for."

"Let me practice spelling. N-O."

Jane smiled sweetly. It looked like a smile, but it wasn't. Ryder began breathing when she stood up without the phone.

"Your bag's packed, Ryder." John held up the pack. "There's winter gear for you on our wing. You can pack some personal items if you wish, but keep it light. We'll be out there for a few days to get accustomed to our gear. The naughties will go when we're back."

"Why's he going with you?" Soup asked.

"Simple," Jane said. "We like him."

Ryder took the pack from John. It was heavy and tight, not much room for anything else. He dropped it on the floor and leaned against the desk.

A corner of wrapping paper was beneath the laptop.

"Give me a few minutes?" he said. "I'll meet you in the horseshoe."

Jane and John traded a glance. They had come to escort him off the naughty wing. Was he coming back?

"He's not going anywhere," Soup said. "Let him scratch his butt before you brainwash him."

Jane and John left him in the room. If he wasn't in the horseshoe in thirty minutes, they'd come back. Cherry was still in the hall. Ryder looked at the bed as innocently as possible. When he looked back, she was gone.

Soup slammed the door. "God, this room smells nice."

Ryder knew what he meant. No matter how much perfume or

fragrance they wore, the nicy smell always hung around. Ryder made his bed. He didn't want anyone messing with it while he was gone. The phone was still there.

"Bo," Soup said, "you've only been here like a month. Maybe you should start eating boogers or something, give them a reason to leave you alone."

Ryder looked at the drones. He couldn't tell them anything, even if they stripped down to their underwear. And it was too much to write down beneath a blanket.

He grabbed the note beneath his laptop.

It had been ripped from the same roll of wrapping paper. The note was written in big black letters.

"*Know your fear*," Soup read. "What's that mean?"

Ryder shrugged. It wasn't *Don't be afraid* or *Know no fear* or *Be brave*. It was *Know your fear*. That was something Cherry would say.

"I don't know anything," Ryder muttered.

❄

"You sure this is it?" Ryder looked at Bradley Cooper.

There was no response. This was where the drone had brought him to meet the group. He was ten minutes early, but the room was empty. Bradley Cooper hovered over to the window, the green eye never leaving him.

There were voices outside.

They were in the horseshoe. The snow wasn't deep, but they were huddled like penguins in the cold, their body heat protecting each other.

They weren't wearing coats.

Ryder had been told to bring his pack to this room, where they would gear up and go over instructions before scaling the mountain. The gear was outside, but no one was wearing it.

He opened the door.

"There he is!" BG shouted.

Figgy sat next to BG. The group glared as Ryder approached.

Their teeth were clattering; their stares were piercing. Backpacks were lined up behind BG, each piled beneath their coats and gloves.

"Better late than never, my boy," BG said. "Gather up."

Ryder wanted to clarify he wasn't late. He was early. But the nicies wouldn't see it that way. He stopped short of the huddle, choosing a sunny spot closer to a small group of producers who were dressed properly. The nicies weren't going to let him in.

Why aren't they wearing coats?

"Do you think you're cold?" BG paused until he had their attention. It was a long time before they tore their hate-stares away from Ryder. "This is nothing compared to where we're going, children. Today your skin will burn and your speech will slur, but this is just uncomfortable. This is chilly. And yes, this is dangerous, but out here your snot won't freeze. Ice will not coat your eyebrows."

He kicked the pack at his feet.

"This will not be fun. But history will remember you. Today we hike to the top of the mountain, where we will camp for the night and return tomorrow. Use this opportunity to harden your will. There is only one rule. Do not quit."

He took the time to look each of them in the eye.

"Gear up."

The clan broke like wild animals, racing for their packs. A few of them went out of their way to bump Ryder. BG watched them dress. When all the scarves and caps and coats and gloves were on, Ryder looked around. There was nothing left. He wasn't given winter gear, only a pack.

"Are you ready?" BG asked.

The nicies responded like marines. BG smiled back but didn't lead the way. He pointed to Ryder, who was beginning to shiver.

"A brother is lacking," he said.

"Let him freeze," someone muttered.

BG took his time finding the one who said it. It was Kraig. BG towered over the boy and dropped a hand on his shoulder.

"You should never go outside without a coat. You won't last two minutes. We're a family, son. Our brothers and sisters' keeper. We work together or fail trying. We're short a coat."

BG stared with intent. The drones captured the moment. The tension and drama ensured a place in the morning's stream. Kraig knew what he was asking. They weren't leaving until he answered correctly.

Without breaking eye contact, he stripped off the coat and threw it at Ryder. Lip twitching, he nodded back at their fearless leader.

"That's the spirit," BG said.

With that, he turned to the mountain. The nicies fell in line, jabbing the snow with long trekking poles. Ryder put on the coat with a secret joy concealed beneath his stiff cheeks. The next two days were bound to be joyless and merciless.

At least Kraig was the one who gave it up.

Faces watched from the naughty wing, hands cupped against the windows, breath fogging the glass. They were warm and bored. The prospect of watching Ryder bring up the rear made their plight a little less boring. They would do introspections, give up a few memories.

At least they were warm.

❄

THE COAT ROTATION continued at five-minute intervals, everyone volunteering to be the next. When Ryder's turn came back around, fifteen minutes had passed before someone volunteered.

The trees blocked the wind, and the snow was easier to navigate. Even with the coat, Ryder shivered uncontrollably. He'd lost feeling in his face. His teeth rattled like pearls on a freight train. He lagged far behind, out of earshot from the conversations. Occasionally, they looked back.

Just get this over with.

He considered turning around. The thought of a warm bed was crushing his resolve. The trip, though, required one step at a time. The others complained when they stopped. Ryder kept to himself.

He began counting his steps like meditation and eventually fell into a rhythm. Thoughts would bubble up and he would take notice, labelling them like Cherry had taught him, then let them drift away like colorful balloons.

He couldn't feel his feet.

Up ahead, the group had gathered. The trees were beginning to thin. Soon they would be exposed as the terrain grew steeper and the temperature dropped. It was getting harder to catch his breath.

"Set up!" BG announced. "We'll camp in the trees tonight; take advantage of the cover. There will be no such luxury on the ice, keep in mind. This is my gift to you."

Maybe the medical staff had advised him to do so, but they were already preparing to crawl in sleeping bags. The tents would be enough to protect them. Someone began breaking sticks for kindling.

"Will there be fire on the ice?" BG called.

There was a groan. They'd be eating dinner cold. Ryder journeyed away from the pack and found a heavy spruce. Away from the woods, its branches touched the ground. Beneath it lay a bed of needles with just enough room for a tent.

He hoped no one saw him.

They hadn't paid attention to him so far. But he had the coat. That meant someone was lacking. He thought about returning it, but no one had complained. They were all thinking the same thing anyway.

Let's get this over with.

He found a small butane canister. He stepped out to gather some snow to melt. The spruce was next to an outcropping of stone. There were tracks in the snow. He'd seen this place before.

Impossible, he thought.

He'd never hiked this mountain in his life. The sense of déjà vu was dizzying. It must be dehydration. He followed the outcropping. Each step was more familiar than the one before it. He had walked this way before, climbed this terrain.

How?

Warmth had begun to glow inside him, like he was built for this kind of weather. He felt stronger, too. His nose grew hot, blood vessels warming the air as he inhaled.

Twigs snapped in the trees. Daylight was quickly waning, and the woods had grown dense and dark. A log lay across an opening, the rotting branches pointing up like weapons. Something was in the shadows.

Or someone.

"Where you running?" Kraig said.

Ryder had lost track of how far he'd gone or how long he'd been walking. It was darker than he thought. He was lucky Kraig interrupted him before it was too late.

"Give me the coat." Kraig was already wearing one.

How far was the camp? He looked around. *And where's Bradley Cooper?*

"You want to pick up where we finished?" Kraig said. "Or do you want to run away? You're good at that."

He crept toward him.

"I don't like you," he said. "*I hate you*, everything about you. You have no self-respect, no discipline or manners. You're broken, all of you."

"You were one of us."

"Not like that. You're all hopeless."

"Then why am I here?" Ryder spit the words, but he really wanted to know. *Why am I here?*

"The other losers are digging a hole. That's right, a giant hole in the horseshoe. When we get back, we're throwing them in it. You too."

Ryder stopped backpedaling. If he ran, he'd get lost. That was worse than what Kraig had in mind. His legs were already numb, so he couldn't feel the fear course through his thighs, but it was twisting his stomach.

Know your fear.

Ryder had been shoved around all of his life. He could take licks. Kraig wasn't anything new. It was just skin and bone. *So why the fear?* It wicked into his chest like poison, swelling in his throat and raising the hairs on his neck. He let those sensations spread and watched where they went, paid attention to the thoughts they bred.

I'm alone.

That was the poison, the thoughts that crippled his will. He'd always been alone. No one wanted him. And people like Kraig reminded him. *You don't belong.*

Kraig pulled his gloves off. "Try not to cry."

"You're too stupid to do anything else."

"I'm good at this. You're good at running."

Ryder could smell that weird nicy smell on him.

"I won't leave a mark." Kraig rubbed his hands. "But I can't promise—"

Ryder took a swing.

Kraig blocked it with his forearm and shoved him. Ryder went tumbling backwards. The back of his head struck gravel. He rolled onto his feet and held up his hands. The world was spinning.

Kraig laughed. "This is going to be fun."

Ryder bent his knees and got low. He was going to shoot for Kraig's legs, tie him up and hang on and hope he would tire out or someone would come looking.

No one is coming.

Gravel cascaded off the outcropping. Kraig stopped approaching. His smile faded. His gaze moved over Ryder's head. It looked like he'd been shot with a tranquilizer. His arms hung at his sides.

The smell of damp hide filled the air. In the dying light, a shadow moved over Ryder. It crept across the snow. An enormous tangle of horns splayed in the shadows.

Hot breath was on his neck.

The cold and rancid fear that had gripped Ryder was replaced by immovable strength and righteous anger. Suddenly he wasn't standing beneath the thing above him.

He looked down on Kraig with vengeance.

The world opened to newfound senses—the smell of perspiration, the tang of fear, the sharpness of perfect sight. He pulled air through warm nostrils that heated the furnace in his belly. Kraig couldn't hurt him anymore.

No one can.

Drones zipped out of the trees. Twigs snapped and Ryder was suddenly thrown back into his small body. He stumbled away, staring up at an enormous beast, an animal he saw in his dreams and hid in his memories. In a flash, he remembered everything.

Ronin.

The reindeer stood over him. Slowly, he turned his head. Ryder saw it, too. Something in the shadows raised a weapon.

"Go," Ryder said. "Go!"

It was too late. There was a dull thud. A web of metallic netting tangled in the antlers and slung over his back. Ronin threw his nose into Ryder and sent him tumbling from the fray.

His roar rattled his bones.

The drones swept in to capture the struggle. Ryder felt his belly swell as Ronin began to inflate. Even with the weight of the metallic net, he could leap farther up the mountain and work out of the trap—

Whump.

This time a stake fired into the stone outcropping. Silver lines fired out like gossamer threads and wrapped around the net and antlers. Another one sank into the rock wall and snagged his back legs.

"No!" Ryder scrambled toward him.

The wires were flexible and unbreakable. The netting shrank. Ryder felt it collapse around Ronin's body, felt the constraints. Double vision threw him off balance—Ronin's vision overlapping his own. He lost track of his body and that of the trapped animal.

This is the dream.

He climbed into the tangle, pulling at the lines. The weight of the metallic netting dropped Ronin on his knees. Hot breath streamed in clouds. Ryder came face-to-face with the giant beast, their eyes meeting, vision flipping back and forth.

Seeing himself. Seeing Ronin.

"I'm sorry..." Ryder said. "Please get up. Please."

Ronin snorted, eyes widening. Despite the countless constraints, he pushed onto all four legs. Ryder's foot was caught in a loop as Ronin lowered his head and charged. The lines stretched to their limits. They sliced the air as they snapped. Little by little, Ronin bulled his way forward, breaking them one by one, dragging the net.

A man watched from the shadows.

If Ronin could get into the trees, he could use their trunks as leverage and drag the net free on the branches.

Ryder reached through the netting as another line snapped. He tugged at his laces and yanked his foot out of the boot that kept him tangled just as Ronin threw his head forward. Ryder fell backwards.

A roar was in his bones as he tumbled into darkness.

16

The reindeer are no longer calves.

It's the last day of the year. The celebration would continue into the New Year. But this year was different from all the previous year ends. There are snowball fights and dancing and youngsters polar-bearing in the open leads.

Elven gather around the herd.

The antlers clatter as they dip their heads. The handlers feed them a blend that will burn the helium bladders faster and hotter. Off to the side and away from the herd, Gallivanter stands beneath the largest of them all.

The last reindeer.

Ronin's growth spurt shocked the breeders. It happened over the course of a decade, a relatively short period of time. The top of Gallivanter's head barely brushes Ronin's knee as he holds out his hand. Ronin curls his tongue around the green cube and grinds it between his molars.

Gallivanter ignores the younger elven throwing up their grabbers—globes hovering to take photos. Neither of them look happy or sad. Intense, the youngsters call them. His green coat spreads behind him. The rest of the handlers, in a show of celebration, display red colors.

"Gather!" Jocah raises her hand. "Gather one and all!"

A single snow-white braid dangles from her head like a rope. There are only a few elven with more years than Gallivanter, but none more than Jocah.

The colony leader announces the first ever end-of-year reindeer games. The ice shudders beneath stamping feet. The crowd parts. A runway stretches across the ice. The handlers give their reindeer encouragement.

"Dasher?" Jocah asks. "Will you do the honors?"

The buck throws back his head and snorts. The elven throw snowballs like confetti as he separates from the herd. With ample space, he backs up several paces, shaking his head vigorously. A deep breath expands his belly. The helium bladder gurgles as his metabolism picks up.

Dasher gallops as his belly inflates. The strides grow longer and lighter. He throws his front legs out.

And soars.

Extra hide billows at the base of each leg to sail on an updraft. The elven celebration reaches a manic pitch as he lands deep down the runway. The herders dial their binoculars to measure the distance. The reindeer rear back to celebrate with kicking hooves.

The games are under way.

One by one, they stretch their bellies and inflate their bladders before launching themselves farther and farther. Each of them is mauled by excited elven. The herders struggle to record the exact distance. Cupid is winning by a nose.

It's Vixen's turn.

She's the smallest of the herd. Her antlers are slim with fewer points. No matter how much they feed her, she maintains a gazelle-like figure. Light on her feet, she draws her breath deep and long.

"Vix-en. Vix-en. Vix-en," the elven chant.

The others had launched like zooming balloons. She shoots like a rocket and glides deep into the night.

They stamp into the runway and lose sight of her. The herders shout for them to clear away, but she's gone far beyond the runway. No one sees her land.

Not even a puff of snow.

A rumble of confusion ripples through the colony. She's leaped so far *that they can't even measure the jump. They don't know whether to cheer or search.*

"Polar!"

The call comes from one of the herders. He's pointing a finger, but no one sees the big white predator. No proximity warning had sounded to send them below the ice. A polar bear is not a friend of the elven. Panic powers the confusion, and elven begin jumping in holes.

Gallivanter grabs the binoculars.

Ronin stretches his neck. Eyes wide, the biggest reindeer of them all has spotted the white-furred beast racing on all fours.

Vixen tries to stand.

Ronin takes three steps. The herd gets out of his way as his belly boils like a sizzling furnace. He throws out his front legs and disappears into the night. There are no cheers like there were for the others. The game is over. As the polar bear closes in on Vixen, it becomes real life.

He lands on four thundering hooves and rolls in a tumbling cloud of snow. The polar bear hesitates but continues the charge. She is hungry and she has cubs to feed. Ronin climbs to his full height and romps in front of Vixen.

His howl brings chills to the elven.

When Gallivanter arrives with a rescue squad, the polar bear is gone. Snow has been pushed aside. Ronin lies on his side with his tongue out and long slashes across his shoulder. Blood pools near his belly. More trails away.

They set up a perimeter with wave emitters and heat beams. Vixen has broken two legs and damaged her ribs from the jump. Gallivanter cradles Ronin's snout. Foam gathers in his nostrils. His nose is red hot.

"My boy," Gallivanter says. "My boy."

❄

RYDER WAS STARING AT A CEILING, not a bunk.

The bed was twice as wide as any bed he'd ever slept in, one he could lay on in any direction and not have his feet hang over the side.

It was in the middle of the room. The sheets were silk. His head, cradled in a plush pillow, throbbed.

Someone was talking.

There was a desk and a laptop and a wide window with thick wooden slats. Thin strips of daylight lined the carpet. A conversation was taking place.

"It was cold," John said.

"No," Jane countered, "it was freezing."

"BG said it's not freezing till it's below zero."

"Then he flunked science."

They shared a laugh. They were talking about the bitter cold and numb lips, snow packed inside his boots—

"Ronin," he muttered.

He fell back onto the pillow, his brain splitting in two. *He came to my rescue.*

"I'm not saying I'm happy we came back early," Jane said. "I'm just saying someone got hurt. I'm not going to say *whooooo...*"

The stream showed a line of hikers scaling a rocky path. The next scene showed a close-up of Ryder. His eyes were closed and the nicies looked worried.

"He's fine," Jane said. "Just a misstep, that's all."

"It was good practice," John said. "If that happens on the Pole, we'll know what to do."

"We'll come home?"

Another laugh shared. No mention of a struggle or a three-thousand-pound reindeer tangled in a steel net. No shots fired. A red line cut across Ryder's palm, the wound fresh where the reinforced netting had struck him.

He crawled to the edge of the bed. His feet barely touched the floor. He pried one of the blinds apart. It was early. The horseshoe was empty and the windows on the other wing were closed. The building was facing the wrong way. He slammed the laptop shut.

Where's Bradley Cooper?

This couldn't be happening. He fell back on the bed, the room going into another slow spin. He was dreaming of reindeer and elven, and now there was one on the mountain.

What did they do to him?

The door opened. BG closed it behind him and observed Ryder for a moment. Figgy was at his side, her toenails clicking the floor. BG was cleaned up, his bushy red hair combed back and the beard groomed. His green eyes peered down from beneath thick eyebrows. He opened the blinds and stared out the window.

"It appears you have a friend," he said. "A very big one."

Friend?

"Yes, this is real," BG said. "You share a connection with a very special animal—a kind of reindeer unknown to the animal kingdom as we know it. Genetically engineered, a species of its own. The last of its kind."

"That's why you brought me here."

All the accidents that had happened in his life weren't accidents. They were always shrouded in mystery, memories he couldn't quite recall. Every time he was threatened or in trouble, something bailed him out. David had found out.

Trouble follows you, someone had told him. Maybe something else was following him.

"Kraig." Ryder chuckled drily. "He did that on purpose."

They'd pulled his memories from the introspection; they knew his dreams, unlocked his memories. BG knew what would happen when Kraig threatened him.

BG wedged his hands on his hips. "Do you know the story of your beginning?"

Ryder had been abandoned in a moving truck and found by a cop on Christmas Eve. That was all anyone ever told him.

"How did the officer know you were there?" BG asked.

Ryder had never asked that question. It was a Christmas miracle he had survived.

"An anonymous call was placed that evening," BG said. "No one ever knew who made it or how they knew you were there. They assumed it was the person who put you there. The report stated it was a man with a very deep voice. It didn't say it was a very fat man."

Ryder looked up. The room was suddenly small and confining. He believed Santa Claus was real. Now he was saying he was the one who called the police. But Ryder had just witnessed a reindeer come to his rescue, had seen through his eyes, had felt his belly inflate and his attempt to fly.

Ryder shook his head.

"It's my business to know, son. You've seen it with your own eyes. Ronin likes you."

"How do you know—"

"His name?" He smiled. *It's my business.* "He doesn't just like you, does he? You dream about him. You always have. You see and feel him. The night you were discovered in the back of the truck, there was a connection between you and the last reindeer."

I can't feel him anymore.

There was an emptiness in his mind, a gap that he hadn't felt before, like a missing tooth. "What'd you do to him?"

"I wouldn't think of hurting him."

"Why are you doing this?"

"I'm curious. And it's time the world knew the truth. I'll start with the reindeer, then find the fat man."

The air was suddenly hot and thin. Ryder couldn't breathe fast enough.

"Reality is what we believe. We see what we want to see, Ryder, but the truth is out there. We owe it to ourselves and each other to find it, to share it. Seeking truth… that's our purpose, Ryder."

"The truth? You sent Kraig after me. You're using me, you're using all of us. This whole place is a lie."

"Where were you before this?" BG blocked Ryder's pacing. "Who cared for you?"

"You don't care about us."

"I'm giving you the greatest gift of all." A smile broadened inside the thick beard. "The reindeer chose to protect *you,* Ryder. He chose you."

"I didn't ask for that. I didn't ask for any of this!"

"We don't ask to be born, don't ask to be who we are. You're too young to understand." He put a firm hand on Ryder's shoulder. "But soon, you'll understand everything."

For a moment, he looked like he was going to hug him. Ryder jerked away. There were no drones in the room. This wasn't for streaming.

"I'm not staying here." Ryder waved at the room. "I'm not one of them."

BG tousled his hair before opening the door. That fake smell hiding under his cologne—the smell all nicies had—was going to be in Ryder's hair, in his clothes.

"You've always been nice," BG said.

❄

CONVERSATION DIED on the naughty wing. Heads popped out of rooms as Ryder walked past them. A few people asked how he was doing and what happened.

You didn't hear? We caught a magic reindeer. Turns out Santa is real.

The room was tidy. Ryder's bed was still made. So was Soup's bed. Arf was folding laundry and dropped a shirt when he saw him. He actually hugged him. It was like hugging a grizzly.

"Where's Soup?" Ryder asked.

"Not back yet."

"From where?"

Arf stared at the floor then put clothes in a drawer. He didn't have to say it. Ryder pushed his hair back. *He went. He actually went to introspection.*

"He didn't come back?"

Arf shook his head. "None of them have."

"What'd you mean?" Ryder's session had only taken an hour. "How many?"

Arf shrugged. He sat on his bed, shoulders slouched, head hung like a lost puppy. "You all right?" he asked.

He'd seen the stream. Ryder explained he'd slipped on some ice and hit his head. Funny thing was he couldn't explain how he woke up the next morning. That meant they'd carried him down from the mountain and put him in bed and he slept through the night. And none of the nicies acted like that was odd. It was like someone flipped a switch and put him to sleep. He woke up with a little headache and that was it. How was he going to explain that?

"They emptied out your drawers," Arf said, "while you were gone."

Ryder's laptop was in the other wing. He didn't bother checking his clothes. He sat on his bed and slid his hand under the pillow. A chill filled his legs.

The phone is gone.

"I heard the rooms are bigger," Arf said.

"It stinks over there."

"Yeah." Arf weaved his fingers into a pretzel. "We're all going over there. It's just a matter of time."

"We don't have to, Arf."

Arf just shrugged. But he was right. BG wanted to turn them all nice. That was why they were at Kringletown. To make good girls and boys.

So why aren't I nice?

Despite what BG said, Ryder wasn't one of them. He could dangle all the desserts he wanted, Ryder wasn't going for it. He didn't feel any different now, even after the mountain or waking up in the nicy wing. He was exactly the same. But BG didn't say he was going to be nice or had turned nice.

You've always been nice.

❄

THERE WAS a list on the board.

A date and time was assigned to each name. Arf was set to go in two days. Everyone would be done before Christmas, and then they would launch for the Pole.

Cherry's name was at the bottom.

He tapped on her door. She yanked it open and looked down the hall. Several naughties were watching. Bradley Cooper hovered next to her drone.

There was only so much they could say.

"Surprised they let you out," she said.

He was, too. When BG had left his room, he had expected him to lock it, but no one stopped him from leaving.

"You still you?" she asked.

"I'm not one of them."

She crossed her arms. "Did you find Santa?"

If Ryder told her what really happened on the mountain, it wouldn't make the stream. And BG didn't tell him not to tell anyone.

"You wouldn't believe what happened."

He started laughing. At first, it was sarcastic and angry, but it evolved into a genuine belly laugh. How could any of this be real? It was so absurd all he could do was laugh. *I have a reindeer who can fly.* He was constantly looking at his hands, like that would tell him if he was dreaming or not. Still, he told her what really happened on the mountain.

Almost.

He told her about Kraig, how he'd wandered off to find a place to pitch his tent. It was the same as the football game, only there was no one around to stop him this time.

"I figured it was something like that," she said. "This morning's stream didn't make sense."

"Yeah, well…"

She frowned. "Something else?"

He juggled the facts and lies. She wasn't going to believe it no matter what order he put them in.

"Yeah," he said. "This giant reindeer got between us."

"A deer?"

"No, a reindeer. And, uh, they used a special net to drag it down. I sort of got caught in the middle."

She waited. "And?"

"We came back after that. I think."

"You think?"

He explained how he hit his head and woke up the next morning, that he didn't remember anything beyond that.

"You were knocked unconscious?"

He shrugged. That part didn't make sense, either. This wasn't the movies where someone took a hit and woke up at a convenient time later. He did hit his head; the evidence was still tender. It was like he went to sleep on command.

"What'd they do with the deer?"

"Reindeer." He shook his head. "*I don't know.*"

She heard him loud and clear. The guilt weighed on his words. He didn't want to talk about it. Wanted to forget it.

"Things are getting weird, even for this place," she said. "No one is coming back from introspection."

"Don't go."

"You think I have a choice?"

Ryder couldn't imagine them dragging her down the hall, but somehow they'd manage it. Everyone else had gone. Even Soup.

"What's going on?" he whispered.

"Same as always." She looked at the drones. "Right in front of the world."

❄

It's deep down here.

And cold.

I'm treading water; it's hard to keep my head up. My feet paddle. I don't think there's a bottom. And I'm afraid to find out. Maybe I can't touch.

Maybe there isn't a bottom.

"Ryder."

He was jostled awake, sucking air deeply and hungrily. His face was wet and warm. He scrambled in the dark, confused, reaching for the walls of a deep and dark hole—

"Hey, shhh." Cherry grabbed his arms.

He wiped his face. The door was open. She was kneeling next to his bed, her whispers masked by Arf's snoring. The drones were dormant and docked.

"What time is it?"

She shined the phone in his face. "Come on."

He got dressed and met her in her room, where the candle was flickering. He closed the door, still foggy, running his hand through his hair damp with sweat, relieved that she had the phone. The cold remnants of the dream still ran over him.

"You all right?" she asked.

He sat on the edge of the bed. "Bad dream."

"Guess what? You're still in a nightmare."

She tried to laugh. He didn't bother. This dream was heavy and clingy. He rubbed his cheeks, eyes puffy. He cleared his throat and tried to walk it off. She gave him space to settle, didn't try to pull it out of him. He noticed that about her, she was good with space. Maybe it was the meditation.

"You got the phone," he said.

She displayed it again. A map lit up. There were no routes, just a detailed layout of Kringletown with labels and locations. There wouldn't be time to explore. He'd slept through any chance of that.

"I waited," she said. "Decided to come get you. Hope that's all right."

She paused. "Want to tell me what really happened on the mountain?"

He nodded thoughtfully while thumbing the map around the screen.

"I've been having these, uh... these dreams for a while now. They're like a... a story, sort of. I think..." He shook his head. He had the feeling he'd always had these dreams, ever since he was little. "I thought everyone dreamed stories, you know? I mean, I have a dream one night and then the next dream would just pick up where it left off."

"That's not normal."

He handed her the phone and paced again, the cold dregs dragging behind him like tin cans. "It's about a reindeer."

She waited for more. "Okay."

"He's a runt who was abandoned by his mother. And an, um, an elven discovers him."

"An elven?"

"You know, like an elf, sort of. You know how dreams are."

She heard the emotion, like it was more than a dream to him. Ryder could still remember what the elven looked like, short and fat with enormous bare feet that treaded over the snow. His round face was buried in a white beard that hung in two ropey braids. His eyes twinkled when he smiled.

And I know his name. He didn't tell her that.

"It was sort of against the rules, what he did. But it saved the reindeer's life."

"A lot of detail for a dream."

"The reindeer kept growing after that. He had this rack of antlers that looked like tree branches." He spread out his hands. "He was very protective of the elven and all the others in the colony."

"There were other what? Elven?"

"And reindeer. They all had antlers too. They weren't like normal reindeer that lose them every year and regrow new ones. They weren't like them in a lot of ways."

He stopped pacing. It was feeling more like a confession.

"They can fly."

Cherry nodded. "Okay."

"They're genetically modified with this bladder that fills up with helium, and there's extra hide on their legs that allows them to glide, sort of like—"

"Santa Claus," she said. "You're talking about Santa Claus's reindeer, the ones that pull his sleigh?"

"Um, yeah. Ronin is the last one."

"Ronin?"

"The reindeer found by—"

"The elven, right. It's just a dream, though, Ryder. There's no Santa Claus and there's no magic reindeer. You know that, right?"

"I know. I know."

She watched him, watched his feet pace to the door and back to the candle. The dream he just woke up from and the ones he'd had since arriving were just so vivid. They weren't just a story.

I can feel them.

Ronin was somewhere cold and dark. Maybe not in a well, but he was alone.

"That was him," he said. "Ronin was on the mountain."

"The reindeer?"

"He showed up when Kraig came at me."

She was at a loss for words. He knew how it sounded. The whole thing was bizarre, the dreams, this place. Maybe she was right, he was still in a nightmare.

"Here's where it gets weird," he said.

"Here? You met an animal from your dream and this is where it gets weird?"

"I think I've known Ronin all my life. I think that's why I dream of him. He sort of... protects me, I don't know why. It just explains why bad things happen to people. I sort of remember him now."

The time when David had trapped him behind the garage, the way he ended up with broken bones and the wall of the garage was cracked. He didn't imagine that.

I remember.

"Remember when Kraig knocked me down at the football game and we heard the howl? That was him."

Ryder remembered the airplane that was soaring in the gray sky before the football game. *Airplanes don't fly over Kringletown,* Mindy the producer said. *This is private land. Nothing comes out here unless BG says so.*

"Let me get this straight," she said. "Your guardian angel is one of Santa's reindeer. Every time you're in trouble, he blows up like a hot air balloon and floats to your rescue, smashes someone with his horns, and then floats back to the Pole."

"I don't know all that. All I know is that when Kraig came at me, he was there. And, uh..."

"Go on," she said. "Don't stop now."

He sat across from her and explained what had happened when he looked Ronin in the eyes, the way he felt the panic and the rage, the anger and strength. How he could see through Ronin's eyes, see his own face looking back. How this was all a trap.

"I was bait."

He raked his hands through his hair. His eyes misted up and he turned away. This was his fault. If he had paid attention to all those other times, he would've run from Kraig, would never have let him come close.

This is my fault.

He wiped his eyes. She'd already seen him wake up with wet cheeks. The mattress sank next to him. Her shoulder was against his; she took his hand. Her fragrance embraced him.

"I think I know where he is."

She held up the phone. Kringletown was easy to recognize. She zoomed on the far side and tapped a label.

"Remember that night I went to the barn? The big doors were unlocked, and inside there were these giant areas—they weren't cages. They were more like stalls an elephant could live in. Why else would BG have something like that?"

"You believe me?"

"I believe there was a reindeer." She squeezed his hand. "And that BG has it. He always has space in his trophy case."

Close enough, he thought.

He wouldn't expect anyone to believe his story, and she hadn't thrown him out. In fact, she was still sitting next to him and—he realized with sudden affection—was holding his hand.

"We go tomorrow," she said, "and see if it's unlocked."

She scrolled around the map. Last time there was a route that took them to the cabin. Submenus popped up when she tapped the cabin, detailing activities such as surveillance, matrix development and memory integration. That last part sounded insidious. BG was collecting their memories; that wasn't a surprise. *But integration? Matrix development?*

Cherry panned throughout Kringletown and found the kitchen and dining hall and library and game room. There were detailed maps of where everything was and how it functioned.

"What's that?" Ryder pointed.

She panned down the nicy wing. The rooms were labelled by name. *Ryder Mack* was attached to a room near the end. There were more amenities on the nicy wing than there were on the naughty wing, and the rooms were larger, but Ryder was pointing at a layer beneath the hallway. He grabbed the label. A submenu popped up and a subterranean map moved to the front.

"Fabrication lab."

It was larger than the cabin lab and almost as big as the entire nicy wing. And that was just one section. There were other rooms labelled cold storage, database, and replicator.

"Where's the entrance?" she said. "Did you see one?"

Ryder had left the nicy wing without looking around. Besides, it was belowground. An elevator would be the way to get there. The thought of sneaking down there sent icicles through his stomach. He just wanted to find Ronin. *And leave.*

"I say we look at this first," she said.

"What about Ronin?"

"We don't know what's going on here. The answer is down there. Here, let's do this. If the phone gives us a route tomorrow night, we take it." She traced a path. "Just like the cabin, we go."

"Why?"

"Because someone wants us to know."

"Who?" He leaned away from her. "Have you ever thought of that? Who's sending us notes? Who gave you the phone?"

"Someone who wants to help." She pointed at the door. "My name is on the board. They're going to come for me. I won't go, but you know they'll make me. BG always gets his way. I don't know what they're doing to us, but no one is coming back, so whatever our mystery helper has in mind, I'm game. We don't have a choice."

She turned off the phone and opened the door, checking the board as if hoping her name had disappeared. She sat next to him and whispered, "I don't want to be nice."

Ryder didn't like the feeling of introspection when he was there, but whatever they were doing now was different. They'd gotten what they needed from the game room. BG's endgame was near. They should do more than find Ronin. They needed to follow the phone. Someone wanted to help.

Or needs help.

17

Jane and John couldn't wait for the North Pole. Every morning they blabbed on the stream, and all the nicies agreed. One by one, they confessed their excitement that always ended in hugs and high fives and sometimes tears. BG deserved a Nobel.

Arf groaned.

He lay on his side with his laptop against the wall. Ryder had nodded off, dreaming about elephant cages and Arctic wind. He woke up staring at the top bunk.

Christmas was a week away.

The phone had been quiet. No maps or notes, no directions on what to do. But he had a plan. First, they were going to find Ronin. It didn't matter what the phone said, they needed to find him before a new rack of antlers was on the dining room wall.

Once they found him, they would free him as soon as the drones shut down at four o'clock. They could have winter gear ready and make their escape. That would give them an hour before anyone would notice. He didn't know where they would go, but they could use the phone to film what they were doing and upload the truth. If they were caught, the world would know what happened to them.

And if he can really fly... He cut that thought out. Reindeer only flew in dreams. *But they don't follow you around, either.*

"I thought you were nice."

Cherry was returning from the bathrooms, drying her hair with a towel. Ryder sat up, confused. He was about to answer when he realized she was pretending.

"I heard the rooms are bigger over there," she said. "What's it like?"

He thought about it. "It stinks."

"Worse than this?" She nodded at their room.

"I'm thinking of going back," he said. "All my clothes are there. Laptop, too. Want a tour?"

She hung the towel around her neck and shrugged. It was a good show. No one would believe it. She'd never said more than a hundred words to him before that. However, no one would really know why she was suddenly interested in him.

"Want to go, Arf?" he said.

"No." He didn't roll over. "I'll wait."

Ryder was struck with guilt. If they found Ronin, how could he leave Soup and Arf behind? Arf wasn't going anywhere until Soup came back, and no one knew where he was. *Still.*

Cherry came back to the room an hour later.

It was a fifteen-minute walk to the other side. Bradley Cooper led them through the spacious foyer. A Christmas tree touched the ceiling, the branches heavy with ornaments and twinkling lights. She wrinkled her nose. The nicy smell greeted them before they got there. The hall was wider than the naughty wing and cleaner. The bedroom doors spaced farther apart.

No one was playing music.

"Did you see the stream?" he asked.

"No."

BG wasn't on it. He hadn't been on the stream since coming back from the mountain. No one had seen him, either. Ryder wondered if he'd taken the helicopter over the mountain again.

"I'm on the end." He pointed at the room.

Cherry's lips were silently moving. She was counting her steps, visualizing what they saw on the phone. The lab took up all the space below them. She was keeping track of her steps in case they passed an entrance. But it was all just bedrooms.

The nicy board was mounted at the end of the hall. A meeting was scheduled for the afternoon. No one was listed for introspection. Nicies didn't do introspection.

Only when you're naughty.

The bedroom was exactly as he left it. The open laptop was asleep and the bed made. It smelled fresher than the hallway, but the clayey smell was seeping in. He wondered if he'd get accustomed to it like he had with Arf's socks.

"Bigger than I thought." She looked around the room, bounced her hand on the bed and pulled open a drawer. "Folded your clothes."

"Someone did."

She looked out the window, nodding to herself, making mental note of the naughty wing, whose window was whose. Ryder touched the laptop. The monitor woke up with a digital note in the corner.

"Look."

Cherry peered over his shoulder and grunted. *"There is only the present,"* she read. "It's Zen."

"Maybe it's Christmas present."

"It means the past and future don't exist, just this moment. As in now, not tomorrow."

"As in don't wait?"

She understood exactly what he was saying. Was their mystery helper telling them not to hesitate when the time came? *Or stop waiting for a map?*

"You going to stay here tonight?" she asked.

"No. Arf will get lonely."

"He's a big boy."

"He is a big boy." Ryder tucked the laptop under his arm. "That's the tour. Want to see the bathrooms? The toilets are made of gold."

She looked out the window one last time. They closed the door and followed Bradley Cooper. Unless there was a secret door in someone's closet, there was no entrance to the basement lab. Still, she counted her steps as they passed the bedrooms.

One door was open.

There was no music or audio from the stream coming out. Cherry was looking down, counting. Ryder glanced inside as they passed. Someone was tending to a stack of folded laundry, placing shirts in an open drawer.

"Soup?"

Blond hair, scrawny build, that was him. But he didn't turn around. Ryder stood in the doorway till he turned to grab a pile of shirts.

"Oh!" He jumped back. He smiled big and wide. "Scared me. What are you doing over here?"

Ryder was too stunned to answer. Cherry's boots squeaked to a stop. Together, they stared. It was him, Soup the Nicy Hater, placing shirts with shirts and pants with pants and socks in orderly rows. Not a single one of them on the floor.

"Dude, the rooms are huge. We could play tennis in here."

Dude? "Where have you been?"

"Just having a chat with Big Game. Everything makes sense now. You know what I mean, right? We talked about things and then, I don't know, I just wasn't bothered anymore."

"For two days?"

"That how long?" He shrugged. "Went by fast."

Ryder shook his head. The smell of nicy was strong. Like fresh-cooked pottery.

"You staying… over here?" Ryder asked.

"Why wouldn't I?"

"Arf is worried."

Soup paused. It was like he had to think about who he was talking about. "He'll be all right. He goes tomorrow."

"Tomorrow?" Cherry said. "Where's he going?"

He returned to organizing his underwear, patting them in place and smoothing out the wrinkles while he hummed a Christmas tune. Everything that had happened at Kringletown was bizarre.

This went over the top.

"Hey." Ryder was startled by a hand on his arm. Jane smiled at him, perfectly. She turned her smile on Cherry. "Giving a tour?"

"No," Ryder said.

Apparently that was funny. "Getting settled?"

"Hey, Jane. I love these." Soup held up thick socks. One was green, the other red.

"You're going to love the boots."

He looked under the bed. His eyes grew wide. He held up a pair of waterproofs and smiled a smile Ryder had never seen on him. He was wearing a white shirt and dark pants.

The uniform.

"Don't forget," she said, "we're meeting in the den for gear assignments. The Pole is a week away. You too." She pinched Ryder.

So many thoughts streamed through his head. He couldn't capture a single one.

"Did Ryder tell you about the hike?" she called into the room. "BG shorted us a coat. We took turns going without one, sort of a teamwork exercise. It worked out pretty well, I think. Don't you?"

Ryder didn't answer. Did she completely block out the part with Ronin? He felt woozy.

"Sounds constructive." Soup stripped his bed and began remaking it, carefully tucking the corners.

"What'd you do to him?" Ryder muttered.

"It's his best self," she said adoringly. "He understands now."

"That isn't him."

"If you strip away your shortcomings, are you still you?" She nodded. "We don't know who we are until we look inward. And once we honestly do that, we put down the things we don't need. We're attached to who we *think* we are."

Soup was whistling as he fluffed the pillows.

"Campbell is his true self now," Jane said.

Ryder waited. Soup didn't erupt. He was deep in a Christmas tune and tucking the bed corner. "Campbell?"

"Yeah?" he said.

Ryder stared. When he didn't say anything, Soup waved him off like he was messing with him.

"This isn't right."

"That's his name, Ryder. He reclaimed it. No more dark corners to hide from, no more suffering. He's a good boy. He's nice."

Ryder walked off. He couldn't look anymore. Something about the scene was disturbing. The hall was swimming around him.

"Don't forget the meeting," Jane called.

Cherry caught up to him. They followed the drones out of the wing and walked in silence. The name, the way he was dressed, the goofy smile and whistling. It was like he woke in an alternate reality. He didn't even call her sweet Jane. But that wasn't the worst part.

He's not wearing the hearing aid.

❄

RYDER NEEDED AIR. Frigid, bone-chilling air.

The horses galloped along the fence, snow flipping off their hooves. His coat hung open, inviting winter inside. He welcomed the shivers.

How far would we have to go to escape? The other side of the mountain?

"It's freezing." Cherry huddled next to him, a scarf around her face. "You should stay in your nicy room tonight."

"No."

Even if there was a door labelled *This way to the secret underground lab,* he couldn't stay there another minute. It was foul. It was wrong.

"What would I tell Arf?" he said.

"Nothing."

"Just let him find out Soup was body-snatched by a nicy."

"Body-snatched?"

"He wasn't wearing his hearing aid! I know BG is a miracle worker and all, but he didn't put a new ear in his head. You saw the way he was acting. That wasn't Soup. That was Campbell." He pointed at the nicy wing. "No one calls him Campbell, and you saw what happened—"

"Ryder."

She put a hand on his arm. Bradley Cooper was grabbing all the footage and he didn't care. Soup's behavior could be explained, maybe. Not the hearing aid. BG couldn't cure that, not in a day or two. Even if there was some medical breakthrough, it wouldn't be seamless, not like that.

"Let's go inside," she said.

"They'll come for you, too."

They had to escape before introspection. He couldn't stand seeing her like that. Neither would she. He couldn't say it out loud. They were all turning nice.

"Why aren't you on the list?" she said.

You've always been nice. BG said it, but Ryder was nothing like them. He wasn't a good boy who did what he was told, so it couldn't be true. *So why aren't I on the list?*

Steel pails rattled in the breezeway. The horses waited at the fence. A large silhouette stepped out of one of the stalls. Ryder could barely feel his feet as he marched toward the barn. The old man ducked into the tack room. The door was still open when Ryder approached.

"Where did he go?" he said.

The room wasn't big enough to hide him. Horses hung their long faces out of the stalls, mashing hay between rubbery lips.

"Where are you?"

Cherry grabbed him. "Don't do this. We don't need attention right now."

He was suddenly red hot. Emotions boiled up from a deep and angry place. All the secrets and the old man was always in the shadows. Why wasn't he on the stream? What was he doing in the cabin?

Ryder pounded on the barn doors, the ones that were locked, the room where Cherry had once visited, had seen cages big enough to house an elephant. His bones rattled. He kicked until his entire body hurt.

"Listen." He put his ear to the door. "Hear that?"

Wump-wump-wump-wump-wump. Something mechanical was turning. He could feel it through the door. That sound wasn't there before.

"Come on." Cherry pulled with both hands.

The drones captured every second. BG was going to see it. He'd throw him in the nicy wing and lock the door this time. The old man appeared in the breezeway like he'd been there the entire time, watching. Ready to draw guns from his long coat.

"Is he in there?" Ryder said.

The old man worked his tongue beneath his bottom lip, pushing a lump of tobacco to the side. Brown specks littered his bushy white beard. He smelled like leather and hard work. He pushed a pair of sunglasses up his nose with the hand with missing fingers.

"Who are you?" Ryder said.

His emotions were running the show now. Ryder planted both hands in the old man's midsection. He leaned in but hardly moved him. A grin wrinkled the scruffy white beard. There were traces of red through it like veins of iron.

The old man grabbed a halter off a hook and turned his back, limping stiffly away. He was almost around the corner when Ryder scooped a snowball off the breezeway and threw it.

It grazed the cowboy hat.

The old cowboy stopped. He spit in the snow. "You don't understand. But you will."

His voice sounded like words spun through a meat grinder. Fear finally dissolved his anger. Ryder felt the full force of paralyzing reality. Cherry grabbed his coat and dragged him out of the breezeway.

"Are you out of your mind?" she whispered in his ear.

Numbly, he followed her across the horseshoe. His emotions had taken charge, but now he understood just how foolish that was. The old man didn't threaten him, didn't even take a swing. It was his voice that raised gooseflesh on Ryder's neck. It was the way it sounded.

Like it was inside him.

"We got to leave," he said. "Tonight."

18

"*Gallivanter!*" *the herders shout.*
The harness jingles. The reindeer at the front tosses his head. Cubes of special feed fall in the snow.
"Here. Take him."
The herder shoves a feed bag at Gallivanter and slides away. Ronin holds his head up. His rack rises above the reindeer. Gallivanter sighs.
"How many times have I told you? The others can feed you."
The last reindeer snorts. His breath hits Gallivanter like hot steam, blowing his beard braids over his shoulders. It's followed by wet nostrils on his cheek. Gallivanter holds up a cube.
"Eat."
The other reindeer gobble all the cubes they're offered. They remember what happened last Christmas. Dasher, Dancer and Cupid were recovering from a slight illness and shouldn't have made the journey. Halfway through the night, they gassed out. Christmas is always a demanding night, but that Christmas the sick reindeer were barely able to inflate.
Ronin had shouldered the burden of hauling the sleigh through the last leg. Without him, they would've been stuck somewhere in the Netherlands.
Gallivanter hugs his snout. "Time to go, my boy."
The reindeer eagerly dig at the snow. The bells jingle. They look back

and wait. There are pronouncements. The elven step back. The call is given; Ronin throws his head back and roars.

He leads the way.

The reindeer gallop across the muted snow; the bells are loud and tinny. One by one, the hooves turn silent and the jingling settles. Nine reindeer soar toward the night sky.

Gallivanter waits for the whine of the timesnapper to engulf them. The elven will remain on the ice. A minute or two will pass before they return, exhausted and satisfied, with an empty sack in the back of the sleigh.

This Christmas will be different.

There will be no accidents to report. No sightings to cover up. But a rule will be broken. A rule that applies to the elven colony, including the reindeer. A rule Gallivanter is very familiar with, one he has broken once before. This is the Christmas Ronin sees a truck on a very cold night.

The Christmas he interferes.

The room was silent.

Ryder turned his head. The sheets on the other bunk were bunched up. Arf wasn't snoring.

He was gone.

Ryder sat up. Bradley Cooper remained asleep. It was a few minutes past four o'clock. Winter gear was stacked on the floor. He hadn't gone to the nicy meeting. That meant Jane and John must have brought the gear to his room.

If you must sleep over there, Jane had said, *we'll take care of you.*

A scattershot of frozen snow blew across the window. It was dark and windy. The barn light was on. Drifts had formed. It had snowed quite a bit since he fell asleep. And there were footprints, too. Like another football game.

Where's Arf?

He had been snoring when Ryder fell asleep and wasn't scheduled for introspection for another day. His laptop was gone, too. Ryder checked the drawers. They were empty.

The bedroom door across the hall was ajar. Ryder pushed it open, peeking inside. It was dark.

And empty.

The board had been erased. The introspection list gone. He ran to the end of the hall, his heart pounding. He pushed Cherry's door open, hoping she would be sitting cross-legged on the floor, shadows flickering across the rug. But the cushion was empty. Candlewicks blackened.

Where is she?

Her bed was made, the pillow smooth and square. He pulled the sheets back and reached between the wall and bed, feeling for the slit she had cut in the mattress. With two fingers, he searched the hiding spot.

There.

He fished out the phone, careful not to drop it. Wherever she was, she hadn't had time to take it with her. Or she'd left it behind for him to find. He touched the screen, hoping there would be a map, at least a clue as to where they took her. There was a message waiting for him. It wasn't a map. It was one word.

Hide!

A surge of adrenaline kicked his pulse up another gear. The room was beginning to spin. Maybe they forgot about him or he was the last in line. He stared at the phone. *That can't be right.*

Two days had passed.

That was why the snowdrifts were so deep, the tracks so prolific. He'd been asleep for two days.

How?

The phone flashed with urgency. He shoved it in his pocket and ran back to his room. Quickly, he put on the winter gear. It would be enough to survive, including food and a tent. He could make it in the mountains for days. Strapping on the backpack, he went to Cherry's room and threw it out her window. The snowdrift was deep and soft and without tracks.

She didn't escape.

He dug out of the snow and put the backpack on, snapping the buckles in place before starting out. He had to get away and clear his head, hide deep in the trees, far enough away that the drones wouldn't find him. He could spy when he had a chance and come back.

The wind nearly pushed him over as he trudged into the open. He leaned into it. His cheeks were scrubbed numb. He plodded through the snow, eyes watering, trees blurry. The horses were in the pasture, galloping away from the fence. The going would be easier once he was in the woods. The snow would diminish. He reached the tree line's moonshadow and was almost out of sight.

His legs gave out.

Creeping death shivered through his body. He fell like a tree. Arms limp, the ground rushed toward him. Face-first, he was buried in the snow.

It was dark. Cold.

He couldn't feel it. His body hummed with a fresh pulse of paralyzing anesthesia. Helpless, he panicked. Trapped in the confines of his own body, he struggled to breathe. Snow melted around his mouth. It packed into his ear, but he could hear the wind howling over him. Each breath was a struggle.

A green light began to glow.

A shadow cut through the bluster. An electromagnetic field vibrated in his teeth. A drone was hovering close to his head, the green eye near him.

What's happening?

He heard footsteps breaking through crusted snow. A hand firmly rolled him over. Icy crystals melted on his eyelashes. The world was dark and blurry.

"Why is he awake?" BG said. There was a pause like he was listening to someone on the phone. "Let's put him in storage. We don't need him."

Snowflakes landed delicately on Ryder's nose. BG was standing in front of him, but he was looking at someone out of Ryder's eyesight. Heavy footsteps were behind him.

BG took a knee and leaned over him. The stink of nicy was on his breath. Ryder involuntarily gagged as BG shoved his hand in his pocket. He pulled out the phone.

"Where'd he get this?"

Whatever chance they'd had to escape was over now. It was all in the open. They would know about the early morning excursions, the trip to the cabin, the maps on the phone.

It was all so over.

BG looked up and nodded. "Okay, all right. I'll send for one of the new boys. The big one. We'll put him on a table for now and sleep him till we get back."

There was a long pause. BG was standing over Ryder alone now. A chunk of time was missing. Snow had dusted Ryder's face. Someone new had joined them. A hulking figure threw Ryder over his shoulder like a sack of laundry. Ryder's arms flopped around as the big boy trudged through the snow. Blood was pounding in his temples.

Arf!

Ryder's tongue was fat. Saliva drooled from his lips as he bounced. Confusion mingled with fear, the fumes of panic filling his chest. Helplessly, he watched the footsteps recede until they reached the building.

Arf carried him to the elevator.

Ryder's ribs were hurting. His gut ached. He managed a groan. Arf wouldn't hear it. *I'll send for one of the new boys.*

The elevator descended deep below Kringletown. When the doors opened, the room smelled like a nicy armpit—a cloying aroma that invaded his sinuses and slid down his throat. He gagged as he was flopped onto a table. Arf looked down on him, with snow melting on a neutral expression. The ceiling was a network of pipes.

I've been here before.

It wasn't the smell that was familiar, it was the maze of conduit above him, the hard surface of the table. Maybe he dreamed it.

BG stood on the other side of the table. It felt like an operation was about to take place. Somewhere a mechanical rhythm played. *Wump-wump-wump-wump.* Panic bloomed in his gut and coldly streamed through his arms and legs. BG closed Ryder's eyes.

He couldn't open them.

A deep humming rose from his bones and filled his head, the anesthesia digging in. Ryder disappeared in the all-consuming darkness.

A black hole of unconsciousness.

19

Floating in darkness.

No ears or eyes, no seeing or tasting or smelling. Ryder reached up to feel his face and had no arms to move, no face to touch. Panic flooded the blackness, cold and electric. As if the very space around him were alive.

A formless void of awareness.

Where am I?

A sudden contraction. Sensation pressed against him. When he turned his attention toward it, colors swirled out of the dark. Where once there was nothing, now there were feet and legs.

Ryder lifted his arm.

The floor was as black as the space around him. There were no other objects, no walls or ceiling. He took a tentative step in one direction then another. No matter where he went, the floor continued. There was no edge to fall from, no wall to stop him.

Just endless nothing.

"Ryder."

He spun at the sound of his name. A form had taken shape. It stood just beyond the edge of darkness. He couldn't make out the details, only the outline of a very short, very round person.

With extremely large feet.

"I apologize. It's confusing for one to experience pure awareness, perhaps frightening. You have no body here, but the illusion of one. It feels strange, though."

Ryder looked at his hands then back to the person. The voice was familiar. He'd heard it before, like he'd heard it all of his life.

"Gallivanter," Ryder whispered.

Laughter trickled out, the kind that bubbled.

"Your dreams," Gallivanter said, "are our story."

Space rippled like heat waves rolling off summer asphalt. He wanted to see him, but every step he took brought him no closer to Gallivanter. He remained in the dark without moving.

"Story?" Ryder said.

"Dreams are stories, and stories have no end. Does the dream?" Gallivanter paused then beckoned. "Remember."

Ryder thought about the last dream, when Ronin led the reindeer on Christmas Eve. They were tethered to a red sleigh, launching into a night sky. Laughter from a very fat man trailed to the ice, where Gallivanter watched the last reindeer lead the others.

He interfered.

"The truth is waiting."

Gallivanter's voice was out there. Ryder imagined his steel-gray eyes from the dream. They were full of joy, pride and wisdom. A reflection of the reindeer against the sky moved across his pupils. And then something different happened.

This isn't part of the dream.

The eyes dried up and the joy faded. The blue moonlight turned harsh and bright. The silhouette of reindeer transformed. Instead, a reflection was looking back at him. Someone was leaning toward Gallivanter, a grin creeping in a tightly trimmed beard of red whiskers.

"Where's my pot of gold?"

Ryder didn't recognize the man at first. He was younger, the beard shorter, his complexion fair and smooth. It wasn't weathered, but the voice was unmistakable. *Billy.*

Figgy, curled up at his feet, looked up with tired eyes. Her muzzle was peppered gray. She groaned. It couldn't be Figgy. She was too old, getting up with a stiff hip to pad her bed before curling up again.

Gallivanter wasn't on ice or looking up at the sky and watching the reindeer pull the sleigh. He was bound to a hard chair in a small surgical room. BG sat in front of him, his grin polluted with bad intentions.

He turned to a computer. The table was littered with equipment, none of which Ryder recognized but struck him as oddly detailed. *This is a memory.*

"Do you know who I am?" BG said.

A pang of fear flooded the dream. For a moment, Ryder thought he was talking to him.

"Tell me what you are." BG looked at the hairy feet. "I don't expect you to answer, given how I've brought you here. You've evolved in a harsh climate, likely the Arctic. The enlarged feet allow for snow travel, the soles built for sliding. The short and wide body, the layers of insulating fat. If I'm not mistaken, I'd say you're an elf."

The computer distracted him for a moment.

"Don't worry, I won't expose you to the world, if that's what you're thinking. Your secrets are worth more than gold, my friend. I saw your reindeer."

BG leaned in and whispered, "He was flying."

Gallivanter's expression changed. His rosy cheeks blanched into gray planks around widening eyes. Somewhere beneath the thick beard, he swallowed a knot. Being captive had not worried him, but the mention of a flying reindeer struck him with terror.

"All these years, you and your kind have been nothing more than a child's secret. Presents under the tree, cookie crumbs and stuffed stockings."

He wagged his finger. *Tsk, tsk, tsk.*

BG punched a command and retrieved a tiny disc. There was something wrong. He picked up the disc with his right hand, pinching it between finger and thumb.

He's missing two fingers.

"I'm a man of science and I'm very good." He took a deep breath. "I'm going to decode your genome, Mr. Elf. I'm going to read your past and download your thoughts. I'm going to know your secrets. All of them."

"What we know," Gallivanter croaked, "is not for you."

BG sat back, slightly surprised. It was the first time he'd heard him speak. It was gruff and grave. But it didn't wipe away the smile. He checked the computer one last time then placed the disc on the elven's temple.

Gallivanter didn't resist.

BG wasn't interested in gold. What the elven possessed was beyond any currency invented by humankind. BG was going to siphon out the real value Gallivanter possessed.

The secrets of the North Pole.

The elven's crisp silver-gray eyes turned into foggy orbs. Ryder saw BG's reflection in the engorged pupils. He leaned back with a curious smile. He was replaced by the memories pulled through the disc. Images spun like a top—a flash of a man in a red coat, reindeer harnessed to the sleigh, cheering, Northern Lights, an endless landscape of white ice.

Images sped across the dream fabric. Days turned into months then years. BG laughing as the room spun into an expansive and elaborate laboratory. His beard thickened and his hair grew. He worked tirelessly with the knowledge he stole then announced his retirement from Avocado, Inc., declaring he would begin his own research in a private lab. And when the world was ready, he said, he would reveal his own discoveries.

My discoveries, he said with a slimy grin.

It was years later when BG stood over Gallivanter, looking like the man Ryder had come to know—the red beard, the leathery complexion. He was wearing a thin, beige gown. The kind of gown a hospital patient would wear. Gallivanter was wearing one, too. It was dark green with red trim, a cheery mix of Christmas colors. The elven, however, was deflated and weathered.

His spirit punctured.

"I promised not to harm you. You've given so much, it's the least I can do."

Gallivanter's expressionless gaze did not change. He was depleted. Nothing his captor could say would change that. He was prepared for the end. Perhaps his only regret was that he couldn't stop him. He hadn't given BG anything.

He took it.

BG pressed his hand on a wall panel. The black surface glowed around his fingers. A window popped out of the wall. It slid out like a filing cabinet. Inside was a thick cushion. With great effort, BG lifted the elven out of the chair. Gallivanter sank into the cushion. Wires and tubes slithered from beneath it and wrapped around his short arms and spread across his head.

"No more wandering."

Toenails clicked on the hard floor. Figgy trotted to his side, tongue wagging. It looked like Figgy—the eyes, the noisy collar—but her muzzle was dark and shiny. Teeth white. She had looked so old when BG first captured Gallivanter. Her muzzle had been white fur. It must be her pup.

It looked exactly like her.

BG touched the black panel again. The drawer began sliding back into the wall. Gallivanter didn't resist. The time to escape had long passed. BG watched it click into place, the transparent door sealing shut. The soles of the giant elven feet blocked the view inside. Cold steam curled around the hairy toes and frosted the glass.

The light dimmed.

BG stored his treasure in a cold tomb. And whistled while he did it. When the door was fully opaque, he bent down and scrubbed the dog's ears. The dog wagged her tail.

There were more transparent doors on the walls. They were empty and waiting. The dog trotted ahead of him, head down and sniffing. Her nose led her to one of the transparent doors. There was a dog inside.

"Come."

The dog obeyed immediately, running to BG's side and sitting exactly where he was pointing. Ears perked and eyes on his master, she waited. *A good dog.*

BG walked with a distinctive limp that Ryder had seen before. He closed the door and entered the lab. It had grown in size and complexity—banks of monitors were on the wall; strange equipment and endless conduit on the ceiling.

Whistling, he went to a smaller room with a pair of what looked like MRI machines. He was barefoot in a gown, legs exposed beneath the beige hem. He sat at a computer nestled between the machines and spent half an hour with the dog at his side. The whistling had subsided. He stood up with slight hesitation and knelt down. The dog licked his outstretched hand.

"Here we go."

He shed the gown. Completely nude, he climbed onto the thin-cushioned mat and lay on his back. A deep breath, he stared at the ceiling. A mechanical whirring began drawing him inside. His breaths shortened as he clutched his sides. Once he was fully inside the narrow tube, a door sealed shut.

This isn't an MRI.

It began to rev up. The engines vibrated the floor and windows. The dog had been watching him slowly get swallowed by the machine. Now she turned to the machine's twin, where the door was already closed.

Wump-wump-wump-wump.

Time sped up. The dog lay down to nap, sat up when new sounds occurred and lay back down when nothing happened. Sometime later—days, maybe weeks or months—the engines slowed. The clanging died.

The computer monitor woke up.

Data scrolled across the screen. When it stopped, the silence stretched out. The dog fidgeted, whining with impatience. He wasn't staring at the machine that swallowed BG.

The door on the twin machine opened.

Tendrils of steam snaked out and slowly revealed a pair of bare feet. The soles were pink and wrinkled. Beads of condensation clung to them. More data ran on the computer.

The twin machine began moving.

A thin-cushioned panel like the one that had supported BG was sliding out of the claustrophobic tunnel. A nude body was slowly revealed, damp and dripping. BG was staring at the ceiling. Unblinking, his chest slowly rising and falling. The dog's whines grew louder, but she didn't leave her place. BG appeared to be sleeping with his eyes open and his hands at his sides.

The computer emitted a sound.

He jolted up, gulping air. Tears streamed into his whiskers, and the dog began barking. He stared at his hands, clenching and unclenching. Laughter bubbled up and let loose.

He pulled a gown over his head and looked at himself in the machine's steel reflection. He stretched and flexed, pulled at the flesh beneath his eyes and wiggled his toes. All while laughing.

The dog sat at his side and watched. It remained quiet until the door on the first machine slid open. Steam didn't waft out. The feet, however, were still there. They weren't damp, pink or wrinkled. The thin-cushioned platform hummed out of the tunnel to reveal a pale body. The chest was rising and falling, the eyes closed.

It's him.

There were two Billys. One was at the computer. One was exiting the first machine. There was a long pause, a surreal moment of contemplation before BG picked up his gray and sleeping body and carried it out.

He walked without the limp.

"Life." Gallivanter's voice entered the dream.

The body was limp and awkward in BG's arms. The head craned back, the mouth hung open as he carried his sleeping form like an overgrown child. A drawer was open in the same room where he took Gallivanter. He placed it on a thick cushion.

"His quest began," Gallivanter said. "Misguided."

Steam licked the transparent door as it sealed the body inside like it had done with Gallivanter's body. With the dog by his side, BG watched the light inside dim and the frost spatter the glass.

The dream sped up. Time raced through days and weeks. The lab evolved and the wall filled up. Feet were pressed against the glass doors, lights dimming on window after window.

"Bodies," Gallivanter said. "They are only vehicles. A body is not who we are. It is not who I am. It is not you."

The maze of conduit on the ceiling pulsed with energy.

A presence slunk into the network of cables that interconnected computers and equipment, the rooms and the morgue that monitored the sleeping bodies. Something seeped through the circuits and worked into the software.

When the lab was empty, data would scroll as if BG were sitting at the keyboard. Words and symbols raced across a monitor. The lab would come to life when no one was there. Monitors on the wall watched everyone aboveground.

"I'm ready to wake. For that to happen, you need the truth."

The activity in the lab reached a fever pitch and suddenly stopped. A phrase typed out on a black screen. *Who are you?*

"The messages..." Ryder's eyes snapped open.

He was back on the table, staring at the ceiling. The smell of the lab had returned. Along with a sound.

Wump-wump-wump-wump.

❇

It was a long crawl from the bottom of a slurry dream.

Numbness ebbed like a receding tide, leaving a dark slate of discomfort. An ache in his ribs. His brain sloshed like wet sand.

The lights were bright white and the room small. This wasn't where Arf had put him. There were other tables in the room with electronic lights beneath them. Slowly, he lowered his feet and waited for his balance. Somewhere a mechanical beat played long strokes. He opened the door.

The lab.

This was bigger than the one below the cabin, but the equipment, the computers, the smell... it was all the same. This was where Arf had put him the first time. Monitors on the wall displayed drone feeds of sleeping boys and girls. Arf was on one of them, nestled into a fat pillow with his arms at his sides. Mouth closed. Even without volume, it was obvious.

He's not snoring.

Suddenly, the air felt thin. Ryder took long gulping breaths and grabbed a chair to keep from falling. It was the chair where BG had been talking to... *Gallivanter.*

There was a curtain in the corner. That wasn't in the dream, but the doors along the walls were. The steady rhythm played from one of them. Through a glass door, he saw exactly what he had dreamed.

The MRI machines.

Outside the glass door, he pulled the curtain aside. There were tables with people behind them, hands at their sides, eyes closed. They were naughties. The last one flushed cold fear into his legs.

Cherry.

"Hey." He shook her gently. "Wake up."

She jostled in place, her lips parting, but her eyes stayed shut. He whispered in her ear. Was she in the same place he had been, that deep, dark place of nothingness where time was absent and space was endless?

Is she dreaming about an elven?

There were computers on each table. He reached for the keyboard, hoping to find something. Words appeared on the monitor.

DO NOT WAKE.

It was the same font as the message that had appeared on his laptop. The words remained for several seconds and vanished. A second message appeared.

BEHIND YOU.

Another room was beeping. When he opened the door, the lights flickered on. Cool air exhaled through the doorway. The floor was empty. There were windows along the walls in columns of three.

He'd dreamed of this room.

The transparent doors were mostly empty in the dream. Now they were frosted and filled with bare feet. Various colors were vaguely visible through the cold haze, people clothed in thin gowns, asleep in a space no larger than a coffin.

The top row was at eye level. To his left, he peered into the one where BG had carried his own body in the dream. The door was clear and the padding was empty.

It was just a dream.

Below that was where the dog had stopped. She'd been sniffing at the seams when BG had called her. It was thick with frost, but there were no traces of bare feet. Ryder took a knee and looked closer. Farther back, he saw a dark form.

A muzzle of white fur.

It was the older version of Figgy, the one he'd seen in the dream, the one curled up and groaning when BG had first captured Gallivanter. Ryder went from window to window, feet only inches from the glass, the details foggy. There were tattoos on some of them, scars on others. The toenails needed clipping. They were pale and ashen. Their faces cloaked in darkness, he didn't know all of them. But he knew who they were.

The naughties.

The most disturbing drawer looked empty at first glance. There were no feet, but there was something deeper inside. It wasn't a dog this time. Tiny fists were curled and the eyes squeezed shut.

It was an infant.

Three short beeps nearly stopped his heart. They came from the far wall. A dark panel lit up. It was the same panel where BG had placed his hand, where he had loaded the elven's body. Unlike the other windows, this one wasn't frosted. Condensation streaked on the inside and beaded on oversized feet. They were almost twenty-four inches long and half as wide. The soles were rough and gray.

Scaly.

Steam snaked around a round body and legs that were short and knobby. The chin was hidden beneath two braids of frayed whiskers. Steam hissed from the window's seams and billowed near the ceiling.

The room suddenly smelled like old skin. Tendrils of mist crawled over a green and red smock.

The big toes twitched.

The second toes followed, bending at the knuckles and popping. Each toe did the same all the way to the little one. They were hairy and long.

The drawer began to move.

Ryder stepped back as it slid out. The elven was almost as round as he was tall, his hair longer than it was in the dream. His equally white beard hid all of his face except for a slender nose, slices of cheekbone and the sunken eyes. The braids were coming apart.

He didn't look alive.

Steam spread across the ceiling and slipped into a vent. Now the fingers began the slow dance—popping and curling. They looked like tiny mittens when fully clenched.

The eyes opened.

Ryder bumped into the wall and slid along it, the edges of the transparent doors dragging against his back. The elven didn't move. He stared at the ceiling with silver-blue eyes as icy as the Arctic Ocean. A groan escaped him like a waking giant.

Ho-ho-ho.

He pulled wires off his forehead and arms. The feet wagged in unison. Back and forth, the momentum carried into his legs. Ripples shook his belly. The entire body rocked back and forth, reaching a tipping point before falling over the edge.

He didn't splat but rather bounced like an exercise ball filled with jelly. Another groan escaped him, the air punched out of him. He lay facing the floor, his giant feet keeping him from rolling.

Ryder watched from the doorway.

The green and red smock had folded over the elven's clenched bottom. His right arm reached back to cover his buttocks then reached toward Ryder. The fingers wiggled impatiently. He cleared his throat. It sounded like grinding ice. Ryder looked back at Cherry still sleeping behind the curtain.

"If you don't mind."

Unlike the dream, where the elven's voice was deep and resonant, this sounded raw and swollen. Ryder stayed near the wall as he approached. The pudgy fingers continued to beckon. His hand was cool to the touch. Ryder pulled and the elven began to spin. The toes grabbed the floor. Ryder pulled harder, tipping him onto wide feet. His balance teetered, but his build made it unlikely for him to fall. Frizzy white hair hung over his face. A swift exhalation blew it off.

Ryder stepped away.

The elven reached back and twisted the hair into cords then knotted them behind his head. A pained smile was hiding in the whiskers and crinkling around his eyes.

"You dream about me," the elven said. "You did."

He waddled like a penguin, throwing his weight side to side as he shuffled tiny steps across the room—feet that weren't made for walking but scaly soles designed for sliding. Gallivanter lifted a short finger on the way to the lab and pointed at a chair.

"Could you?"

Ryder helped him climb onto the chair and watched him balance a keyboard on his belly. His fingers were too short to type, but his hands darted at the keys with musical rhythm, all while he grunted and muttered.

"Keyboards." He grunted. Or maybe he laughed.

Whatever was on the monitor leaped into the center of the room. A three-dimensional display of data rotated from floor to ceiling. Gallivanter hopped off the chair and stood in the middle of the data storm, pointing and moving packets with hand gestures.

There were still spots on his forehead where the wires had been attached, but the gray flesh had already become rosy. He was beginning to thaw. He yanked a holographic panel out of the interstellar data projection. Waving his hand, the panel rotated through a series of photos—faces, names and personal information.

Ryder was still frozen. "What's happening?"

"My manners are lacking," he said, "but time is short, one sees. A very small window to do what we need. You dreamed our story, Ryder Mack. That much is true."

Gallivanter looked over his shoulder. A bright eye peered through a thicket of white hair.

"Dream?" Ryder shook his head.

"*Our* story."

I can't dream a story. But here he is, the one from the dream.

"I'm still dreaming," he muttered. It was the only explanation. Elven were fantasies. *And so are flying reindeer.*

"You are not," Gallivanter said. "My body has been asleep, but I have not. I have been awake a very long time, Ryder Mack."

Ryder remembered seeing the energy pulse through the conduit on the ceiling. Was he talking about BG's mind interface? The little discs that were used in the introspection could read thoughts. BG was using the same technology to monitor the elven while he was in cold storage, the wires on his head reading his thoughts. Gallivanter had simply reversed the flow. Instead of BG taking his thoughts, Gallivanter had connected with the computer network. He'd sent the messages.

He was in the computers.

"Limitations, there were," the elven said. "I could only go so many places, do so many things without a body. Even with the help."

Gallivanter wagged a finger at the computer he was on. Something stirred behind them. Rolls of wrapping paper fell off a shelf, golden bells and green holly leaves on one side. A drone hovered out of a cabinet. Ryder's heart shrank. But the drone didn't aim its blinking green eye at him. It grabbed a gadget off the table and delivered it to Gallivanter.

Even with the help.

He had been controlling the drones, shutting them off and looping the footage in the early morning hours. They'd given the phone to Cherry. *And delivered the messages.*

Gallivanter fitted the gadget on his hand and pushed the holographic profiles to the side then pulled open a new set of data. A string of light bathed him in eerie red light. New connections were made. One of the profiles expanded.

Billy Big Game.

"His obsession began on the Pole." Gallivanter continued working. "He stumbled onto me, he did. I take the blame for that, careless. It wasn't the first time I had been seen, but captured. That was."

Gallivanter flung more profiles, images of boys and girls standing with their arms at their sides. It was them, the naughties and the nicies. A list of data was attached to each one of the images.

"Very unfortunate, his background in biology. My knowledge unlocked secrets to synthetic life. He used that, you see. He used that."

Figgy was an old dog in the dream when BG had first captured Gallivanter. That wasn't a different dog later on, but it was younger. BG didn't heal her. He put that old and tired dog in the cooler.

After he copied her.

Those weren't MRI machines. They were building new bodies. BG wasn't limping when he came out. Soup didn't have a hearing aid. They were better versions of themselves.

Nice.

"They don't know what they are, they don't. They have memories of childhood, they believe they grew up, their memories tell them. They believe they are exactly who they have always been. But they just woke up, they did."

"Why?"

"He wants good boys and girls—"

"To do what he wants."

Gallivanter stopped what he was doing. "Cryogenically preserved, all of us. Even William is a perfect simulation of himself, one that he controls."

But BG's original body wasn't in the morgue like the others. His cell was empty. But everyone was there—Soup, Arf, Jane. All of them. Somewhere on the nicy wing their replications were sleeping; they would wake up with perfect teeth and that smell.

Soup was right. They're fake. They're all fake. And now he is too and doesn't even know it.

Ryder fell into a chair. He could barely feel his legs.

"This," Gallivanter said, "is why we hide."

He continued changing the profiles, ending each one by highlighting a floating button that said sleep before going to the next one.

Ryder walked across the lab and pulled back the curtain. Cherry was still sleeping. She didn't look any different. Ryder leaned over and sniffed her hair. Smelled like incense.

"The last ones," Gallivanter called. "When he's finished, he will put them in the box and take their clones to the Pole. That cannot happen."

She was warmer than normal. Her complexion looked clammy. He brushed her hair and felt her forehead and noticed the little button attached to her forehead. He was about to pluck it off.

Gallivanter held up his hand. "Do not wake her."

Ryder was about to argue. If he pulled the button off, she wouldn't be under the influence anymore. But she'd wake up and see all of this. Ryder was still standing, barely—maybe because of the dreams, because he already knew the story.

The last ones.

Ryder left her side. Gallivanter turned his back and didn't see him step onto the silver disk next to him. He was immersed by the data and, unexpectedly, space seemed to expand. From the outside, it didn't look any bigger than a shower stall or phone booth. Inside, the data space went on forever.

He didn't understand any of the symbols or how they were connecting, but the profiles were simple. That was what he wanted to see. *Sleep* was highlighted on the ones Gallivanter had already programmed. The others still said *active*. *Wake* was glowing. Ryder flipped through them, and Gallivanter didn't stop him. He reached the very last profile.

It's me.

He had awakened on the nicy wing after the mountain, after Ronin had been captured. He was asleep for almost a day. But nothing about him was different. His teeth weren't perfect, his attitude was still bent. The reindeer kiss still on his cheek. His body wasn't in cold storage.

You've always been nice, BG had said.

That was why he smelled nice. The first day he arrived at Kringletown, Soup and Arf could smell it. Ryder never noticed.

Data scrolled next to his image, a record of when he slept and when he was awake, when he'd been good or bad. And his memories, they were there too. That was how Gallivanter did it. He uploaded the dreams into his awareness.

ACTIVE, it said.

He looked at his hands.

"Was I not real?" Gallivanter said. "When I sent you dreams? When I sent you messages? Body, no body, I am who I am, as are you."

Ryder stepped out of the data. The sudden contraction of space caused the floor to shift. He stumbled to his knees and got up, woozy. *I'm dreaming. I have to be still dreaming.*

"They will sleep and we will walk out." Gallivanter held him steady. "I cannot do that without you."

The nicies were tucked into their beds. Gallivanter was about to put them in a deep state, like they had done to Ryder when they carried him off the mountain. They'd turned him off. Gallivanter was about to do the same thing, but one person was awake. The monitor showed an empty bed with the covers thrown back.

BG was walking down the corridor.

"I won't leave her."

Ryder pulled away. He was going to pluck the button off Cherry's temple and carry her out. If Gallivanter wanted his help, he wasn't going to do it without her. He went to her side. The magnetic disc latched onto her like a magnetic leech.

"Please." Gallivanter was too far away to stop him. "We'll come back, my promise. We'll return for them, all of them. No one will be left."

"She helped you. She helped me! You'd still be in that drawer if it wasn't for her. You can't do this." His head was spinning. "We're not leaving her."

BG was crossing the foyer and reading his phone. He seemed relaxed and oblivious to what was happening in the lab. There wasn't time to argue, but Ryder wasn't negotiating. He needed her to wake up for a lot of reasons. More importantly, he needed to make sure he wasn't dreaming.

Because elven don't exist and reindeer don't fly.

Gallivanter glanced at the monitor where BG was nearing the elevator. Perhaps he understood what Ryder needed. Dreams or not, leaving Cherry behind was too much. He went to the table and touched the panel.

Her eyes fluttered.

She didn't recognize the ceiling or the smell. Ryder knew that experience, of waking from black nothingness to reconnect with reality. Her nostrils flared. She struggled to understand where she was and how she got there. Where did time go?

She saw the lab, the computers and the glowing data disk. And then the short, round elven with the puffy white hair and frayed beard braids. Gallivanter waited patiently. On the monitor behind him, BG had reached the elevator.

He took her hand. "Trust me."

She stared helplessly as he helped her sit up and put her feet on the floor. Pins and needles shot up her legs. Ryder found her boots. Gingerly, she took a step. Gallivanter wobbled to the elevator.

A sound went off.

On the monitors, everyone was still asleep. BG was sprawled on the floor. A puddle of coffee crept toward his cheek. Ryder helped Cherry into the elevator. She moved slow and steady, mouth open.

"Wait!" Ryder said. "I forgot my boots."

They were under the table where he woke up. Gallivanter groaned as he raced across the lab. On the way back, he stopped near the data disk to put them on. They couldn't see what he was doing.

"Hurry now," Gallivanter called.

"Coming."

He jumped on the elevator with the plastic ends of the laces tapping the floor. Just as the doors closed, he heard hissing in the cold room.

Gallivanter didn't recognize the sound.

20

The elevator went sideways.

Cherry held onto Ryder. She wasn't blinking. Gallivanter looked back with kind eyes. Barefoot, he wiggled long toes with tufts of white curly hair.

"You're..."

Gallivanter nodded.

She closed her eyes. A shaky sigh poured out of her. The elevator arced in an upward path. She leaned against the back wall and pinched the bridge of her nose.

"How did I... where are we..."

"A lot's happened," Ryder said. "We're getting out."

The elevator slowed. The doors opened and Gallivanter waddled out. "Dress for cold," he said. "I'll meet you outside."

He was going in the opposite direction of the naughty wing, moving like an overwound windup toy wearing nothing more than a thin gown.

Ryder grabbed Cherry's hand and began running. She kept up, reluctantly. They turned onto the naughty wing and she stopped. He went to his room and started throwing on Arctic gear. He had the snowsuit zipped and was lacing the first boot when she finally followed.

"There's another suit." He pointed. "Hurry."

She watched him tie the bootlaces. He was almost done and she hadn't moved. "I remember talking to Jane," she said. "She said they were ahead of schedule... and then... and then I was looking at you and, uh..."

"Gallivanter. His name is Gallivanter."

"What's happening?"

"We have to go. Just put on the gear so we can..."

The truth was he didn't want to explain. If he thought about it, he would freeze up and stare at his hands like her. He had to keep moving, keep looking ahead. He would figure it out later. There wasn't time to process, not now.

Would there ever be?

She wore a blank expression. She wasn't moving until something made sense.

He sighed. "BG knows how to copy us. That's why Soup wasn't wearing a hearing aid. It's why nicies smell weird, something to do with synthetic cells. We start off as naughties and he turns us into nicies. *Good girls and boys...* remember that? He controls them."

Cherry turned away like a fish struggling to breathe air. She flexed her hands and stared. Just like he'd done.

"You're not one of them," Ryder said.

He didn't tell her any more. She didn't need to know what he was, and she didn't ask. *Keep moving.*

"Where are they?" she asked. "Where are the..."

"The naughties? They're asleep. We'll come back for them, but we need to go."

He pulled on his cap and started unpacking gear for her, throwing the suit and coat on the bed, unlacing the boots. She moved like she'd just come out of cold storage, legs stiff and sluggish. He dressed her.

"Are they all nice?" She swallowed. "The naughties?"

"Almost. Gallivanter put them all to sleep."

"Then why are we hurrying?"

He zipped up her coat and pulled her gloves on. The light on the barn had come on. It was still dark. The sun hadn't risen yet. A round figure was waddling toward the barn. Ryder pulled the window open. Snow blew across the desk.

"Where we going?" she asked.

He didn't answer that. They were leaving Kringletown. That was all he could think about. But they weren't leaving before they went to the barn.

❄

Snow scrunched under Gallivanter's broad, bare feet.

Winter greeted the early morning with blustery breath; the elven's thin shirt fluttered. Ryder and Cherry followed his wide trail, huddling against each other. When they reached the barn, Gallivanter hit the slick concrete and slid through the breezeway.

He cut to a stop at the big barn door.

By the time Ryder and Cherry caught up, he was balanced on his toes like a ballerina, standing almost as tall as them. He waved a pattern at the warehouse doors like a magician warming up. The weathered trim darkened in front of his hand, a panel Ryder had seen in the cold room, the same panel BG had touched when he put the elven in the wall.

A black mirror oozed from the wood grain. A reflection of bushy white whiskers filled the square as Gallivanter put a finger on the surface. A lighted trail followed his markings, glowing like swaths of Northern Lights. The panel glowed green.

The doors popped inward.

A mixture of hay and wet hide exhaled from the dark. And a strange and familiar sound echoed.

Wump-wump-wump-wump.

Gallivanter hung his hairy toes over the entrance. A wide set of stairs led downward. Light beamed down from the rafters. A dusty floor led between high-walled enclosures with barred windows.

Wheelbarrows, steel buckets and flat shovels were lined against the walls. Despite the smell of manure, they looked more like cells than stalls. He hopped down the steps.

Something moved.

Gallivanter shuffled across the gritty floor. Once again, he rose up on his toes. There was a black panel on a stall, but he didn't trace it this time. He stood on his toes with his hands up and waited.

A bright pink muzzle emerged through the bars.

Nostrils flared, snorting. Sniffing. A mournful moan cried from the dark.

"My boy," Gallivanter whispered.

Memories rushed into the room. Ryder reached for Cherry before he tumbled down the steps, but she was gone. Instead, he clutched a handful of course blankets. A cold floor was biting his cheek. He was toothless and tiny.

And crying.

Cheeks wet, he let loose a shrill cry. Wrapped in brown blankets, he couldn't find words to help escape the cold. His desperation echoed in the hollow vacancy of a moving truck. A mournful moan answered from a distant rooftop. The thud of hooves approached. Snorting nostrils reached into the truck and tickled his cheek.

The reindeer kiss.

Ronin had abandoned his place at the front of the sleigh; he broke the rule not to intervene. There were exceptions to that rule.

He made this one.

Ronin had been abandoned. Left behind. Made fun of. He wasn't going to let that happen again.

The wet muzzle was on his cheek again. Pink and warm, almost red and hot. Ryder wasn't an infant in the truck anymore. He stood in front of the cage, dark eyes looking through bars. Ronin was inside a tight enclosure, with wires attached to him. There was conduit on the walls.

A moan shook the room.

Ryder rubbed his nose and felt his knees turn to jelly. Eyes wet, cheeks warm and salty. His throat swelled with words trapped inside. Cherry was next to him. Rubbery lips tested her touch.

A blaze of colors decorated the floor. Gallivanter was tracing the cage's panel. The pattern glowed for several seconds then faded to black. He did it a second time and then a third time. Furry brows stitched together, he studied the room.

The rhythmic thumping was coming from an enormous cubicle in the far corner. Ronin withdrew from the bars and vanished into the dark recesses, the pink snout barely visible.

"What's wrong?" Ryder asked.

Gallivanter sprang like an Arctic fox, throwing himself sideways and rolling like a snowball gathering momentum on a mountainside. The barn doors clapped like a bear trap.

The thwump of a spear gun echoed in the rafters.

The unforgiving spike of a steel post sank into the floor. Willowy vines whipped from the top, tentacles shooting toward the bouncing elven. One by one, they snapped and wrapped around objects and fell to the ground—bound up with buckets and shovels.

Gallivanter disappeared into the shadowy depths.

Another spike stuck near Ryder's feet. Straps suddenly whip-snapped around them, wrapping their ankles and wrists, winding around their waists. Additional bindings slithered up their backs and wound around their necks, scaly and cold.

Ronin kicked the walls. The rafters shook.

Ryder struggled. The binding strap tightened as he twisted. Cherry couldn't breathe. Her eyes bulged.

"Relax," Ryder wheezed. "Don't fight."

When she stopped flailing, she drew a deep, trembling breath. Slow and easy, he reached out, careful not to stress the binding around his wrist, and found her hand. She closed her eyes and focused.

Something moved near the thumping cubicle.

The lights cast a shadow from a wide cowboy hat and stretched over a harsh limp. The old man sighed with patience thick with arrogance and studied them from beneath the dark rim with a long-barreled weapon in his hand. It was the strange gun Ryder had seen in the tack room.

The one used on the mountain.

"It's you."

Ryder curled a fist without straining. It was the limp. BG had put himself in the cold room after he was cloned. But he didn't stay there. The drawer was empty. He had crawled out with a bum hip.

The real Big Game.

Stooping with a grunt, he picked up a stone and unwrapped the flat strap. It slithered back into the spike.

He waited.

The strap around Ryder's wrist loosened. William pushed the rock into his palm. His lips worked around a lump of tobacco. He sighed a wintergreen breath, eyes dark beneath the cowboy hat.

The rock grew warm.

The strap slithered around Ryder's fingers and drew them tight. The rock was now hot. It was burning a hole into his palm. Ryder yanked but couldn't let go. The lash around his neck closed off his next breath.

"Don't—" Cherry choked.

Ryder thrashed, soundless. Breathless. The smell of burning skin clogged his nostrils. The stall shook as Ronin bellowed and bucked. The floor tremored.

And then the burning stopped.

The rock bounced on the floor, cold and harmless. There was no burn, no scar. Like nothing happened. Like he imagined an orange coal had melted the skin. He could still smell it.

William spat.

"No more games, old friend." He scrubbed Ryder's hair. "I don't know how you did it, and I don't care. I'll make this quick. Come out or the boy suffers. Don't drag this out. I will win."

He glanced at a phone then dropped it in a coat pocket. His desperation was twitching in the corner of his eye. A cold wave passed through Ryder. The old man had made him believe the rock was a hot coal. *What else can he do?*

A form shuffled in the shadows.

Gallivanter stood in the dimmest edge of light like he had in the dream. His toes gripping the floor. The old man chuckled, fingers tightening on the metal barrel of the strange gun.

"You locked me out of my system and put my family to sleep. But I know you, old friend. You know that. You weren't leaving without him."

The weapon reported at his side.

A spike bit into the wall and spit out spidery straps. Gallivanter rolled into the dark. Tools clattered in his wake, tightly wrapped.

William grunted. He shuffled forward but was reluctant to step too close to the shadows. Gallivanter kept him cautiously at a distance.

"What were you going to do, leap off and forget me? Did you think I would just go away, forget everything? I can't let you go, old friend. I'm too close. And you're too late."

The shadows were extinguished by every light in the barn. The cages went farther back than expected. The old man had been waiting for the right moment to illuminate the rest of the room, hoping to draw the elven out. Somehow, Gallivanter remained hidden in the litter of daily chores.

"Mmm."

William picked up a stone thoughtfully. Impatience clenched his jaws. There was no escaping the barn, but the elven was elusive. The old man wasn't giving up, but he didn't have time to waste, even with Ryder and Cherry tied up and Ronin locked away.

He had changed the combination.

That was Gallivanter's hurry. Everyone had been put to sleep except for William. He couldn't be controlled by the system. He wasn't a clone, wasn't connected to the computers. There wasn't a profile for him. Gallivanter wasn't too late to free Ronin.

William was ahead of him.

He took Ryder's stocking cap and swept up a handful of grit then sprinkled it over Ryder's head. Dust and sand fell into his hair. Ryder felt a sneeze coming on. The particles, though, crawled beneath his coat. Ryder gritted his teeth.

Bugs.

"You're jealous," he said through stiff lips. "That's why you woke up. Billy was getting all the attention."

William took off his cowboy hat and pushed his hair back. His hand never left the weapon. His breathing wheezed at the end of each exhalation. He searched the room's depths and sprinkled another handful of sand over Ryder's head. The imaginary bugs stampeded down his stomach.

Ryder closed his eyes.

He couldn't react, didn't want to give Gallivanter a reason to surrender. He was their only chance. *It's just sand. It's not real.*

"Billy's not you," Ryder said.

William's eyes narrowed. He dusted his hands.

"You messed up," Ryder continued. "Thought you could clone yourself, just transfer the memories, but that didn't work, did it? The memories were the same, but Billy isn't you. A copy isn't the same. He looks like you, but he isn't—"

"Quiet."

Ryder's throat went numb. The binding hadn't tightened. He was able to breathe, but his vocal cords no longer responded. William had complete control.

The old man put a hand on Cherry's neck. Ryder's fist didn't get far. The strap cut off his air and, all at once, the bugs sank their stingers into his belly. The bindings held him as he thrashed. A strange sound gurgled in his throat. Panic couldn't get past his tongue; it rumbled in his chest. Saliva bubbled in the corners of his mouth.

"I will put an itch behind the boy's eyes and let him scratch them out."

The agony suddenly escaped Ryder, bursting from him like a broken pipe. His cry filled every corner of the room. Ronin's cries and stamping hooves drowned him out.

"One!" William called.

Ronin slammed the walls.

"Two!"

Ryder couldn't contain the suffering. It poured from him, blotted out the rhythmic thumping, blurred the movement around him. One sound, however, cut through the chaos. It wasn't William announcing the end of his countdown or Gallivanter calling out his surrender.

It was a mechanical click.

The bugs suddenly vanished. Sand was stuck to his cheeks. William looked at him then the cage. He took a step back. Ronin went silent. The black panel on his cage was glowing green.

The door popped open.

William kicked it closed and traced the panel. The pattern lit up and turned green again. Confusion gave way to anger. He repeated the command.

"Denied," a voice reported. "Old man."

Soup!

The door exploded off the hinges. It narrowly missed William, cracking on the steps and rebounding toward the ceiling, clipping rafters into pieces. The walls groaned. From the recesses of the cell, a rack of antlers appeared.

A blur leaped from deep down the aisle. Gallivanter was bouncing toward them. William didn't hesitate, firing off binding stakes as he retreated. The elven threw stones and tools, straps falling harmlessly as he closed the distance.

Ronin bounded from his confinement and stretched to his full size. Cables and wires that were attached to him fell free. Nostrils flared, his chest crackled like the belly of a wood furnace. The cowboy hat had fallen to the floor. Ronin sighted the old man and swung his head, raking the antlers across the wall and flinging debris.

William unloaded his weapon, straps intercepting the shrapnel before it knocked him to the ground. Ronin leaped with the ferocity of a polar bear protecting her cubs, his rack plowing through the rafters. Snow trickled through cracks in the ceiling.

He stretched out, landing just shy of the old man. The tip of his antlers snagged his coat. The old man shrugged it off with one last burst of fire, dropping the weapon as bindings tangled Ronin's legs. The stake dislodged from the concrete floor and cut the air as Ronin tossed his head. Boards shattered; bales of hay exploded.

Gallivanter sped past the bucking reindeer, barrel-rolling toward their captor. William threw open the door of the noisy cubicle. The rhythmic pounding grew louder and a familiar smell escaped.

Ronin reared up. Sparks flew off the door. Snow trickled through the ceiling. A blizzard of hay filled the room as the reindeer trashed the benches, flung wheelbarrows and kicked holes in the walls.

Gallivanter called out.

The great beast stopped. He stamped the floor, rage still boiling, breath streaming from red-hot nostrils. It took a minute to calm down. The elven waited. The old man was trapped.

He was in an impenetrable room. Perhaps it was a safe room or an escape route. There could be a door on the other side. That, however, wasn't the problem. Ryder knew what was alarming the elven. It was the sound that came out of the cubicle and the familiar odor that escaped.

It smelled nice.

※

THE BINDINGS WENT SLACK.

Hay floated down like a gentle flurry. Spotlights fell wherever light fixtures still worked. Trails of snow trickled through the ceiling.

Ryder held Cherry tight, afraid to let go. The hot coal in his hand, the bugs on his stomach. It didn't matter that it was imaginary. He closed his eyes and felt her breath on his ear, her pulse against his cheek.

A hulking silhouette moved over them. A warm muzzle nudged Cherry back.

"It's all right," Ryder said.

She held out an empty hand and let him sniff. He licked her palm then nibbled at the strap around her wrist. Ryder and Cherry unwrapped each other, letting the straps fall lifeless on the hay-scattered floor.

"He won't harm you again."

Gallivanter threw William's coat to the side and held up a phone. It was the same type of phone that Cherry had, the one he'd glanced at before the bugs climbed down his shirt. It was the same kind of phone BG had used when he made Figgy do tricks.

Figgy is a clone.

He wasn't responding to BG's commands; he had to do them. There was no choice. He was programmed. *Could he be made to believe he was doing them because he wanted to?*

Gallivanter stared at Ronin. After a silent pause, the reindeer stepped through the carnage and grabbed splintered timbers with his antlers. Gallivanter guided him to the safe room where William had escaped. They propped the timbers against the metal door.

"You were right, what you said. He put himself in storage. It didn't take long to know he is not his memories. So he woke up." Gallivanter's tone was as grave as ever. "So he did all of this."

The barn groaned. Snow flurries swirled in beams of light.

"What?" Cherry stood in the stall.

A light fixture swung over large bundles of cables that were feeding obscure machines. They had been strapped to Ronin. The rhythmic thumping that was coming from the cubicle had stopped.

"Hurry," Gallivanter said.

"Are you just going to leave him in there?" Cherry said. "After everything he's done?"

"We'll return for him and the others."

"What about Soup?" Ryder said. "He's awake."

Gallivanter didn't understand what Ryder was saying. He hadn't heard Ryder wake Soup and Arf up in the lab when he went back for his boots. He couldn't just leave them in those drawers. What if they didn't come back?

"He was the one who opened the stall," Ryder said. "You heard his voice, Gallivanter. That was Soup. I woke them up before we—"

"You shouldn't have—"

"If I didn't, we'd still be tied to the floor and Ronin would be in the stall. It doesn't matter; we can't leave them. They're awake."

Waves of snow sifted through the cracks.

Gallivanter gestured at the doors. Ronin cleared the way, sweeping debris from the steps. His rack barely fit through the breezeway. Cherry and Ryder helped the elven up the steps and followed him.

Morning had arrived.

The sky was depressed and gray. The wind scoured the horseshoe, throwing plumes against the building. They shielded their eyes, struggling to catch their breath. Gallivanter led them into the middle of the horseshoe and nodded at Ronin.

Unspoken words passed between them.

"Stay," Gallivanter said. "I will find them."

"Let me," Ryder said. "I can go faster."

The elven held up his hand. The wind parted his hair and exposed weary eyes beneath furry brows. Without another word, he kicked sideways and rolled across the horseshoe. He reached the building before they could blink twice.

Why didn't he do that earlier?

Ryder wouldn't have been able to keep up, that was why. It was strange to wait without a green eye watching them. There would be no stream in the morning. Or the next. No one would throw food in the kitchen or score touchdowns.

Kringletown is over.

They huddled against Ronin. The barn cried out. It wouldn't be long before it gave up and the weather buried what was inside. Ryder put his hand on Ronin's neck. The hide was musky and coarse.

Ronin's ears twitched and turned. He scanned for predators, but he was no prey. Muscles tensed in his broad chest and across his flank. Another blast of winter forced them closer.

A shotgun-crack and the roof fell.

Ronin suddenly stepped back. He lowered his head and thrust his rack at them. The antlers expertly snagged their coats and tossed them like toys. They were already a safe distance from the imploding barn. They were white-dusted and dizzy when they looked up.

Ronin turned around.

The barn buckled like a bulldozer was driving through it. Wooden shards rained down, and debris showered an explosive collapse. The barn wasn't falling.

It's being torn apart.

Antlers appeared where the breezeway had been buried. An object blasted out like cannon fodder. Ronin reared up and swatted it away. It landed with a frozen thud, bent and broken.

The cubicle door.

Antlers stepped out of the wreckage. From across the horseshoe, Ronin's clone emerged. Even from that distance, the thing's smell was thick and pungent. Freshly baked. William followed his newest creation into the morning light.

The clone shook off debris.

Specks of hay and splinters were thrown into the wind. It released a gut-shaking howl. Ryder swallowed acrid panic. The phone was still in his coat pocket. The old man must not have an extra one. If he did, Ryder would know it.

I'd feel it.

Ronin scuffed the frozen ground and widened his stance. His hindquarters shivered. William reached for the clone's rear flank. He didn't respond, didn't snort or dig. Ryder and Cherry, half-buried and far away, watched William reach back and swat.

The clone bolted.

Snow flung in its wake. He surged forward, front legs extended, flaps of hide billowing where his legs met his torso. It was a long leap aided by a partially inflated helium bladder. Head down, antlers aimed, he flew like a weapon.

Ryder threw an arm over Cherry.

The clash of true bone antlers echoed off the mountains. Horns locked, a snowstorm kicked up. In moments it was impossible to tell them apart as they circled, heads down, horns locked and angling for leverage.

One of them was thrown.

Legs flailed as he rolled onto his back. He was barely on his hooves when the victor charged. Their horns once again locked like locomotives on a collision course. The downed reindeer was driven back, his hooves carving tracks in the ground. Turning and circling, it happened again.

The victor tossed him against the building this time.

William watched. His coat was ripped and fluttering. The cowboy hat lost in the rubble. He raised a hand. The victorious reindeer turned his head, muscles bulging along his neck. When the old man dropped it, the clone tossed Ronin one last time.

"No!" Ryder scrambled.

Ronin tried to get up. The clone put his front hoof on his chest. Ryder plodded through the snow. The clone swung his head around, sweeping the snow with an array of antlers—

The world tumbled and burned.

Ryder gulped for air but couldn't squeeze it into his chest. A deep bruise spread across his ribs, a dull lump of pain sinking in his stomach, the sky smearing into a monotone of watercolors. Cherry was next to him. Her voice distant and worried. She looked over her shoulder, wiping the snow from his face.

"What do you want?" she shouted.

A shadow fell over them. Ryder crawled onto his knees, drool hanging like fishing line. Oxygen was finding a way into his lungs, wheezing past a knot in his throat.

"You only exist because of me." He nudged Ryder with his boot. "My first son's not going anywhere."

He flicked two fingers at the clone. Ronin struggled as the clone put him on his back, both hooves pinning his chest to the ground. Antlers on his neck.

"No one wanted you." The old man sighed deeply. "You were in a truck in the dead of winter. You wouldn't have lasted five minutes."

Ronin howled.

"You mattered to me, though. No one thought much about the boot prints at the scene or the hoofprints that led up to the truck. It was just another Alaskan mystery. But I knew there was something special about you. I saw something no one else did."

He spit in the snow.

"I was right, you understand? That was never in question. I had the elven, had his memories. I knew what was hiding on the Pole. I wanted to show the world, that's all. I needed more than an elven. When I heard about you, I knew the last reindeer had come for you." He glanced at Ronin. "I brought you here, Ryder. I *made* you my son."

Ryder's body wasn't in the cold room. But there was an infant. Only one.

That was why he was so different from the other nicies. He smelled like them, but he wasn't perfect. He couldn't be. He was the first one. William had put him in the cold room, but not before he cloned him. He'd sent Ryder back to foster care and let him bounce from home to home, where he found trouble. Where he needed help.

And help would arrive.

And when William was ready, he brought Ryder back to Kringletown, where he would need help one last time. *Welcome home.*

"I'm not your son."

"Oh, but you are. You're every bit of it. I built you. I watched you grow up, paid for the damages you left behind, compensated foster parents for their trouble. I may be absent, but I am your father."

"I am not your—"

William kicked him before he got up. Cherry swung on him. He leaned over, tobacco stuck between his teeth.

"Call the elf."

Ryder painted the snow red. He wiped his mouth. William grabbed his coat and shook him, shoving Cherry when she tried to stop him. Ronin had stopped struggling. His tongue hung from his mouth. Black eyes stared at Ryder.

"Gallivanter!" William shouted. "My patience is thin, old friend."

He strolled toward the cloned reindeer. Ronin's chest rose in long deep breaths. When William neared, the clone looked up like a good dog and waited for him to call out the next trick.

"I will count to three. If you have not surrendered"—he kicked Ronin's hindquarter—"the beast suffers first. Then the children."

Ryder tried to get up. Cherry stopped him. If William didn't knock him back down, the clone would swat him across the yard. Ryder couldn't take another hit like that. William held up a finger.

"One."

Ryder felt his coat pocket.

"Two."

He slid the phone out. The screen was black. He pressed the button, hoping there was time to boot it. Hoped there was something on it that would stop what was about to happen. If something put him to sleep, then the clone could be stopped.

"Three!"

The phone lit up just as William lifted his leg. He was about to drive his boot into Ronin's ribs when he was buried in a cloud of snow. The clatter of antlers was followed by a heavy thump. William went twenty feet before landing heavily on his back, his breath forced out in wheezing surprise. Mewling and roars followed.

A reindeer charged out of the melee.

Head down, his antlers were pointed at Ryder and Cherry. The hooves pounded the frozen turf. Nose burning with determination, his belly began to swell. He aimed the network of boney antlers at their hunkering forms. The air shimmered around the antlers and hummed as he drew near. Ryder threw his arm over Cherry.

His coat yanked up.

He was snatched from the ground and tossed. Losing his grip, he swung for Cherry, for the ground, for anything before the antlers found him again. For a second time, he landed hard, only this time it wasn't on frozen ground. Muscles writhed beneath him. The world went silent.

And the mountains were far below.

21

Wispy fog streamed past him, silent and still. As if he were looking through a window and the clouds were outside. Corded muscles writhed beneath him; short hairs bristled under his hands. Legs yoked over a swollen belly, Ryder grabbed a fistful of hide. The clouds weren't outside.

I'm in them.

Ronin's head bobbed up and down, neck straining in a silent gallop. Specks of frozen precipitation shot past. There was no wind howling in his ears; no bitter cold scouring his cheeks. The air warped around the antlers. Ronin tipped his head and put one black eye on them. A hoarse bark escaped his throat. He went back to pedaling the wind, a missile piercing the sky.

It's a magnetic field.

The antlers had shifted the blurred space when he turned his head, reshaping the spitting specks of ice and billowy clouds streaming past in foggy ribbons. A magnetic force field protected them from the thin and frozen air. Warmth seeped from Ronin's hide like a furnace was burning below.

Cherry rested her chin on his shoulder.

Her breath was in his ear. He put one hand over hers and

squeezed. This was too surreal to relax. This could be a game room illusion. It could be a dream. But neither of those events had filled him with wonder like this.

The last thing he remembered was being on the ground when Ronin charged. They had cowered in the snow just before the world started spinning. A long wound glistened along Ronin's flank, the hide damp and matted.

They were still climbing.

Ronin's belly huffed and bellowed wider and hotter with each breath. Below, patches of green land streaked past occasional openings in the cloud cover. Ryder's legs ached, his hands firmly clenched against the reindeer's back. Ears pinned back, Ronin silently galloped higher. They rose into the thick interior of the clouds, where they were swallowed. Once hidden, he stretched his legs and glided. His belly fully inflated.

Ryder turned around. Cherry's cheeks were ruby and scuffed, nose cold and runny. Beyond her, the back end was empty.

Gallivanter was still at Kringletown.

❅

THE FURNACE WAS STILL WORKING.

Ryder woke with bristling fur on his nose. A frigid breeze was sneaking down his coat. His legs were painfully aching like a wishbone was breaking. Cherry lay across his back, her fingers laced around his stomach.

The clouds were icy and cracked.

He wiped his eyes. Cherry groaned as he pushed upright. Those weren't clouds. They were soaring in the open. The black sky was above and snowy dunes below. Open leads exposed cracks in the ice that spidered over the Arctic Ocean like a network of veins.

The Pole.

Ronin was pawing at thin air, his strokes short and rapid. His breath was a rattling tailpipe. Wind was leaking through the magnetic field like an icy draft sneaking through a cracked windshield.

The antlers were flickering.

Ryder rubbed the reindeer's ears. Ronin gave a hoarse cry and his belly expanded. They rose higher, but it didn't last. They were dropping as the panting grew louder.

"Stay down," he told Cherry.

Ryder hugged Ronin. She hunkered down behind him. There was nothing but ice. They were dressed for the Arctic, but it was still so cold.

The ice was several feet below them when Ronin stretched his legs out. The flaps of hide billowed between his legs. They soared up as his belly inflated one last time. And then little by little, they leaked back down.

His front hooves sprayed snow.

It splashed through the magnetic field. Ryder held on with his eyes closed, listening to the dampened impact of four hooves plowing through deep snow. The magnetic field vanished. Frigid air cut through him. He gasped for his next breath as a wave of snow fell over them.

They crashed.

Ryder dug his way out with choppy breath and numb cheeks. Cherry was crawling toward him, her hair gray with a fresh dusting of winter. He held her as she stumbled and sank. They ducked behind a cresting dune.

"You all right?"

He pulled her against him. His eyelashes crackled. They squatted deeper into the snow. A path had been carved like a snowplow was searching for the road. They worked their way toward it and saw the massive antlers.

"Ronin."

Together, they rushed to the reindeer's side. The wind cut away all the feeling in Ryder's hands. It felt like someone was pinching his ears and nose. They dropped against Ronin's belly, the furnace still warm. But like a balloon from a long past birthday, it was losing air.

Ronin raised his front leg and pulled them deeper into cover. He curled his head around them, tongue slowly lapping the snow from their stiff pant legs. Ryder wrapped his arms around his furry snout.

"His nose is cold."

A clod of fear dropped in his stomach. The weather was scrubbing the world into a barren landscape of white nothingness. They weren't dressed to survive. And Ronin was exhausted and hurt.

How did he make it this far?

Ryder crawled over to Cherry and pressed her into the nook of Ronin's neck. He put his arms around her and pulled Ronin's shaggy chin against them. The night sky was deep, black and bruised with swirling bands of green and red. The Northern Lights decorated the nighttime like ribbons around a gift.

Ryder couldn't feel his body.

Everything that had happened in his life and here he was, trapped somewhere on top of the world with Cherry in his arms and a reindeer around them. Fear suddenly flushed from him like an ocean breeze cleansing something wrong and rotten. He felt clean. He felt okay, just to be here and now, watching something as magical as this. They had escaped Kringletown.

There was no other place he'd rather be.

"I'm not scared anymore."

He nestled deeper. Cherry was curled beneath him, her chest rising and falling. She was practicing her meditation. Ronin's belly rose and fell in long, easy breaths that matched hers. Together, Ryder fell into the same rhythm.

As one, they breathed.

Peace fell on them as a soft and comforting blanket. It didn't matter what had happened or where he was from, if none of this made sense. Whether this was a dream or not. The night sky watched them accept the cold hand of winter with a million starry eyes. If anyone found them, a smile would be frozen on his face. He liked that idea as dreamy thoughts spilled across the landscape of his mind. He felt the colors of the Northern Lights and tasted the touch of spitting snowflakes.

He heard singing.

It was high and joyful. It blended in harmony. Voices were carried on the wind and sifted into his head like fairy dust.

Cherry shuddered beneath him.

Fresh snow cascaded beneath his collar. The warm wall of furry hide pulled away. Ronin stretched his neck and pawed through the snow until he found the hard purchase of ice.

He stumbled onto all fours.

Suddenly exposed, Ryder and Cherry shielded each other from the wind. They squinted against the squall of frozen bullets pelting their cheeks. His vision was blurred.

"Ronin!"

The reindeer seemed to falter with weakness and indecision. There was nowhere to go. He didn't need to protect Ryder anymore. He'd done enough. It wasn't fair for him to use his last breath trying to save them when they could just be together.

His antlers vanished.

Ryder fought the ice crystals bleeding through his eyelashes and smearing his eyesight. He peered between split fingers.

"Where—" The wind momentarily stole the words from Cherry. "Where did he go?"

Ryder was half-frozen and abandoned in the coldest part of the world without a spit of land in sight. A reindeer had flown them there and now had disappeared right in front of them. Maybe he was dreaming.

That didn't explain why he still heard singing.

22

Going up.

The elevator pulsed every half second as if not sure it could make it to the surface, recording a slight drop before going up several more feet. Darkness turned gray as he rose higher, causing the pulsing hesitations to spike deeper, thumping dull pain as it reached the light of morning.

Billy's eyelids flicked open.

The surface below his cheek was hard, cold and slick. He rolled onto his back and stared at the ceiling. The taste of iron slid to the back of his throat.

The headache continued.

The elevator was within reach. A deep inhalation stung his lower lip and whistled between his teeth. He pulled back scarlet-painted fingertips. The tip of his tongue revealed an angular opening between two teeth.

A pearly piece on the floor.

What's my name?

He knew this was home, that there were kids. The drone was in the corner like an escaped balloon. It was like he didn't have a name.

And never did.

There were several sublevels belowground. He was going to the lab sometime early in the morning. It was still dark, but the sun was up. Something was wrong.

Something bad.

Rot sank deep in his belly. He leaned over and dry-heaved. He went to his hands and knees and continued, twisting his empty stomach until a string of saliva dangled.

What have I done?

That thought felt different. He usually felt like there were two parts of himself, one talking to the other. Now it was just him. Something was missing. The inner voice was quiet.

It was missing.

He fell on his back, panting. His past was hidden in the dark recesses of his mind like monsters under the bed. He couldn't remember what he'd done or what he was going to do, but the urge to weep swelled in his throat.

He was probing his chipped tooth when a bone-crashing clatter echoed from outside. It sounded like trains colliding. He propped his weight against the wall. A profound numbness settled like grains of frozen sand. He shuffled to the foyer.

Out front, the circle driveway was empty. Snow was tracked with shallow ruts from days ago. Icicles hung from a mountain of antlers. The collision came again, followed by a hoarse cry that jarred loose a memory of an oversized reindeer struggling in a tangle of binding straps.

Ronin.

He leaned on a table. A vase shattered on the floor. Ronin was a distant memory, a car disconnected from a locomotive of thoughts and no longer part of the trip. Like a memory that didn't belong to him. But he was there, he was part of it. He had trapped the reindeer, had lured him onto the mountain.

He kicked through the vase. The office door was ajar. The mountain was flaming with morning light. He stumbled to the glass wall, pressed his hands against the cold and smooth surface, and watched an enormous reindeer gallop across the horseshoe. Snow flipped from his hooves as Ronin lowered his head. Multiple points of a massive rack raked through the snow as he charged two figures hunched low to the ground.

He's going to impale them.

Instead he snagged one of them like a giant coat rack sweeping the back of his heavy coat. Arms and legs waving in panic, he tumbled like a lead kite and was followed by the girl. Ronin lurched beneath them as his belly swelled. The strides grew longer, the hooves gliding and stirring the snow. The boy fell onto his back first. The girl behind him.

And then they were off.

Long strong legs reaching for the sky, loose hide billowing like sails. Ronin surged toward the mountain.

And over it.

A sense of relief filled him. It started at his toes and rose to his throbbing cheek with tingling joy. Ronin was free. He had escaped with two of the children.

Someone else was still out there.

The barn looked meteor-struck. Shards of debris had showered the horseshoe. William watched Ronin soar out of sight. There was another reindeer at his side.

My older brother, William. My mentor. My sibling.

Billy looked at his hands, turning them over as if the truth were written in the creases. The sick feeling squeezed his empty stomach.

My brother?

He had never questioned his reclusive sibling. Their past seemed so ordinary, the memories bleached by time. Now as he looked out, the old man felt like someone else. *Why would we have the same name?*

William walked to where the children had been hunkered down. The hitch in his stride was more pronounced in the morning. He dropped to one knee and picked something up, dusting it off before pocketing it. The reindeer didn't move.

A clone.

They'd brought Ronin off the mountain and immediately began

building a matrix. Billy didn't think it would be ready for another day, but there it was. Waiting for a command.

The old man marched stiffly toward the remains of the barn. An opening was blown in the side of the chaos like a tractor-trailer had escaped. William limped into the shadows.

Billy followed.

Without a coat, the wind sank its frozen teeth into his belly. A sharp inhale stabbed his exposed tooth. The clone swung around at the sound of the door, snow dropping from the rack. Puffs streamed from his flared nostrils as Billy approached. A peculiar smell grew stronger—a fuzzy odor that clung to his tongue.

A memory bobbed to the surface.

A room with large drawers and glass doors. The soles of bare feet facing out from a dark recess in the wall. Billy sitting at computers and pecking at keys, writing commands in elaborate scripts uploaded to a large noisy room, scripts that were orders. Commands. Programs that told the children what to do, how to behave.

Good boys and girls do what I want.

Billy knew what made boys and girls nice. But that wasn't him sitting at the computer. It felt like William. Billy looked to his hands. The barrier hiding his memories dropped another webby veil. The rhythmic sound of machinery. Waves of heat in a tubular oven. Three-dimensional webs of neural pathways spontaneously stringing together, each connection linking thoughts into concepts and memories.

Me.

His knees were weak. It was a memory of coming *out* of the replicator. Billy remembered inventing the replicator. He remembered using it to create Figgy. Now he remembered crawling out and picking up his own body. He'd carried it to the storage room and put it in a drawer.

No.

He fell in the snow. Memories swirled in the light. The world spun viciously. Billy wanted to find the truth. He took in children who needed a home. He was a philanthropist who used his mind and money to make the world a better place. He was building something on the other side of the mountain that would show the world he wasn't insane.

I'm a lie.

He stumbled into the rubble. The walls and rafters had collapsed. The distinctive odor of synthetic stem cells, the clayey odor of his very own flesh, wafted out.

"What have you done?" he said.

William jerked around. He peered out from the special room where the clone of Ronin had been spun up. They stared at each other with hesitation. Shivers danced on Billy's chin. His fingers twitched.

He remembered an accident that took two fingers from his right hand. It had happened on a climbing expedition. He'd spent the night with tourniquets around his knuckles. Billy remembered the agony lasted for months.

But Billy had all ten fingers.

"Get to the lab," William said. "Wake the children."

He finished gathering things into a bag and buttoned a thick coat. Billy didn't follow him. The compulsion that had yanked him around all of his life had been cut. It was just words now.

"You did this to me," Billy said.

William replaced the cowboy hat with a fur-lined cap and nodded for several seconds. Understanding was coming into focus. Something had changed between them.

"You've always known, Billy."

"You lied to me."

"About what?" William turned. "We're brothers. We have the exact same DNA. It's no different than coming from the same womb. Now stop arguing and—"

"You lied to me!" Billy was quivering. "You made me do those things. That was you! Your voice in my head, your demands. I didn't want this, William."

He grunted. "You're upset I gave you life. You're upset I made you ageless, made you the envy of the world. Do you understand what I'm saying? You and the dog were the first ones." He jabbed his finger at the ground. "You are an impeccable creation!"

William's face was flush, his eyes dark. He minced tobacco between his teeth and spat with force.

Creation.

"No one has the right to question their existence," William continued. "You were born like the rest of us, but I gave you purpose. I gave you direction. What would the children give to be you? Think about that, what would they give to have such riches, to have purpose, brother? You are the envy of the world because of me. If it was my voice you heard, it was because you were listening. If it was my direction you felt, it was because we are alike. Don't whine about your life. You are what you are, brother. You're no different than the rest of us."

William threw a bag over his shoulder.

"I want you to remember what we're doing. We saved children, we gave them a home. And we created life. The truth is near, brother. And the elven is trying to stop us."

"Gallivanter."

"We never should've monitored his thoughts, that was our mistake. We had everything we needed. We should've locked him up and forgotten him, but it's too late for that. He's awake, brother. And he put you to sleep."

"We?" Billy tongued his chipped tooth. "*We?*"

"We're in this, there's no way back. We move forward. The truth is out there."

"I see the truth, William."

"Don't let him put thoughts in your head. We've been working for fifteen years—"

"Him? Putting thoughts?" Billy laughed sickly. It was the first time he could remember his head so uncluttered.

"This is his fault." William swept a heavy arm at the destruction. "Ronin escaped because of him, you understand? Everything we've worked for is gone, over that mountain, and I'm sure they didn't stop there. If he reaches the Pole, he'll destroy our life's work. We are on the verge of discovering a centuries-old myth. Don't let him destroy that."

Billy scanned the horseshoe, the building, and destruction. It felt so foreign now. He didn't want any of it.

"What's my name?" he said.

"What?"

"My name, William!" he shouted. "What is it?"

A frown knitted the old man's brow. He hiked the bag over his shoulders and snapped the buckles then reached into his pocket. A shadow stretched behind him. The reindeer clone snorted. The thing dropped to its knees.

Billy clutched William's coat. He wasn't getting on the reindeer, wasn't going to follow Ronin. He knew what the old man was planning. He once wanted the same thing.

Not anymore.

A shiver of gooseflesh turned his bones to metal, muscle to stone. An electrical pulse lit up. Billy was as stiff as an ice carving, fingers still clawing the coat. William held up his hand. Cradled between two fingers and a thumb was a black phone.

The screen was alive.

"I don't have time for this." He buttoned the top of Billy's shirt. "I would fix you when I get back, but I'm afraid you won't last that long. I'll start over, print another one when I get back. It won't be you, though. I think you know that."

He climbed onto the clone's back. The space warped around the antlers. A strange energy almost pushed Billy over. The clone anxiously pawed the frozen turf. Something hissed like a gas leak. The belly began to swell.

William patted the beast.

The antlers hummed and the air wrinkled. With a great growl, the clone leaped forward and nearly jerked the old man over the backside.

Two steps and they were airborne.

❄

THE SHIVERS WENT DEEP.

Bones turned into titanium and quivered like cold steel struck with a mallet. His skin withered across his cheekbones. The biting cold burned. His whistling breath stabbed his chipped tooth.

Thoughts slowed.

Churning in a flurry of panic, one by one they fell like bricks until only one remained. *I'm going to die.*

Could he die if he was never born? Life began in the replicator. He was a copy, a clone. No different than the reindeer. These childhood memories weren't his.

Did he have to be born to be alive?

William was right. His mind wasn't right. He couldn't remember much, like his memories had been thrown behind a fence and he was peeking at them through a knothole. Somewhere beyond the barrier were all the things he'd done, every awful thing hidden from him. Those were his memories, the things he'd done. Whether William made him do them or not, he'd still done them.

Tears left hot tracks on his cheeks and disappeared in his beard. They gushed from a well of guilt and shame, a salty brine seeping through whiskers and coating cracked lips.

I want to live.

The bone-quivering cold turned warm, as if his organs were melting. Hypothermia had begun. It wouldn't be long now. He would end up a statue staring at the naughty wing. A fitting end.

"Hi, Bill." One of the boys was in front of him, hands in his coat. "You shouldn't go outside without a coat. You know that."

He was joined by another boy, who stood eye to eye with Billy, perhaps even a few inches taller. A snarling scar patched his left cheek and misshapen ear.

He knew these boys. He should know their names—he'd brought them here; he'd fed and clothed them—but the memories were behind the fence. The big boy leaned in. A faint whiff of body odor followed.

"Is he okay?" the big boy said.

"He's sleepy, that's all."

"His fingers are blue."

"He didn't wear gloves. You should wear gloves, Bill."

The big boy threw Billy's arm over his shoulders and heaved him off the ground. The world jostled as he plodded through the snow. They were halfway across the horseshoe, the building drawing closer with each step, when the big boy spun around.

"You coming?" he called.

The smaller boy was looking at the mountain. He marched toward the door, his eyebrows knitted, lips set in grim frustration. The big boy followed him inside.

Billy's lips began to quiver as they stepped into an elevator. His pulse quickened. They were going to the lab. He was afraid the fence barricading the bad memories would come crashing down and all at once he'd face the things he'd done. The doors opened to a hallway instead of the lab. It led to a glowing room.

"He's like ice," the big boy said.

He gently placed Billy in a rocking chair and draped a blanket over his lap. The room moved like the deck of a ship. Stockings hung across a mantel, festive decorations of holly and garland above them. A warm fire crackled. Somewhere beyond the fence, there was a memory of telling a story.

The boys warmed their hands at the fire. They mumbled to each other, looking over their shoulders every once in a while. Something in the hall grabbed their attention. The smaller boy tickled the end of Billy's nose. It turned into an itch.

The silence of their departure was filled with popping embers and settling ashes. Billy melted like a block of ice. Sensations returned on sharp edges that squeezed his fingertips. He was able to curl his toes.

The urge to weep threatened to drown him.

He was still unable to move. Webs filled his head. His memories, disconnected and full of holes, were still mostly hidden. His life didn't make sense.

I gave you purpose, William had said.

Footsteps scuffed the floor like coarse sandpaper. Billy stared at the fire and waited. A very short and very round person approached the chair next to him.

A long green coat dragged behind him.

He threw an absurdly large and hairy foot onto the stool and hefted his rotund bottom into the seat. A sigh leaked through the thick whiskers. His beard lay over his belly in two tightly braided ropes.

A memory hopped the fence.

Flashes of an Arctic winter. Conifers spotted the barren land, their limbs heavy with snow. In the distance, a larger-than-life reindeer rooted for lichen. A thrill of excitement rode a wave of adrenaline through Billy's bloodstream. He had come to the Pole in search of big game.

And stumbled onto the biggest of them all.

Sighting a mutant reindeer with a long-range weapon, he leaned on the trigger. Before the neutralizing dart erupted from the barrel, something moved into his line of sight.

Gallivanter.

He didn't know the elven's name at that time. He didn't even know what he was seeing. Just that he wanted them. The reindeer searched the elven's hand, nibbling treats from his palm.

Billy fired twice.

From that distance, there was a delay. Billy waited for a response. If there was none, he would take another aim. The first round missed, but not the second one.

The elven fell.

The reindeer sniffed then nudged him before lifting his head. His roar echoed in the distance. Billy felt it. The reindeer looked around, giving him enough time to unload a second shot. The beast swung his head with remarkable speed. Nothing happened. Billy took a third shot and a fourth. Each time, the reindeer swung his head.

He was knocking down the darts.

Billy would keep firing until the thing missed or he ran out of ammunition. It seemed to be jabbing the elven to wake him up, snagging the green tunic with an antler but having to turn his head to block incoming fire. Little by little, the elven was moved behind a tree.

Without hesitation, Billy reached for a new and untested weapon. One that was compassionate and more effective than a bullet, leaving game unharmed. Unlike the sleeper dart, it discharged like a cannon.

The canister spilled its contents as it neared the target. The reindeer had tossed the elven into the air as if to catch him on his back. The entanglement straps reached out with webby lines. Instead of snagging the animal, the elven was wrapped up.

A second roar shook snow from the branches.

The elven was incapacitated and anchored to a tree. He was waving an arm at the reindeer, shooing him away. All the reindeer's efforts to free him would keep him there long enough for Billy to unload another web. He took aim, finger on the trigger.

And then it happened.

The animal began to inflate, its belly filling like a balloon. Billy watched a reindeer soar into the clouds like a prehistoric animal forgotten by time. He sat in stunned silence, waiting to wake up. When he decided he wasn't dreaming, he approached his catch. The bearded elven was enveloped in a mess of entanglement straps.

That's when it began.

Gallivanter watched the fire. When he nodded, a warm sensation melted on top of Billy's head like an egg spilled into a frying pan. It seeped through him, sweeping away the paralysis.

"Not your memory," Gallivanter said. "Not you."

Billy rubbed his face. The air was suddenly thick and hot. He drew quick, stabbing breaths. "But I did... other things."

Gallivanter stroked the beard braids.

"I couldn't stop. He was too..." Billy trembled. *Too strong.*

"Your memories belong to William, most of them. He made you what he wanted. Hid you from yourself."

A good boy.

He remembered looking at the elven shortly after bringing him home, remembered confining him to a chair and extracting his memories. The urge to weep returned. Those were William's memories.

"Who am I?"

Gallivanter looked at him. The eyes wrinkled in the corners and twinkled in the center. He hopped off his perch and waddled over, patting Billy's hand.

"You are this."

Billy wiped his eyes. He didn't have to have a name to exist, didn't have to be born to be alive. *I am this.*

"Can you forgive me?"

Gallivanter shuffled toward the exit. "I will show you."

Billy was slow to get up. His legs were newborn. He trundled into the hallway. Gallivanter was in the elevator. It went up, the smooth sound of hydraulics easing to a stop. There was chatter on the other side of the doors. They opened to the foyer and the chatter stopped.

The children were waiting.

23

Ryder was afraid to move.

After all, the North Pole wasn't a land. It was a sheet of ice floating on the Arctic Ocean. They weren't going to survive long in this weather, but one wrong step and they could plunge through an open lead into dark water.

They would only last minutes.

Ronin's footsteps were disappearing. The bitter wind blurred his vision. The tracks were quickly eroding.

"Cherry!"

He barely felt her slip from his grasp. She was shuffling in the same direction Ronin was last seen moving, swinging her arms in front of her.

"Stop—" He choked on a mouthful of frigid air.

And then she was gone, too.

Unlike Ronin, he watched her disappear. She didn't plunge through the ice. She just vanished. First her arms and then the rest of her, like she'd walk through a veil that didn't part but rather absorbed her. Ryder reached his arm out.

His mitten vanished.

He stuck his arm out again; this time it disappeared up to the elbow. Before he could pull it back, something grabbed him like something taking bait from below the ice.

Silence.

That was the first thing he noticed. He hadn't fallen into the belly of a sea monster. Cherry was holding onto his arm. The scenery hadn't changed. The sky was still dark and the stars numerous and bright; the snowy landscape went out to the horizon. It was bone-breaking cold.

The wind is gone.

It was like a window had been rolled up. Their breath streamed out in thick clouds that hovered in front of their faces. There was a slight blur behind him, a watery wall that warped the view.

"What is it?" she said.

A liquid wall hovered in space. He put his arm through it. "I can feel the wind on the other side."

Ronin had come this way. The snow had been trampled around them like a stampede had swept through the area with no indication of where it came from or where it went. The prints were wide and deep, a mixture of hooves and snowshoes.

Footprints.

"You hear that?" Cherry said.

He slowed his breathing. It sounded like… *like singing.* It was all around. They moved a few steps and stopped. The celebration grew closer. The hair on the back of his neck stiffened. The air had that funny watercolor look to it again.

"Ryder!"

Cherry pointed back from where they had come. An object was falling from the sky. At the last moment, it threw out four legs and glided over the snow, galloping to a stop and shaking a rack of antlers. Someone fell off.

William.

The old man gathered his coat around his neck. He was prepared for the fierce weather, buttoning up and pulling on a second pair of mittens. The wind pushed him away from the cloned reindeer. He leaned into the gale and worked his way back, using the clone for protection. He reached into a pocket. A chill more frigid than the water below the ice trickled through Ryder's legs.

The phone.

Ryder had dropped it before Ronin had thrown them on his back. Now the old man cradled it in the thick padding of his mitten, pulling it close to see. Ryder didn't know how it worked.

He just knew what it did.

Cherry shoved Ryder behind her. The old man waved the phone side to side. He looked directly at them, lifted his hand and squinted. The loose ends of his coat flapped like a kite snagged in a tree.

Chilling fear had filled his legs and was replaced by red-hot coals, but not the imaginary kind the old man had made him believe. He'd been running his entire life, searching for where he belonged. Now he knew the truth of who he was and why. The old man couldn't take that away from him. No one could.

I'm not afraid.

"There's nothing!" Ryder shouted. "You're alone, William!"

The old man cocked his head.

Cherry kept Ryder from moving forward. Her lips drew a grim line. Crystals had formed on her eyelashes and had begun to melt. Ryder felt a smile jab his cheek. Determination creased her forehead.

"He can't hear you." The voice came from behind them.

Two elven were in the trampled snow. One was bearded with a giant bush. Their enormous feet were half buried. They smiled while Ryder and Cherry searched for words. The pause was long and silent, the strangeness wrapping around them and squeezing.

"We're inside the dome." The elven who said that wore a long gray braid that pulled the hair from her doughy, grandmotherly face.

"Back-reflecting technology," the bearded elven added, "allows us to be unseen. The field generator is in the center, you see, and we adjust the radius—"

"Nog."

The grandmotherly elven touched his arm. Nog went silent, lips still parted as if he might continue.

"We've been waiting for you," she said.

Ryder and Cherry looked at each other. This was what the game room felt like. Vertigo weakened his knees. Reality had flipped upside down.

"Nog and I decided to present ourselves first. This is quite a bit, we realize. A bit overwhelming. So take your time, and don't worry about William and his reindeer."

The old man had wandered farther away.

"What Merry means to say is that *she* decided to show ourselves first. Honestly, I think it'd be better if we went Band-Aid on this. It's not like time is abundant right now, and the wandering gentleman out there isn't going to last long, not like that—"

"Nevertheless." Merry took his hand. "There's no good way, children. It is Christmas Eve. We're busy at this time of year and there's been a lot to celebrate. We don't invite your kind into the colony, you see. Only three in the last two hundred years."

"Where is he?" Ryder blurted. "Where's Ronin?"

"He's safe, child."

She twittered her fingers and urged them to come closer. Nog stepped aside, his wide feet stamping the snow like snowshoes, making space between Merry and him.

"What about William?" A look of concern wedged between Cherry's eyebrows. The old man was struggling. The wind shoved him down. "We can't let him freeze," she said.

"That won't happen," Merry said.

"He will find what he needs." Nog lifted a defiant finger. "The true Christmas spirit."

After all he'd done, it was still hard to watch the old man like that. He was cold and suffering. Most of all, he was lost.

Merry and Nog held up their hands, both with wiggling fingers and merry smiles, their cheeks rosy and eyes sparkling in deep folds. Ryder and Cherry took their hands. With their backs to William, they faced another watery wall. They were standing in the space between two incognito domes, Nog explained.

"Don't you think we should show them first?"

"*You* do."

"*We* should."

Merry was warm and soft and full of wrinkles. Nog was a step ahead of them. When he got back in line, she nodded. Their hands tightened as if the roller coaster were climbing over the first drop.

"Children," she said, "the real North Pole."

The air shimmered like a vertical pond of water was suddenly disturbed by a pebble. The distant horizon wavered and the dunes of snow quaked. And then like turning a knob, a correct frequency was found and the window was clear. A roar of celebration surprised them.

Elven were everywhere.

They sang and shouted, cheered and laughed. The volume was deafening and so full of joy that it felt like a bonfire had been ignited with gasoline.

They wore long coats and short coats, some with caps and others without. Beards that touched their toes and faces smooth and round, a concert of partygoers mingling in controlled chaos. There were fast avenues where the ice was exposed and the elven slid on bare feet. There were congregations crowded together and barely moving.

Snowballs were launched like beach balls, and snow fell like confetti. Elven popped out of the ice, and others leaped into open leads of water. And they were singing.

They were all singing.

Presents brightly wrapped floated amongst the crowd, passed along like pails of water, each making their way toward a giant red sleigh, where elven kept count and directed traffic. Enormous snow creatures were at the end of the lines, taking the gifts with thick arms and placing them in a big sack, their heads turning like turrets. They were abominable things made of snow.

Ryder felt the ice begin to tilt.

He and Cherry staggered. Merry and Nog held them upright. His balance was suddenly elusive. He didn't get dizzy in dreams.

"It's real," Cherry murmured.

"My dear, you flew on a reindeer," Nog said. "Of course it's real."

"It's just so, so... *magical*."

"Not magic. Science. Magic is phenomena not yet understood—"

"Nog."

He cleared his throat. "Not magic."

"That feeling you have right now," Merry said, "is why we remain secret. You're not ready to see. William took our knowledge for the wrong reasons. There are others like him."

Ryder didn't know if he'd ever get his legs back. In the game room he knew it was an illusion, that he could leave and go back to the way things were supposed to be. And in a dream he woke up. Reality was always waiting.

But this is reality.

A hoarse call rose up. A herd of reindeer was gathered in a circle. They were facing in with bushy white tails flickering out. Their antlers clattered as they crowded together. Somewhere in the middle a greater set of antlers rose up.

Ryder took a tentative step.

His legs were stiff and numb. Merry tried to hold him back, but he stumbled ahead, dragging them through the barrier with him. It felt thick and wet, raising every hair follicle on his body as he passed through it. He emerged on the other side still dry.

All at once, everyone stopped.

Presents held stiffly, snowballs cocked and ready, no one moved. They were caught in the act, holding as still as Arctic hares. Even the snow creatures were motionless, as if they were natural features conjured up by a storm.

"Everyone!" Merry called. "I'd like to introduce—"

The stampede drowned her out. Sliding and marching, rolling and jumping, cheering and singing as they rushed toward them. Ryder and Cherry drew closer as short arms and little hands mobbed them.

Merry and Nog tried to control traffic, but it was futile. The fat little bodies crushed together, pulling at their coats and grabbing at their hands. Touching them and cheering. Gray-haired elven seemed just as thrilled as the bouncy younger ones.

The abominable snowmen got control.

They parted the crowd and stomped their way toward them. Gently, they moved the swarming elven a safe distance away, allowing a few at a time to reach them.

"Christmas, everyone!" Merry's amplified voice magically rose above the din. "Remember it's Christmas. We need to continue our work. Please, everyone."

A collective groan rippled through the crowd. Little by little, they peeled away and picked up the presents. Three younger elven slipped between the snow creatures and tossed a gleaming cube in the air. As it hovered above them, they wagged their tongues and threw up fingers.

"Enough selfies." Merry ushered them away. "You have work."

The reindeer hadn't moved.

The tips of great antlers were barely visible. The snow creatures cleared a path. Ryder and Cherry walked down the icy red carpet with straggling young elven on both sides of the abominable barricade.

The reindeer snorted.

Two elven were feeding them and adjusting harnesses on their bellies. They seemed immune to the hysteria, focused on the reindeer instead. Ryder held out his hand. Wet nostrils walked up his arm and sampled his neck and hair. A coarse tongue raked his cheek before the next one in line did the same, purring with approval.

"They remember you," one of the handlers said.

She gave them green cubes. Little by little, the center of the gathering was revealed. Ronin lay on folded legs. He lifted his head slowly, like his antlers were cast iron. Eyelids lazily revealed watery eyes. Ryder fell on his knees.

The reindeer closed around them.

"You're special," the handler said. "You have the kiss."

Ryder touched his cheek where the birthmark was. "I... remember..."

"He never forgot."

A musky scent of wet fur and grassy breath smothered them. Ryder leaned against Ronin's neck, the fur warm and tickling. Cherry did the same on the other side. They ran their fingers over his long snout. A deep satisfied groan rattled deep inside Ronin. The adrenaline that had fueled Ryder tapped out and a deep restfulness fell over him.

Reindeer breath sprinkled down like magic.

"You share a connection." The handler's voice was comforting. "One that will always be there. One that might feel..."

Ryder could feel her lean closer to whisper.

There was an explanation for all of this—like how a reindeer flies, or the way he saw through Ronin's eyes, or that elven really do exist—but he didn't want to call it science. Not just yet. They shared a connection, one that seemed to connect their thoughts and senses. There was only one word for that.

"Magical," the herder whispered.

The sky was dark and still. Colorful ribbons dashed against an endless backdrop. From outside the ring of reindeer and imposing snow creatures, a song rose up. Surrounded by the impossible, Ryder rested in the best place in the world—the strong neck of a reindeer.

The greatest of them all.

❄

BELLS.

Melodious bells gently carried Ryder to wakefulness. The ground jolted.

"Not this year." Tinsel, the elven herder, stroked Ronin's muzzle. "You've done enough for one night."

That didn't slow him. Ryder and Cherry fell back as he made it onto his front legs. The antlers swung around as he stretched his neck and let out a long mournful wail.

"They'll be fine," Tinsel said. "They know the way."

Reluctantly, he dropped back down, a growl rumbling in his throat. There was nothing he could do about it. He didn't have the energy to stand. Tinsel soothed him until he laid his head down. Snow puffed out in long streams. His eyelids dropped once again.

"Come," Merry called.

Nog helped Cherry stand. Merry waited patiently for Ryder to take her hand. Ronin's eyes were already wandering beneath his eyelids, watching dreamy green cubes dance like sugar plums.

"Thank you," Ryder whispered into the fluffy ear.

He stopped from hugging the big snout resting peacefully. This was the presence he'd felt all of his life. No matter how lonely he felt, there was someone out there watching over him. Ryder told him that he didn't need him anymore.

Secretly, he didn't want to let go.

The elven were no longer scattered across the ice but grouped tightly around the sleigh. None were waiting for Ryder and Cherry as the snow creatures escorted them. Occasionally, the younger ones snuck a selfie. Everyone else was focused on the most important night of the year.

Cherry and Ryder laced their fingers.

The sleigh was larger than it appeared from a distance. The eight reindeer were tethered to the front, mouths buried in feed bags, stamping the snow impatiently, bells ringing on the harnesses. The sack was bulky and tied shut. The strangeness of all of this threatened his balance again, telling him to wake up. There weren't sleighs on the North Pole or sacks filled with toys.

And reindeer don't fly.

The bench was padded and a control panel looked like something from a spaceship. A mug of cocoa steamed from a cup holder, little white marshmallows bobbing in foam. Cherry pinched his arm and he winced.

"Just wanted to make sure you're real."

"Why wouldn't he be?" The voice was deep and resonant, as if a bassoon could talk.

His beard was as white as snow and thick as a blizzard. His red coat was worn and thick, white specks of snow stuck to the fuzzy surface. A strong fragrance of nutmeg surrounded him.

This was not the cartoon from movies or coloring books or

holiday calendars but a real man with scuffed mittens and a ruddy nose, eyes as deep and blue as Arctic ice.

He's real.

Ryder didn't say it. He'd said that enough already. Even though they'd flown on a reindeer and waded through an ancient race of jolly elven, seeing the fat man was the most dizzying thing of all.

"Santa."

A low rumble of laughter tumbled from his thick beard, an abrupt but distinctive one. His eyes twinkled like stars were born from them. An elderly woman was next to him, sprigs of gray hair escaping her winter cap. She took his arm and they smiled upon them gently.

"It's been a troubled road," he said. "But those hardships have made you who you are."

He shed his glove and touched the tips of their noses. A faint smell of cinnamon tickled their nostrils.

An elven approached with an electronic tablet and reminded Santa what time it was. He acknowledged him with a nod and turned to the waiting crowd, lifting a hand above his head.

"Merry Christmas!"

They cheered and leaped. The ice shuddered. Snowballs were launched. Elven hugged and danced, and Santa's laughter was buried beneath the celebration. They took the feed bags from the reindeer.

More elven joined the one with the tablet and ushered Santa to the sleigh, muttering updates about weather and routes. He slid onto the seat and listened intently, having a sip of cocoa.

"Are you coming?"

He turned a twinkling eye to Ryder and Cherry. They had turned solid with wonder, had become observers watching reality dress up like a dream. Santa patted the bench.

"Life in the ice isn't for you," Merry said. "He'll take you home."

"We don't have a home."

Cherry beat him to it. They couldn't go back to Kringletown. The ice was as good as any other place they'd been.

"You do now."

Mrs. Claus adjusted Ryder's cap and tightened Cherry's scarf before guiding them around the sleigh. Elven held their hands to keep them steady, boosting them onto the front seat and then handing Mrs. Claus two steaming cups of cocoa. She put them in cup holders and winked.

She fussed with Santa's coat, pecking him on the cheek with a smiling kiss and silly laughter. The elven cheered like children and cleared a path in front of the sleigh. Santa waved with a thick mitten.

"Would you like to do the honors?" he said.

Ryder and Cherry didn't know what he meant. Santa gestured to the reindeer, their heads turned and waiting, clouds streaming from their nostrils.

"Now Dasher, now Dancer..." he started.

The two reindeer in front faced forward; muscles rippled over their hindquarters, white tails flickering. Ryder looked at Cherry and swallowed. He couldn't remember the rest.

"Now Prancer and Vixen," Cherry said.

Santa threw his head back and put his hand on his belly. "Ho-ho-ho!"

They finished the names together. Ryder managed to squeak out the last one but then, unexpectedly, heard Santa add one that wasn't in the popular refrain that everyone back in the real world knew and loved.

"And Ronin to lead them all!"

The sleigh jerked forward. The reindeer dug into the snow and sped through a storm of celebratory snowballs and cheers. They jostled in the seat until Dasher and Dancer lifted off the ice. Two by two, the rest of them followed. Their antlers glowed and warped the atmosphere, surrounding the sleigh with a protective bubble where the wind couldn't reach them.

They soared on a smooth trackless path, circling above the mass of elven. Santa waved back and wished them all a good night. Ronin was a dark figure on the ice. A sorrowful moan reached them. Ryder waved with a lump in his throat. All was blurry when he heard the last reindeer call to them.

And then they were gone.

They had exited the incognito dome that kept them hidden from the world. Alone on the North Pole where they lived in the ice, their stealthy technology keeping them secret. How long would it last? And what would happen when they were finally discovered? After all, William found them.

It can't be much longer.

"He's been watching you." Santa flipped a switch and leaned back with his cocoa, tossing a sideways smile at Ryder. "Ever since he found you."

"He doesn't have to anymore."

This time, Ryder meant it. This was where the last reindeer belonged. Maybe it was time for someone to protect him.

Santa reached for a button. When he pressed it, a high-pitched whine sounded from the rear of the sleigh. The stars blurred and the earth too. They had entered a time-warping field that would allow them to travel the world in a blink of an eye. Santa began laughing.

"Just try to stop him."

24

Visibility was getting worse.

William had tested the phone in these conditions. All of his technology was built for this day, the day a reindeer would lead him to a hidden society of elven and a fat man in the sleigh.

This was a mistake.

He'd given in to desperation, the final pieces falling apart when Ronin escaped. *When Billy questioned me.* He hadn't expected him to be so resistant, to be so remorseful. Billy was his clone. He had the same DNA. William had implanted him with his own memories, had guided his thoughts. Yet he had changed so quickly.

How?

Gallivanter wiped him clean, hid his thoughts, implanted new compulsions, or something. *What's my name?* William didn't know if Billy was rejecting his name or really couldn't remember it. *He doesn't have a name.*

How long had Gallivanter been lying in wait, planning his emergence from cold storage, lurking in the network until the time was right? William had taken precautions, set up redundant firewalls, scanned for intelligence anomalies, cloned the elven over and over, and interviewed them extensively to build a predictive model of what he might do to attempt to escape. All of those Gallivanter clones with his memories and experiences and, still, he'd pulled it off.

No matter how many clones he cranked out, William would be alone. They were merely bricks he'd used to pave a broken path to the Pole. Now he was truly alone.

"Hey!"

He shouted at the reindeer clone. It didn't have a name. He hadn't named any of the elven clones, just gave them numbers to keep track of them. The reindeer clone was no different. A tool didn't have a name. A hammer was a hammer.

A clone was a clone.

"Hey!"

Could he leap back to Kringletown? Did he have the energy? He had Ronin's stamina because he was a perfect duplicate of the last reindeer. *Of course he can.* He wasn't quite sure if he had Ronin's memories; there hadn't been time to scan him. It shouldn't matter if he did. He would listen, he would obey, whether the phone was working or not.

Billy stopped listening because Gallivanter changed him. And the phone still worked on him.

William assumed that was why Billy had stopped obeying. What if something else had happened, some sort of identity crisis that crashed the protocol? That was the mistake he'd made in the very beginning, confusing memories for consciousness. William had expected to wake up in a new body when he cloned himself. Instead, Billy woke up and William went into cold storage.

Ryder reminded him of that.

"Come here!"

Distracted by the Northern Lights, the reindeer clone stretched his neck and looked up. Perhaps he couldn't hear him.

Why won't the phone work?

William leaned into the wind. He saw the clone's legs tense and the stomach bloat. He had heard him after all, anticipating William's need to escape. He was ready to climb onto his back and warm up inside the electromagnetic field.

But then it launched.

William was still on the ice. The Arctic air crystalized in his lungs as he fell on his knees and searched the dark sky for the clone's return. A dim figure receded into the background of green and red ribbons. He was going to leave him. His reindeer clone was heading home without him.

When William looked up again, there was a faint glimmer of hope. There was something else up there. The reindeer clone was following a long train of reindeer pedaling the air.

Is that...

"Hello."

William turned stiffly. He wiped his eyes and shielded his vision.

Long coats whipped around oversized feet. Ruddy faces thick and placid. Watching him as he tried to stand. He fell on his face, inhaling a mouthful of snow and coughing coldly. A pair of hands lifted him up. Sullen expressions looked down.

"You've been looking for us," the elven to his left said.

"Congratulations," the bearded elven said gruffly. "You're only the fourth human to enter the colony in two hundred years."

William climbed to his feet and stumbled. They kept him from falling again. He tried to speak, but his tongue was swollen and his lips numb. The female elven patted his hand.

"One step at a time, William."

They guided him toward nothing. The Arctic ice went all the way to the horizon. *Where are the rest of them?* Twice he nearly gave up. His legs were wooden pegs.

"Just a few more," she said.

And then the wind stopped like a switch had been pulled. One second, it scoured his face. The next it was gone. His inner ears ached in the silence. And the world was no longer a barren sheet. There were hundreds of them.

Maybe thousands.

They were awkwardly staring along with giant snowmen. And

one very big reindeer. An angry growl splintered the silence. Ronin stood up and lowered his head. Elven crowded around him, but they weren't protecting him from William. Ronin lifted his head and howled like he'd done on the mountain.

"We usually celebrate now," the female elven said. "The sleigh is off and the children are safe."

"We're a little disappointed this year," the bearded elven said.

"Not because you're here."

The elven parted like a snowplow forced them aside. Sensation began returning to William's face and legs. His thoughts were little cubes of ice tinkling inside his head. He went coolly numb again when he realized what she meant.

His life's work spread out before him. He knew everything about the elven and the truth about Santa Claus. He knew their technology and their secrets. All he ever worked for had been proved right. And no one would ever know it.

Because I'm staying.

25

They watched the sky.

A knot doubled up Billy's stomach. Gallivanter twined his fingers over his stomach, a smile resting on his face. Billy couldn't decide if the smile was satisfied or cynical. Some moments the elven seemed to barely have the energy to stand.

He always had enough to smile.

The elven hadn't said much for most of the day. They had been very busy getting things back in order, making rights out of wrongs. There would be no more nicies, no more naughties. No more Big Game.

Just us, Gallivanter had said.

It was past midnight when they stepped into the horseshoe and began watching the sky. Gallivanter didn't say what they were doing, but Billy knew. It wasn't long before the silence was splintered like a cement block dropped on a frozen pond. It echoed in the distance and cascaded down the mountainside.

Gallivanter's smile grew.

An outline appeared over the mountain. Billy hadn't expected such a grand entrance. Stealth was what he expected, but there it was in the open for anyone to see, a team of reindeer circling around and drifting into the horseshoe with a jingle of bells and clopping of hooves. The rails of a large sleigh slushed to a stop.

Gallivanter began walking.

The reindeer turned their heads. Billy wondered if they were glaring at him or watching the elven pick up his waddling pace as he neared.

Do they know what I did?

Gallivanter nearly vanished in the dark, but the ripple of bells meant he had reached the reindeer, hugging each one of them as they dipped their heads, snorting and sniffing. Gallivanter's greetings were emotional and heartfelt.

Unmistakable laughter bellowed from the sleigh.

It made Billy dizzy. William had pursued the Christmas legend for so long. That obsession was over, William was gone, and the fat man was only a couple of hundred feet away from him. He nearly melted into a puddle of awe.

He's real.

William had left on the cloned reindeer and never returned. Gallivanter didn't seem concerned. It was as if he expected him to chase after Ronin.

He will not return, the elven had told him.

Despite the evidence—the elven, the flying reindeer, and the sleigh that flew over the mountain—he still reserved his doubts for the sake of sanity. It was better to believe this was all a hallucination, that he was not a product of a synthetic cloning machine. But the evidence was, once again, irrefutable. He didn't have a choice.

He believed.

He was distracted by his thoughts, struggling with recurring doubts, when two figures climbed out of the sleigh. The reindeer were still out there with the fat man's baritone voice joyfully greeting Gallivanter.

The two figures slowed.

Billy sensed their disbelief, imagined their confusion, could feel their swelling anger. Ryder looked back at the sleigh. He wasn't expecting to find Billy waiting for them. They looked back again, reconsidering their return to Kringletown. They'd been lied to enough. Was the fat man bringing them back to the same life?

"I'm sorry." Billy raised a hand before they turned around. "For everything, I... I can't express..."

The ache in his chest broke off the rest of what he was going to say. Whenever he stared directly at what he'd done, it hurt too much. He was shaking. How was he going to rebuild their lives?

I can't do it alone.

The standoff was broken by a jingling of bells and a trail of laughter then a crackling of time and space. The reindeer and sleigh had vanished. A waddling figure approached them. Billy's chin quivered. He had assumed the elven would return to the Pole. After all, he was finally free to do so.

Gallivanter the Wanderer.

"Oh, it's good, catching up with an old friend." Gallivanter looked up at Ryder and Cherry. "It's been a very long trip, I know. One doesn't simply brush an experience like this under the ice. We have work."

Corded braids swung from his chin. All those years in cold storage and he'd seemed to recover not in months or years. It was less than a day. It would take most people a lifetime to overcome the mess William had made.

But Gallivanter was not human.

He tugged on a beard braid. "It's time to wake them."

"Why?" Ryder stared through Billy. "You know what he did to us, to you. You know what's on the other side of the mountain, don't you? Why would you wake *him*?"

The truth was going to be easier for some to digest than others. After all, Ryder was different. He was special, and not because there was a reindeer protecting him.

He's naughty and nice.

He was the clone who grew up in the world, untainted by William's inner voice, allowed to suffer and believe he was unimportant, that he didn't matter.

More human than the rest of us.

"Put him in the cabin," Ryder said. "I don't want him anywhere near the others when they wake up. He did this, Gallivanter. This is all because of him."

Gallivanter stroked his braids and turned thoughtfully. His tireless exuberance dissolved into one of calm understanding. Perhaps he'd underestimated Ryder's reaction.

"Could you excuse us for a moment, Billy?" Gallivanter said.

Billy swallowed. "No."

They were surprised by that. Even Gallivanter turned toward him.

"Ryder's right. This is my fault," Billy continued. "I-I mean, it was William's doing, but it-it-it was my hand. I don't deserve their trust or to be forgiven. Not now or maybe ever. Please don't lock me away."

"Like you did us?" Ryder said. "You put us in the cold for how long, Billy? Months? Years? You put them to sleep because they weren't good enough. Good boys and girls do what you tell them, right? You deserve to be in one of those drawers."

Billy drew a long shaky breath. "You're right."

A grim line set Ryder's lips as he looked down. A conflict of thoughts wrestled in his head. Cherry was expressionless. Hardened by shock or unresolved anger, his words went through her like a summer breeze through a screen window.

Gallivanter waddled behind them. With a few muttered words, he guided the kids inside. Billy remained in the cold. Whatever they decided, he would accept. He was free to suffer.

Without William's voice.

The door opened and the elven gestured. They went to the elevator and waited. It was after midnight. The nicies were already asleep in their beds.

Not the naughties.

When the elevator arrived, a breath of synthetic odor wafted out. He hadn't been down there yet. Hesitantly, he followed the elven inside, stress involuntarily pulling the corner of his mouth. Each step felt like walking toward a cliff, the world rushing past and a dark unknown waiting to swallow him.

"I woke you for a reason."

Gallivanter took his hand. Billy grabbed at the wall as the elevator descended. His throat swelled. Gallivanter's smile did not waver. His eyes were gentle and forgiving, as if nothing needed to be forgiven. All was exactly the way it was supposed to be.

When the doors opened, the lab buried him beneath an avalanche of sounds and smells. He struggled for his next breath, clenching the back wall of the elevator as his memories breached the fences and rushed into awareness. Everything he'd done, he had to face it. All of it.

All of them.

Gallivanter stayed with him, watching him, holding his hand. Perhaps it would be better if they did put him in a drawer. It might be easier that way. And he deserved it. But then a sound reached him, one reaching back through all the years to when this started. There was the sound of cold storage doors decompressing and drawers sliding out. More voices joined the others, sleepy and confused.

Billy slid to the floor and buried his face.

He heard a voice unlike any of the others. Once he heard it, the tears came.

"We need you." Gallivanter put his hand on his shoulder. "For the healing to begin."

It was the cry of an infant.

26

Madeline watched from the back of the train.

There were no seat belts in this car, just row after row of children fighting over the windows. The chaperones tried to get control, but it was hopeless.

Madeline was not part of it.

These were children from foster homes. It was the first time any of them had flown on a plane or boarded a train. The first time they had seen reindeer.

Steel wheels walloped metal rails. They were heading for the mountain. They didn't really know where they were going. This was a secret trip that very few lucky winners experienced.

"Tickets!" The conductor appeared.

Madeline slunk in the corner. Despite her anxiety, a smile pounced across her lips. She had doubted this trip and had nearly turned around when she arrived at the boarding station, where a fountain made of antlers used to be. Ghosts of her past had followed her onto the train.

But the sight of the conductor put her at ease.

The children faced the front as he closed the door behind him.

His suit was royal blue with gold buttons and his hat formal and stiff. His beard was thick and dark and nicely trimmed over his cheeks.

"Tickets, please! I need to see your tickets."

The children waved golden tickets. Each one had their name embossed in black letters on shiny paper. They had arrived by mail with a return address that said *Santa's Village*. They were cordially invited and advised not to lose them.

"One at a time, please."

The conductor examined each ticket through spectacles balanced on the end of his nose then stamped it with a nifty tool. The children showed each other what it looked like before pressing their face on the cold windows.

"What do we have here?"

He took a knee next to a girl quietly weeping. Her hair was tied in two pigtails, one with a green ribbon and the other one red. She muttered through hiccups.

"Wait." The conductor patted his coat and front pockets then lifted his conductor's hat and searched the lining. "Is your name... Gabrielle?"

She nodded.

"All tickets accounted for!" He marched to the front of the car. "All passengers booked for a trip to... to, uh..."

"Santa's Village!"

A smile grew somewhere under that black beard and high-beamed behind his spectacles. With a jabbing finger and a stomping foot, he let loose a laugh that stampeded through the car.

Madeline covered her mouth when it reached her.

"Who would like to see it snow?"

The children raised their hands and shrilly agreed. The conductor brandished a handkerchief and began cleaning his spectacles like he forgot he'd asked a question. He held them up and cleaned them again then promptly balanced them on his nose.

"Then let it snow."

The children looked out the window. There was snow already on the ground, but it wasn't falling. The conductor couldn't control the weather, but a snowflake did fall. It landed on Madeline's shoulder.

Snow drifted down from the ceiling.

The children cheered. They scraped it off the floor and stuck out their tongues, snowflakes fat and thick. Madeline could barely see the front of the car. The train entered the trees and the rails were sloping upward, tilting their weight slightly back in the seats.

When the fun had reached critical mass—children climbing over seats and adults joining in—the conductor called out and the children, miraculously, sat down. The snow stopped and the relative quiet was broken only by the imperfections of the rails.

"Who would like to hear about the boy kissed by a reindeer?"

The boys and girls raised their hands. Once again, the conductor cleaned his glasses. When they were back on his nose, the cabin lights went up and the trees disappeared. Some of the children and one adult shouted in surprise. The train had entered a tunnel.

They were inside the mountain.

"There once was a boy much like all of you." His voice resonated over the echo of the steel wheels and the engine's whistle. "On Christmas he sat at his window and waited for Santa. And each Christmas, he fell asleep. But one very special Christmas, he'd become lost and wandered about searching for his way back home. That was the year he was found by one very big, one very special reindeer."

"Ronin," Madeline muttered.

"This very brave reindeer hoisted the boy upon his back and flew him to the top of the world, where a very fat man and his family of elven welcomed him."

The darkness of the tunnel was replaced by an icy sheet that appeared to expand the horizon. The children's attention was drawn out of the windows and words of awe were pulled from their mouths. Madeline was unsure if the image of the North Pole was projected on the tunnel wall or in the train's windows. It didn't matter.

She shuddered.

"The elven prepare for one special day of the year," the conductor said. "That's when the reindeer gather and the sleigh is loaded. That's when the snowmen help and the reindeer fly. And everyone works together to make it the greatest day of the year."

Reindeer appeared to fall from the sky. Elven gave them feed of a special blend to help fill their helium bladders. A sack was in the back of a sleigh, and a very fat man in a red suit sat in the front seat. Snowmen loomed over the herd, helping pass along presents.

Madeline silently mouthed their names.

"And when it was time to leave, the very special reindeer flew the boy back. The boy rubbed his nose and said thank you. The reindeer's nose was so hot that when he pressed it to the boy's cheek, it left a mark he would never forget."

The train continued chugging. The children pressed their faces to the glass. They pointed and shouted, staring in wonderment.

"Why didn't the boy stay up there?"

Lisping wonder escaped through a gap in a little girl's front teeth. The conductor leaned over and touched her cheek. "Because this is his home."

"Well-well, why do elfs stay there?"

The conductor began to clean his glasses. All at once, the tunnel went black. The North Pole vanished and his voice rose out of the dark.

"Who said they did?"

Daylight knifed through the cabin. The children leaned back, their eyes growing wider. The train shot out of the other side of the mountain and into a bowl, as if a giant had scooped out the middle of the mountain and built houses out of gingerbread and twirling sticks of red and white candy canes. The roofs were pointed and steeply slanted, the doors short and wide, steps shallow and curving.

The streets were paved with brightly colored gumdrops. Elven waved as they passed, crowding the candy-paved streets with fat bellies and hairy feet. Some had braided hair, beards that tickled their toes or pulled over their shoulders. They wore long coats and short ones, shirts that didn't quite cover their bellies or reached the ground. The children waved back, not realizing that if they looked very closely at the elven's eyes and the shapes of their noses, all of them looked exactly the same.

As if they were all twins.

The train whistled and began to slow. The station was up ahead. The children bounced in their seats as the engine sighed with the final turn of steel wheels. The road was wide and welcoming, filled with excited elven around an enormous reindeer, who reared back.

"There he is!" A girl pointed.

A howl shook the timbers of Madeline's memory, dropping an incident of the first time she'd heard that sound. Suddenly the drones were overhead and Ryder was on the ground.

The howl echoing from the trees.

The children were greeted by the elven and other residents of Santa's Village, men and women dressed like people from a time forgotten. Madeline peeked from her corner at the window, recognizing them by the way they walked or the way they talked.

It had been eighteen years.

Some of the children approached the reindeer. A teenage boy stood next to the enormous animal, passing cubes of pressed food to the children. The reindeer took them from their hands with rubbery lips.

Madeline smiled this time without covering up.

She waited until the children's chaperones left. They thanked the conductor profusely and emotionally. He had no idea how much this meant. They had no idea that he knew exactly how much.

He watched the scene outside with the wonder of one of the children. Madeline imagined he did this every time the train stopped, sneaking pleasure from watching them hug an elven for the first time or feel a reindeer's lips.

A reindeer's kiss.

So absorbed by the scene he didn't hear her slide out of the seat and approach. Suddenly remembering he was the conductor, he turned to greet a chaperone he'd somehow forgotten. She pulled her hair behind her ears. The color of her hair had darkened since he'd seen her last. The conductor's expression dissolved as recognition filled his eyes.

"Cherry."

He threw his arms around her. She hugged him back, leaning on his shoulder. His smell, distinct and faint, mingled with a name she hadn't used in such a long time. A life she'd left long ago.

Not everyone transitioned smoothly.

Many of them had left Kringletown to start lives of their own, to forget what had happened, to begin again. Some of them had sold their stories to the media, but they fell through the cracks of urban legend, living in the blogs of conspiracy. No one ever believed children were being cloned and an elven had been in cold storage.

Or stories of flying reindeer.

"It's been so long," he said.

"Eighteen years."

"It feels longer."

She sniffed back emotion, afraid she might cry. The elven were leading the children into the village, where they would play amazing games and ride amazing rides. A Christmas tree towered in the center of the village. The teenage boy was still with the giant reindeer, a line of children waiting to feed him.

"The beard looks good."

"This mop?" He pulled on the sideburn tab and peeled it off, adhesive clinging to his cheeks. He cringed like it hurt, rubbing the crimson birthmark on his cheek. Whether that was something he was born with or something that had happened to him in the back of the truck, she liked to think it was from Ronin.

A real reindeer kiss.

"I'm sorry," she said. "I should've told you I was coming."

"No, no. I'm glad you didn't. I would've been nervous if I knew you were back there, or said something embarrassing."

"Well, then I'm not sorry. And I don't want to get in your way. I know you have things to do. I can wander around on my own. Looks like you've added a lot to the village since we…"

She snuck a glance down the road. It hadn't changed that much, really. Not since she last saw it. That had been shortly after everyone woke up, after the naughties met the nicies and the originals greeted their clones.

Cherry didn't climb out of cold storage, so she didn't know just how strange it felt. But when Bill took them over the mountain to see what William was building—the village, all of those Gallivanter clones, and all the nicies who left Kringletown—it was too much for some of them.

"Meet me at the tree," Ryder said. "In an hour."

He stripped off the conductor uniform. She laughed behind her hand. He was wearing an elf costume under it, fighting a cap over his curly locks. Once dark brown, streaks of gray were at the temples.

"Promise me."

She nodded. "Go."

He wanted to kiss her. She wanted him to. Instead, he shook her hand then shook his head, embarrassed, whispering to himself, "Idiot."

He didn't ask her why she came back. If he did, she wouldn't have an answer. She didn't know what had compelled her to return after all these years. She'd always wanted to, just didn't have the courage. This year was different.

She didn't know why.

He darted down Candy Lane. Thankfully, he didn't tell anyone she was there. She preferred to introduce herself to her brothers and sisters when she was ready. Not all of them would be happy to see her. She had left them and never talked to them again. She needed to ease back like an old pair of pants she wasn't sure she'd fit into.

She waited on the station platform.

The air was crisp and clean. She closed her eyes and breathed it in, deep and cleansing. A sudden wave of emotion swelled in her throat. It all seemed like a dream. A flying reindeer and elven on the

North Pole. Santa Claus in the sleigh as the world spun beneath them.

A lab where bodies slept.

She was one of the few who didn't have to greet her clone. Still, she couldn't stay after that. She didn't know if she wanted to weep for lost innocence or the fact that she ran from it. Ryder wouldn't come with her; he'd begged her to stay. He wouldn't go with her, had said he needed to stay and face the nightmares that were yet to come.

To make bad dreams good.

Hot exhaust blew on her face, grassy and humid. She leaned back as the long face reached for her. The massive reindeer snorted.

"Hello, Raker," she said. "Remember me?"

Ronin's clone sniffed her open palm. They had called him Ronin's clone for a long time. Gallivanter suggested the name Raker. It didn't have a special meaning, just a name of his own. He started out as a clone, but he was as real as any reindeer. A reindeer who deserved his own name.

"Want to feed him?"

A teenage boy brought a bag of compressed alfalfa to the platform. He was wearing puffy brown trousers and suspenders over a long-sleeved shirt. Madeline pulled one out and offered it while the boy scratched the tufted beard beneath Raker's chin.

Phones weren't allowed in the village. There was no reception or Wi-Fi anyway. Nothing recorded ever left, but stories were told each year as children came and went. It wouldn't be impossible for her to know the reindeer's name, so it didn't surprise the boy when she said it.

But no one should know the boy's name.

"Thank you, Ben."

The boy searched her face. "Have we met?"

He wouldn't find the memories he was looking for. There were still children waiting to feed the reindeer. She rubbed Raker's nose. The boy turned his head to invite the children over.

A distinct crimson birthmark on his cheek.

"You wouldn't remember," she said.

And then he was off, chasing Raker after other children wanting to shower him with treats. Ben was slender and awkward standing there, but elegance came out when he moved. Like a boy who never played sports.

Who only caught touchdowns.

He had grown up with the truth. It wasn't something thrust upon him in the middle of adolescence. Once upon a time, he was found in the back of a truck by a reindeer who refused to play by the rules. He was brought to Kringletown, where William made him a twin brother.

A twin brother who was eighteen years older.

He didn't know he'd been asleep all those years. He was raised in Kringletown by adoring brothers and sisters, a doting adoptive father and an elven caretaker. Madeline didn't need to remind him of the times Aunt Cherry had fed him with a bottle or searched for his pacifier.

She'd left long before he would remember that.

She wandered the village, getting lost along the colorful cobblestone paths, squat houses with flower boxes and icy ramps that led up to front doors. William had spent years building the place. He needed somewhere for all the Gallivanters he was cloning, and a place to hide the nicies who weren't quite right. If he couldn't find Santa, he could make his own colony.

He never came back from the Pole.

No one ever answered what happened to him. The last she remembered was seeing him stumble on the ice. Raker had been with him but returned to Kringletown. Gallivanter said William stayed on the Pole, that the elven kept him there. They couldn't let him go, not after what he knew.

Not after what he did.

She spent the afternoon huddled near the food court, sipping hot chocolate and listening to the children. Occasionally, one of her brothers or sisters would walk past, their glances lingering, but no one stopped to ask who she was. And she didn't volunteer. It was like treading on thin ice, not knowing if those were cracks she was hearing behind her and everything would fall into disappointment. Her first visit back had been a good one.

No need to push it.

The bell started ringing at nightfall. A pleasant gong that echoed throughout the village. She followed the flow, the sliding elven and the giggling children. They were all heading toward the Christmas tree that was five stories high and smothered in ornaments and blinking lights with a twinkling star on top.

They were all there.

The children and the adults all gathered in front, exhausted from a full day of wonder. On a platform were a large chair and a mountain of presents. Madeline leaned against the corner of a building and watched the elven lead a very fat man front and center.

A chill crawled down her back.

The memory of riding in the sleigh reappeared in vivid detail. For a moment, she thought perhaps they'd brought Santa Claus down for this special occasion, but his laugh gave him away. He belted out a *ho-ho-ho* that raised a cheer from the crowd, but it didn't fool Madeline. A laugh like that was unmistakable. It came from the fat man's belly, full of joy and promise. This was an imposter.

An imposter she recognized.

Still, she watched the children line up and the helpers hand out presents. A big black dog sat next to Santa, a floppy red hat tied to her head. She watched the presents and licked the children when they were close enough to lick.

A dog that was almost forty years old.

Ryder was at Santa's right hand. Jane was there too, and John and Soup. Arf was unmistakable, large as life and hunched over. His twin was next to him. Which was which—clone or flesh—was impossible to tell from a distance. Perhaps if she was next to them, she could smell the distinct odor that separated one from the other.

Still, she couldn't help but smile.

"They believe."

An elven was beside her. She was too lost in thoughts and worries to notice. He wiggled his toes. His hands laced on his belly, where two braids rested.

"Do you?" he asked.

"I did." She cocked her head. "Once upon a time."

"No one said *the end*. Perhaps the story isn't over."

"It's not a story if it's real, Gallivanter."

"Life is a story, child."

They watched the last child receive a gift. The fake Santa laughter rang out and the elven clones cheered and danced. Raker waltzed out of one of the alleyways with Ben at his side, the enormous rack of antlers bobbing with each step.

"You look good," she said. "I think you've lost weight."

"How dare you, Ms. Cherry Stone." He patted his ever-round stomach.

"It's Madeline now."

"Ah. New name, new life."

"Well, you know. Life is change."

Santa climbed off the stage with the aid of his helpers and hugged the children on his way through the crowd, high-fiving and ho-hoing as he went. Raker howled as he neared. Figgy trotted behind him.

"Have you forgiven him?" Gallivanter asked.

She watched the fake Santa climb onto the reindeer's back and the crowd back up. The elven formed a ring of safety so there would be no accidents. Figgy barked to help secure the perimeter.

Santa's beard was phony and so was the belly. Beneath the white locks were a neatly trimmed red beard and an ageless body. He raised a gloved hand and wished them all a good night. Raker's belly inflated.

And they sailed into the night.

Gasps and gawks followed. It looked so real that they believed it. But it was real. That was a flying reindeer. Rumors were spread that it was the best magic trick in the world, and no one could explain how they did it. But Madeline knew better. Sometimes the truth was disguised as a lie.

And sometimes a lie is just a lie.

He patted her hand. "I'm glad you're here."

Ryder the Helper was still on stage as children were ushered around the tree. There was time to explore before they went to their rooms where hot chocolate was waiting and an elven would tuck them in.

"I've been thinking..." Cherry turned.

Gallivanter was gone. Disappearing as magically as he appeared. But she knew how he felt about magic.

She was going to say that she'd been thinking about coming back for quite some time. No matter how far she travelled or where she looked, peace was always out of reach. And there were the dreams that haunted her, the ones of her childhood and the things she left behind. The pain left unhealed. She came back to face them, to confront Bill. A part of her wanted to forgive him.

It was just hard.

The walls from childhood were meant to protect her. She wanted to tear them down. This was the place to do it, the place where they had been built.

She also came to see Ryder. But one step at a time. She would have to take the walls down a brick at a time. *Baby steps.*

She snuck off and found a quiet path. Her room was in the middle of the village. It was on the third floor of a gingerbread house with shutters made of icing and sugar cookies. The door was locked. It had been open earlier in the day when she dropped off her luggage. She didn't have a key. *Nothing needs to be locked in Santa's Village*, she had been told.

There were footprints on the threshold.

They weren't footprints but a distinct pattern of cloven hooves. A reindeer had been here. Bill must've seen her hiding behind the building and landed when everyone was at the tree.

But why would he lock my door?

She followed the tracks down a wide alleyway. When they disappeared at a dead end, she found them on the other side of a narrow cut-through and followed them to the edge of the village that met the cold wall of the mountain.

The houses were different there.

They were larger, without gumdrops and icing shutters. The smell of hay came from a quaint barn. The tracks that were at her door crossed the street but didn't go to the barn. They went to a little blue house, where a candle burned in the window.

Madeline stopped in the middle of the road.

In the distance, the elven were singing. Snow fell in soft waves, clinging to her hair and melting on her cheeks. She held out her hands and let them land softly. There, alongside the blue house, Raker hid in the shadows. His antlers barely fit in the narrow space. He snorted and pawed the snow, turning his head toward her.

He leaped.

Straight up into the night sky he went so quickly that, unless she was looking, she never would have seen him. It wasn't just a leap across the village, either. He soared over the rim of the mountain. Bill the fake Santa wasn't with him. He was unattended. She crept closer to see what he was doing.

"Cherry?"

Ryder came out of the blue house. His coat was unbuttoned and his boots untied. She caught the smell of incense.

"I think... Raker just escaped." She pointed up.

"I just put him up and fed him." He gestured to the barn. She could see him now, his antlers bobbing in the shadows of a deep stall. He looked at them as if he'd heard his name.

"I just stopped inside to change," Ryder said. "You were supposed to meet me earlier. How did you find me?"

She looked at the hoof tracks. They were outside a window. The reindeer had been peeking inside his house. A fit of laughter hit her. It started as a trickle and transformed into gut-punching hysteria.

"Are you okay?" he said.

She held onto him. Weak and exuberant, she let the joy take over and prop her up then fell into his arms weeping and laughing. They stood in the road as elven song serenaded the night and snow littered their shoulders.

And the walls started to tumble.

"You want to go inside?" he said.

Arm in arm, they climbed the steps. They talked late into the night. So late that elven song turned to elven snoring and not a creature was stirring. It would be many months later when she would tell him that a very special, very large reindeer was still watching out for him. He didn't believe her.

But that wouldn't stop Ronin.

TOYLAND: THE LEGACY OF WALLACE NOEL (BOOK 7)

Get the Claus Universe at:
BERTAUSKI.COM/CLAUS

❄

Toyland: The Legacy of Wallace Noel (Book 7)

CHAPTER 1

A funeral isn't a fun way to start. But this isn't your usual Christmas story.

Great-aunt Annie was a hundred and thirty-six years old. You read that right. That's not how long people live, but you heard what I said about this story.

We didn't call her Great-aunt Annie. We just called her Awnty Awnie because she wasn't great. I mean, she was great. Just didn't seem old. Eternally young. But, like I said, this story starts with a funeral.

By the way, no one ever called her Aunt Annie. It was Awnty Awnie, one word. *Awntyawnie*.

What I remember most about her, besides the infectious high-pitched laugh and her doughy hugs, was that she was a wonderful storyteller. Probably the best ever. That's where Piper gets it.

When Awnty Awnie started a yarn, everyone listened. Neighbors, pastors, little kids, dogs. You knew a story was coming when she patted her knees.

"There was this time..."

They were all Christmas stories about reindeer and snowmen, elven and Santa Claus. Stories you never heard before. She believed them. And so did we.

Then one day forgot them.

Before she passed, she forgot our names. Even Pip. There was one story left, though. One she never told.

It began after the funeral.

Everyone was in their dress-ups. Pip wore what four-year-olds wear: frilly dress and sparkly red shoes that tapped the floor. Tin had just started driving a car, whatever age that is. She wore a dress, too. Not sparkly shoes, though.

Awnty Awnie's house was as old as she was. The paint was peeling and the foundation cracked by a giant oak tree. Awnty Awnie didn't care. Once upon a time her house looked like a greenhouse.

She loved nature.

Pip's mom was planning to auction off the house with all the stuff in it. Her collections were in piles, boxes and cabinets, under beds and behind couches. There were newspapers, magazines, yarn, hats, and stuffed animals everywhere.

She loved her stuffed animals, too.

Pip and I climbed the steep stairs to an old, stuffy attic, where she played with Awnty Awnie's stuffed toys. Pip would've told stories till it was time to go home if her mom didn't start crying.

We went back downstairs when Oscar called. He took care of paperwork for Pip's mom. Stepdad stuff. I don't know why stepparents are always the bad guys. Tin and Pip had different dads. Tin's dad wasn't a bad guy, just sort of not around. Pip's dad was bad-bad. Their mom left him before they got married. Then she met Oscar.

He was a keeper.

He came over to help, but still he couldn't understand why Pip's mom was crying. A walnut was just a walnut, not the thing she'd carried home from school when a bunch of girls teased her and Awnty Awnie chased them off with a broom.

"Just let the auctioneer have it all," she said.

She had a box full of memories to keep her crying for a month. Tin didn't want to let the memories go like that. She didn't have as many memories as her mom did. If she didn't keep going, Awnty Awnie's last story would've have been lost forever.

Tin found the footlocker.

It was metal and dented, with leather straps and rivets along the seams. It contained a heap of random stuff—wooden shoes from Holland, leather bolo ties, pan flute CDs—along with plastic binders of black-and-white photos. The pictures weren't that interesting, really, just trees and flowers, hills and buildings and things.

"I didn't know she travelled," Tin said.

"Neither did I," her mom added.

There was a lot they didn't know. Mom found an old leather-bound journal with newspaper clippings glued to the pages.

"Who's Wallace?" Pip said.

She read the journal's cover. Pip was only four, but she was precocious. She even knew what *precocious* meant.

"Look." Tin held up a photo.

It was grainy, but they could make out what looked like a very tall treehouse. Oscar was the one who called it a fire lookout used by foresters. The man in the photo didn't look like a forester.

He had a very round belly and a thick gray beard. He was wearing a white T-shirt with suspenders. But, oddly, he was wearing a floppy hat. The photo was black and white, but it didn't look like a Santa hat. It had a little bell and looked more like something an elf would wear.

He was hugging a giant stuffed panda bear. It stood nearly as tall as he did. Mom flipped the photo over. Awnty Awnie's handwriting was in blue ink. *Wallace and Pando, 1908.*

"That's a Noel Bear," Oscar said.

I knew what a Noel Bear was. Of course I did. I didn't know who Wallace Noel was.

All those stories that Awnty Awnie told had, in one way or another, come from a beat-up metal footlocker, a journal and a collection of black-and-white photos. But her last story is this one.

If you ask me, it's her best.

Click here to get Toyland: The Legacy of Wallace Noel (Book 7)

YOU DONATED TO A WORTHY CAUSE!

By purchasing this book, you have donated to the care and adoption of abandoned and abused animals since 10% of the profits is annually donated to Dorchester Paws, a non-profit organization that provide animals with food, shelter, and medical attention until they find a home.

ABOUT THE AUTHOR

My grandpa never graduated high school. He retired from a steel mill in the mid-70s. He was uneducated, but a voracious reader. As a kid, I'd go through his bookshelves of musty paperback novels, pulling Piers Anthony and Isaac Asimov off the shelf and promising to bring them back. I was fascinated by robots that could think and act like people. What happened when they died?

Writing is sort of a thought experiment to explore human nature and possibilities. What makes us human? What is true nature?

I'm also a big fan of plot twists.

bertauski.com

Printed in Great Britain
by Amazon